The
Beauty Thief

RACHAEL RITCHEY

The Beauty Thief

Copyright © 2015, 2016 Rachael Ritchey

All rights reserved.

ISBN: 0692374981
ISBN-13: 978-0692374986

*Second Edition

References made from the "Great Book" are paraphrased from verses of scripture out of the Bible. The "Great Book" and its references are a work of fiction created by the author and should not be confused with actual Bible verses.

To my daughters, Kass and Onna

Your beauty lies not in
how you look or what you wear.
It is in the depths of your heart
where character and courage reside.

Chronicles of the Twelve Realms

The Beauty Thief

Captive Hope

CONTENTS

Betrothed 1

Five Years Later 6

Eliya on the Way 14

Family 23

Castle Taisce 32

A Celebration and a Curse 44

Midnight Visitor 58

Shock 66

The Journey Begins 77

Watch Your Step, Princess 87

No One is Perfect 99

Plans Change 105

Conleth 114

Unmerited Rancor 124

The Blow's Affliction 132

Truth in a Story 140

To Forgive or Not to Forgive 149

Weariness 158

Arrival at High Castle 167

Paramount Unity 176

Rubinthynium 189

Beauty Comes with Age 202

Weathering the Storm 211

Ambush 222

Tracking Thieves 235

The Mighty One is Over All 247

Forming Plans 257

Piercing Perfection 266

Send Help 274

A Princess for Gold 283

Captive Audience of One 293

The Trail's End 300

In the Belly of the Beast 309

Total Lunar Eclipse 319

Epilogue 333

CHAPTER ONE
Betrothed

It was intolerable. How could she be expected to endure this? The urge to stomp her feet and throw something was overwhelming, but Caityn had the presence of mind to realize only a toddler would behave in such a manner. The disparity between her need for an emotional outburst and age enraged Caityn further, but she kept her body in check; it was by sheer force of will alone.

"I hate being a princess! I'm tired of always being told what I can and cannot do. I want to make my own choices, and it seems to me I should be allowed to make this one myself. I'm thirteen now. Why can't I choose for myself, Mama?"

The whiny timbre of her voice did nothing to mask her agitation. She was fortunate not to see her mother's face in that moment, or her temper might have boiled into a tantrum belying her words.

"Daughter, as much as you think being a princess is difficult and drudgery, you have no idea how the world around you really works." Queen Ismene faced Caityn and placed gentle hands on her shoulders. "I know you are capable of making your own decisions, but my point is plain, dearest. Every person must take orders of some kind or another. Even your father has rules to live by.

"We all have roles in life which we must fulfill. But, whatever your role, it is not who you are as a person. It is merely what you do. Now stop this fussing and listen, Caityn. 'Princess' is not who you are; it is your job. Who you choose to be, my love, is entirely up to you." Ismene paused to let her words sink in. "Now, Caityn. I can read the look on your face. This does not release you from your responsibility. You still must marry the man your father chose for you. Pick up your protruding lip and come sit by me on the bed."

The young princess glowered at the back of her mother's head as she watched the always graceful queen glide across the room. Caityn's feet, though, refused to budge. She was unsettled over the whole conversation and couldn't bring herself to comply.

When the queen sat, their eyes met. As if willed to move only by her mother's mind, Caityn approached the edge of the bed, but she refused to sit, crossing her arms over her chest. "I still don't see why I have to marry some stranger, some . . . some old stuffed-shirt!"

"Caityn, I will not have you insulting the High Prince with such childish name-calling. Besides, he's only five years your senior. Be glad your father didn't wait for a prince of the realms to choose you. Do sit. I'd like to tell you a story."

She finally gave in, sitting almost a foot away from her mother. Caityn wanted to make it clear she sat of her own choice, not out of obedience. It startled her when Ismene wrapped an arm around her waist and pulled her close.

Without wasting any time, Ismene began her impromptu tale. "Once upon a time there was a little princess who loved horses. She was all of three years old but begged her daddy to let her ride his stallions. Many times she implored and many times the king refused. She was persistent, and one day his 'nay' changed to 'yea.'

"The princess was thrilled, and her father was pleased to fulfill her wish. He took her to the stables to meet her new equestrian friend.

"One day during her riding lessons, her dear papa had a meeting to attend and couldn't watch her as she mastered her new skill. But on this day, she had a new audience: a quiet young boy who stood on the fence.

"Now, she was a brave one, if not a little headstrong, and she tried to make her sweet horse go faster than was prudent. She did not listen to her training master. She did not listen to her nursery maid who loved her so dearly, and, sadly, the little princess took quite a tumble.

"My oh my, there was such a ruckus! But, quiet and calm, the boy from the fence carried you home.

"No one stood in his way as he trudged up the hill—he was a prince, you see. And it was quite a sight, a ragtag group from the stables. They huddled protectively around you and the High Prince."

"This story is about me?"

"Yes, sweetheart. You've always had a mind of your own, and you can see, 'tis not always in your best interest."

"I still don't see why I have to marry somebody I've never met."

"Don't you see? You have met. The boy at the stables—he is your betrothed. He proved to your father and I he had a good head on his shoulders, not to mention a chivalrous heart."

Caityn threw herself back on the bed. "Oh! Some prince who can carry a three-year-old is the ball I am doomed to be chained to for the rest of my life!"

She felt the bed move when Ismene stood, but she didn't bother to lift her arm from her eyes. In truth, it was the only thing holding her tears at bay.

"Really, Caityn, don't you think that's a little dramatic, even for you?"

Caityn's distress caused anger to lace her voice like poison. "Not in the least." She popped up from the bed and stood rigid. "Can you even imagine what 'tis like to be told you have no choice of who you will marry?"

"Sweetheart, have you forgotten? Your father and I were betrothed. I never met him until our wedding day."

"Mama!" The endearment was drawn out in exasperation. "I mean, I don't even like boys. Well, not really. Well, I don't know what I think of boys, but marriage? I don't even want to think about it! I don't want to marry anybody!"

"Even when you're fuming mad, I love you. This attitude, though, needs to change. Hmmm . . . think of it this way. You need never worry about whom you will marry. Instead, you can focus on all the other wonderful parts of being a young woman with a bright future ahead.

"Besides, thinking seriously about marriage right now is unnecessary. Your father and I only wanted to tell you of this to give you time to prepare for the future. We didn't want to spring it on you at the last second, so to speak."

Caityn couldn't keep the hurt out of her voice. "I don't think it would matter when you told me. I would still hate it."

She stood stiff as Ismene reached out her arms. Her mother's embrace and gentle strokes upon her head were working their magic. Caityn felt her resolve soften a bit. Ismene whispered, "Caity, you will always be you, even though you are the Princess of Taisce with a very important job to do. No one and nothing can change who you are. This will always be your choice."

CHAPTER TWO

Five Years Later...

Caityn plunked herself down on the window seat of her room where she leaned against the wall and rested her head. A chill ran up her spine as the feeling of being watched invaded her consciousness. She'd felt it so often over the years she'd learned to ignore the dread.

In a move of defiance against the uncomfortable feeling and propriety, Caityn propped her feet up on the seat in an unladylike fashion but didn't care one wit how it might look. Her mother wasn't nearby, and manners didn't seem to matter so much in the privacy of her own room anyway.

The prince must have been held up on the practice fields with his men. Caityn was expecting her betrothed for tea, but if he didn't come soon, it would be cold. He wasn't late, but her anticipation of any encounter with him grew with each passing hour.

Two days from now, she would wed the High Prince of all the realms. But the thrill of marrying wrestled against the sadness of leaving her home. Taisce was all she'd ever known. Her family and her people were precious, and the thought of leaving them made her stomach churn, but she found comfort in knowing she would be with Theiandar.

Theiandar. He had certainly come as a surprise.

She gazed out her bedroom window, thinking on the events leading up to this week, and surveyed the majestic land of her birth. She saw the distant, snow-peaked mountains and the twisting river, but superimposed upon her view were the memories of first meeting her betrothed.

Caityn closed her eyes and let the images of the past take over her tumultuous thoughts. She could picture the day they'd met when she was sixteen, but she'd not then realized he was her betrothed. She had not discerned who he was at all, except to say that she was drawn to him. He'd seemed familiar, but at the time, she hadn't known why.

Sixteen year old Caityn had known him only as the captain of a guard unit in the High King's army. His men had called him Raz. Caityn recalled seeing the twenty-one-year-old captain training with her father's men, and she'd thought him handsome. But, of course, like many shy sixteen-year-old girls, she kept it to herself. Instead, they'd formed a bond of friendship over their mutual love of horses.

The conversation they'd had after their formal introduction a year later had been horrifying. As soon as the awkward moment had begun, everyone else had cleared out, leaving them standing alone in the great hall at Taisce. Theiandar had lowered his voice anyway. Her embarrassment was beyond anything she'd ever experienced before, but watching Theiandar struggle to explain, his speech flustered and face red, had softened her anger toward him.

The only moment which caused her a second of doubt was when he'd laughed at her after she said, in honest bewilderment, "But . . . your name is Raz." She'd almost slapped him; the startling desire had been strong.

He'd rambled on about how it was a nickname the other soldiers had given him. "Raz means secret. They thought me pampered and devoid of manliness, as though it was a secret I had yet to discover. Maybe they were right, but the nickname stuck. Now I hope it implies I've learned the secret."

His apology for laughing in surprise sounded sincere, but she was still upset enough to let him sweat while she stood in silence, contemplating his words and actions over the last year. Up until the formal introduction, he'd never once implied he was the prince or her betrothed.

"Cait, I realize I've embarrassed you, and I regret it most deeply. You must know I've come to care deeply for you. It never occurred to me you were unaware of who I was . . . I mean am. Please show me mercy, my beautiful Caityn. Can you find it in your power to forgive me?"

She remembered nodding but couldn't recall if she'd said anything in reply.

He'd said, "You are the most gentle and beautiful creature I've ever known. Forgive me still, for I wasn't sure of the merit of this betrothal when my father reminded me of it. But I have relished these several times here with you. They've assured me of my father's wisdom in arranging our marriage. Honestly, I'm amazed he knew me so well. He chose exactly who I would have chosen for myself."

He'd raised her hand to his lips. The soft press of his kiss, the courtly bow of his head, and the passionate longing in his eyes all worked to melt the stony anger that had attempted to invade her heart.

That was a year ago, and she had to chuckle at herself now. She knew in her heart of hearts this man was the one she desired to be with for the rest of her life. High Prince or servant of a king—it didn't matter.

***

Her door stood slightly ajar. Adair gave a brief rap on it, but received no response, so he pushed the door open on silent hinges and leaned on the doorframe, admiring his younger sister. Caityn's head was bent in quiet prayer. He smiled knowing she was much more than a russet-haired beauty. Her charm and loveliness radiated from the inside. There was no denying how people of every station were drawn to her.

A tad regretful at interrupting her, Adair cleared his throat and grinned as Caityn swiveled around.

"Adair, you're home!" She ran to embrace him with childish abandon. "I was expecting Theian for tea, but you'll have to do. Look at you with this shocking beard! When was the last time your face saw a razor? But never mind! I was afraid you wouldn't make it back in time."

He rubbed the blondish-red hair on his chin and looked at her with a bemused expression in his blue-gray eyes. Adair took her shoulders and held her at arm's length.

"Absurd child! I'd have to be locked in a dungeon with no way of escape before I'd miss this occasion! How could I possibly pass over the wedding of my best friend to my best sister?"

She rolled her eyes and grasped his hand. "Look who's absurd now. I'm your only sister."

Adair's amused smiled spread wider as she dragged him to the table set for tea.

"Ah, yes. Of course, there's no reason you can't be the only and the best." Adair winked. "Besides, if I had to choose between you and our dear baby brother, you know I would choose you first." He paused with a mischievous look in his eyes. "But only because you're marrying my friend!"

At this, she reached over and punched him in the arm. "Very funny, Adair. And you know as well as I do, if Brennan heard you calling him a baby, he'd call you out for a duel."

He smiled. There was no denying it. Their fourteen-year-old brother, though lovable, was a bit of a hothead. The siblings were quiet for a moment while Caityn served the tea with expert ease. She sipped and Adair held his cup aloft.

"In all seriousness, you are the best sister a man could ask for."

Caityn's smile was bemused as she shook her head. "That's kind of you to say. I don't deserve praise, especially from you — the big brother I always teased and tormented."

Adair leaned back and raised his arm over his head. "Oh, we both know I only got as good as I gave."

Caityn hid her mischievous smile behind her cup. "Yes, I suppose that's true. I'm still trying to decide if I should forgive you or pay you back for the time you stuck a mouse in my pocket and set the cat to chase. Remember how she clawed me up one side and down the other? I suppose you're lucky Mother didn't have you mucking stalls and doing every dirty stable chore for a week! I was left with kitty scratches all over my arms and neck, and you ruined my best day dress, frightening me and half the household staff, I might add. Mother was likely relieved no one was truly hurt."

Adair couldn't help but laugh at the memory. "You looked hilarious, all flailing about. Besides, working in the kitchen for a week was more than enough punishment. Your honor and dress have been recompensed, I think."

Caityn's genial laughter filled the room. "Yes, I suppose kitchen duty is going to have to be enough. But do be wary dear brother." A sly wink followed the sinister tapping together of her fingers.

* * *

"How can this be? I'm not the cause of the sweet sound echoing down the hall." Theiandar stepped in to the room in time to see both Caityn and Adair turn to observe his entrance. "Should I be jealous?"

He approached the table and Adair rose, his height almost matching Theiandar's six-foot frame. The two men grasped arms in greeting.

"Welcome home, Adair. Cait was just telling me earlier she was worried you wouldn't make it back for the wedding. How was your time down seas?"

"It was fantastic, but that's a story for another day. I doubt Caity would forgive me if I usurped all your time with far off tales of adventure."

"Well, we must ensure no such usurpation occurs." Before Theiandar had even finished his sentence, he was bent low over Caityn's hand. "I'm jealous, Princess. My wish is for all your smiles and laughter to belong to me alone."

"I'm sorry to say, but it would be a selfish desire and one I certainly couldn't commit to, my lord. How dismal and lonely to horde joy all to oneself."

"Ah, then I count it joy to know you are willing to give me even a little of your smiles and laughter." His voice dropped to a whisper. "Though only because I know all your heart belongs to me."

As Theiandar sat down, his eyes never left Caityn's face. Adair was forgotten. His bemused voice interrupted the couple's distraction.

"Keep your whispering together for after the wedding and in private. Didn't your mothers tell you? Tis rude to whisper secrets in front of people."

Theiandar laughed and slapped his friend on the shoulder. "I'm happy to yell from the rooftops what I told this lovely lady. I only thought to save your ears from the intensity of my passion."

He shot Caityn a jovial smile as Adair rolled his eyes just like she was wont to do. This commonality between the siblings made Theiandar laugh again as they sat enjoying the time together. Not one of them thought anything could change this kind of happy moment or rob them of future ones. All Theiandar could think about was that in two days, just two days, this beautiful girl—no, woman—he fixed his eyes upon would be his bride and, forever, his wife.

No man deserves such a gift, he thought. *But I'll do my best to love and protect her like I do the Twelve Realms. No, more. I would give everything for both, but without her . . . I can't imagine my life without her.*

He was surprised back to the present when Caityn took his hand. "Is everything well, Theian? You seem to be a thousand miles away. Where has your mind wandered?"

Her indulgent smile was intoxicating. He stared at her, memorizing all her perfections, because even the imperfections were perfect to him. Eventually, he moved his gaze back to the window.

"Not far, really. In fact, my mind was right here, with you."

Theiandar looked back at Caityn and regarded her quizzical expression, while he placed her hand in the middle of his chest where she could feel the rhythmic beating of his heart.

"It was here. *You* are here, and I can't get you out . . . not that I would ever want to. I love you, Cait. In all honesty, I'm getting impatient for you to be my wife."

Adair was forgotten yet again, and as much as he loved these two, he must have known he was not wanted in this moment. With the same stealth in which he'd arrived, he took his leave. Neither Caityn nor Theiandar could have known how their obvious adoration for each other left him longing to have a love like theirs for himself.

CHAPTER THREE

Eliya on the Way

"Keegan, get my horse! Honestly, you are the slowest groom in the entirety of the kingdom," Eliya snapped. "Everyone else is already astride." *I'm sick to death of traveling this road.* "At this rate, we'll never arrive at all."

High Queen Zoe cantered up to where Princess Eliya waited to mount her horse and frowned. "Eliya, I realize you are tired and sore from the last few days of travel, but the way you treated poor Keegan was unkind. He is doing his job and the job of another man who only yesterday became ill."

Eliya bowed her head and stared contritely at her boots. She hadn't suspected her grumbling had been loud enough to get her mother's attention. Eliya knew she'd done wrong, but she experienced difficulty mustering up any real remorse. It was regretful her mother witnessed the episode and meant Eliya would have to apologize immediately in order to satisfy her mother's sense of right and wrong. She gave a curt nod without looking up.

It did her no good to postpone the apology, though, because her mother sat by, waiting to witness this new exchange. Less than a minute later, Keegan once more approached the gentle mare to fit the saddle in place. Eliya squared her shoulders and did her best to look regretful in the midst of a contrived apology.

"Keegan, please do forgive me for my curt and rude behavior to you a few minutes ago. I was unduly harsh and was not aware you are currently performing two jobs."

Keegan bowed low and replied, "Milady, apology's not necessary, though I accept it grateful-like. I be only sorry I don't move more quick, seein' as I would do anything to please Your Highness." He bowed again and with her slight nod of acknowledgment, he returned to finish saddling the mare.

Eliya looked up at Queen Zoe with a trace of a smile and took her mother's outstretched hand. "Thank you, Eliya, for doing what I asked. I know you did not care to do so."

"Oh, Mother, you know me well. I feel better in my heart for having said it, even though I didn't mean it like I should have. Tis strange how asking forgiveness of others can bring healing to our own hearts."

Eliya couldn't mistake the pride in Zoe's smile. "My sweet girl, you find the wisdom in each lesson I set before you. It is hard to ask forgiveness, but it is worth it when we've wronged someone."

She beamed at her mother's praise. Within a short amount of time, Keegan helped her mount her horse, and High King Dante's entourage was ready to move toward the home of King Othniel of Taisce.

Eliya was still coming to terms with the fact that soon she would have to share her big brother with this woman she'd never met. It was hard to swallow the idea, because she always thought of herself as his favorite girl in all the world. *Of course,* she mused again, *maybe it wouldn't change with a marriage.* Then again, her mother had told her of what a marriage was supposed to look like. Her own example from her parents' marriage was also enough to cause doubt. Unfortunate in this regard, Eliya's chances of staying top girl in Theiandar's affections were slim. After all, he grew up with the same parents. It was obvious he would have the same subtle knowledge imbued. They rode through the shadowy forest, and her hopes dimmed once again.

* * *

High Queen Zoe was uncomfortable and sore. She knew with certainty she was getting too old for this kind of travel. The only thing keeping her spirits up was the knowledge that in two days her son would be marrying his bride. She had never met Caityn, but Theiandar had expounded on her merits many times over the last few years. Zoe, too, would come to love Caityn.

They had been traveling from High Castle for five days now. Before nightfall they would arrive at Castle Taisce and have real beds to sleep in. The thought made her sigh, which caught her husband's attention. From his position riding alongside her, he reached his long arm over and momentarily took her hand.

"Zoe, are you well?"

"Oh!" She laughed a bit self-consciously. "Yes. Tis silly, really. I was thinking about the marriage. Then my mind wandered to arriving at the castle, which brought me to thinking about sleeping in a bed." She laughed again. "I find it amusing how thoughts can jumble together in such a way and lead down rambling paths."

High King Dante smiled at his wife. "I can agree with you, although I think women must have stranger mind ramblings than men. I think I would have arrived at your conclusion with a few less steps in between."

"Ah, yes, men and their simple minds." Zoe enjoyed teasing him. "You do realize that is why you are easy to please?"

"Ha! You jest, my dear, but 'tis only the truth. I am easy to please. I think not all men are, but you have found yourself a man who is content to ride next to you for days on end, even to the end of the world."

"Such poetry! I should blush at it, my lord." Zoe smiled at her husband before peering over her shoulder at her daughter who rode behind them. She then spoke to Dante in hushed tones. "I think our youngest is not happy about the reason for our travel. She is a bit sulky, and I caught her verbally lashing out at one of the grooms. While we anticipate this new love and remember our own, I think she's afraid she's losing something."

Her husband was quiet a moment while pondering her words. "I did notice the rather serious conversation you had with her earlier. It looked like you resolved it without incident." Dante looked over at Zoe but could see she was not satisfied with his response. "She is only sixteen yet. I'm sure her emotions are just something she will have to learn to control. I wouldn't worry about her, my dear. She isn't likely to browbeat anyone else today, and she will come to love Caityn—as will you, I'm quite sure."

"Thank you for trying to encourage me. I am feeling a bit

nervous about meeting her as well. Tell me, what is she like? I realize your acquaintance is not as extensive as Theian's, but you have a different perspective."

Again, Dante was quiet as he chose his words carefully before speaking. "She is beautiful to look at, with amber-colored hair, long and shining. Her eyes, I think, are blue-gray and quite captivating. Her skin is smooth and naturally tanned. She is a tad under your own statuesque height, and her presence is not meek in the least. I would have to say her nose is not quite straight, but it is not unpleasant."

"Oh, you're such a man! I want to know more than her looks. Tell me what she's like on the inside. Tell me who she is as a woman."

Dante laughed. "Oh! I was sure I was doing just that, but let me try again." He cleared his throat. "When I first remember meeting her, she was such a wee thing, maybe three years old. She had tumbled from her horse while in training, and our own son carried her to the castle. I happened to watch as Theiandar handed her over to Othniel. Zoe, Theian was inspiring, even then. He was completely out of breath and looked as though his arms might fall off his body, but he was also elated. I could tell he felt like he'd conquered the world by carrying her up the hill."

"My dear, you're running off course. I would like to hear about Caityn. Of course, I always love to hear our son highly spoken of, but him I know!" Zoe's smile was contagious.

"Too right, love. As I was saying, she had fallen from her horse. As soon as she was in her father's arms she calmed quickly. The next day, though, after being cleared by the physician, she was right back on the very same horse. Having seen this, I believe she is certainly courageous. And over the two or three times I've had occasion to meet her since then, I've found her to be gentle, seeking wisdom, patient, and compassionate. If anything, she will be an asset to the kingdom, a faithful wife to our son, and even a great friend to Eliya."

Zoe smiled at him, her heart once again relieved by his words. Their son would have a beautiful wife—one truly beautiful, not just a pretty face. For Zoe, this had always been her utmost desire for her son's marriage. Now that it was happening, the same hope bloomed for her only daughter.

As her thoughts drifted in the direction of Eliya's future mate, her eyes wandered across the countryside they had entered. It was fully noon and almost time to stop for midday meal, which was good because she was ravenous.

* * *

The group stopped for the noon meal, and Princess Eliya slid off her horse with more bounce in her step than at the outset of the day. Even though she ached in places she didn't know existed, it was refreshing to be out in the countryside.

Her home, High Castle, was situated on a hill next to Solfen River, but the area all around was fairly flat and somewhat mundane. This place, Taisce, had true majesty. The land's backdrop was mountains looming before them as though they were giants at rest. She was captivated by this view to the north as soon as they cleared the forest. Here, the air felt fresh and cool.

Eliya walked a short distance away from the group, certain she would hear those great peaks speaking to her if she could get far enough from the sounds of the people and animals. She closed her eyes and felt the soft breeze roll over her neck and cheeks. The wisps of wind pulled at her raven hair and tickled her forehead.

Listening intently, Eliya thought she heard the sound of a creek nearby. She opened her eyes and looked back to see everyone busy. Instead of bothering them, she decided to take a look for herself.

She could tell the sound was not far. She headed through the tall grass toward a copse of birch trees. The sound of gurgling water grew louder. Eliya took cautious steps through the brush as it became thicker and more uneven. When she reached the water's edge, she froze. She thought she saw or heard something on the other side, though nothing seemed to move except the grass in the breeze. Eliya relaxed and looked closer but still saw nothing. After a moment, her eyes traveled back down to the bubbling brook making its way lazily through the stand of trees.

She bent down to touch the water, but before her fingers skimmed the cool, wet rocks at the edge, a hand shot out and grabbed her arm. Eliya's breath caught in her throat.

"My lady." His voice was a deep rumble, sending shivers down her spine. "Why have you wandered from the group?"

Her immediate desire was to quell the rush of fear by which she'd been overcome. She didn't answer right away but looked down at his hand, still wrapped around her upper arm.

In an abrupt manner, he dropped his hold and bowed his head. "I'm sorry, my lady, but while this is part of the Twelve Realms, 'tis one of the more dangerous parts. You shouldn't leave the group unattended."

Because her pride was smarting and her heart was still racing, she didn't reply right away. She also forced herself to ignore the intensity of his deep blue eyes.

"I can take care of myself, thank you very much. You certainly didn't need to accost me to prove how dangerous it is here." A quick survey of the area around the creek revealed nothing, except to prove to her that they were alone. "I was fine until you showed up. What's your name? I recognize you from my brother's guard, but I don't know you."

She stared at his downturned face and could see the color rising in his cheeks. She must have embarrassed him. *Well, good,* she thought. *Serves him right.*

He looked up, only to stare straight into her eyes. It confused her when he gawked and didn't answer. Eliya self-consciously touched her hair before her growing confusion morphed into frustration. "Well, soldier, out with it. What's your name? I should have you punished for unduly grabbing me." Eliya raised her eyebrows with mock severity. "You're lucky I'm only curious."

He gave his head a slight jiggle to clear his thoughts. "I'm Gavin of Taisce, Your Highness. I apologize for causing you any distress. I truly was entirely worried for your safety."

"Well, Gavin of Taisce, you are forgiven, although if it happens again I may have to enlist the help of my handy dagger." She couldn't hold back her puckish sarcasm.

Gavin laughed. He'd caught on to her humor, but she had no idea the joker in him wanted to offer an equally sarcastic reply. The thought of further banter was cut short, though, when Gavin's head swiveled to scrutinize the bushes on the other side of the brook.

Some protective instinct must have overcome him as he stepped around Eliya and scanned the distant terrain. Eliya sensed the change in him and stood still, looking out into the woods. After a time, Gavin spoke in a low voice. "Please walk straight back to the camp, my lady. I am right behind you."

Eliya, caught up in the serious timbre of his voice, didn't hesitate to obey. Without a second thought, she flitted out of the copse of trees and across the grassy plain. The questioning look on her father's face didn't go unnoticed when she arrived at the camp, breathless and a bit disheveled. He made no inquiry of her whereabouts, though, for which she was grateful.

She watched Gavin return some minutes later. He went straight to High King Dante's general. Shortly after their brief conference, they were all loaded and on their way, everyone anticipating a good night's rest ahead, safely behind the castle walls.

CHAPTER FOUR
Family

Theiandar and Caityn, along with her family, waited at the top of the keep's entrance stairs for his family to arrive. Caityn was nervous as she clasped her hands in front of her belly. Theiandar noticed her unease and reached out, taking her hand in his to give it a gentle squeeze.

"Don't worry, Cait. My family won't eat you alive. Besides, you already know my father, and he has to be the most intimidating and impressive one of the bunch."

She looked up at him. "I'm sure you're right, but I can't help being nervous. What if your mother disapproves of me? What if your sister and I don't become friends? There are only two years between us, and we'll be living in the same castle. I don't know how I'll handle it if your family dislikes me."

Theiandar's good-natured laugh echoed off the castle wall as he placed his arm protectively around her shoulders.

"You have nothing to worry about then, because they will love you as I love you."

Caityn gave him another timid smile and was silent as her gaze returned to the tops of the buildings opposite them.

Nervous anticipation clouded her vision as she waited for the imminent arrival of her soon-to-be in-laws. She knew Theiandar meant well, but the disquiet was persistent.

They did not have long to wait. The caravan marched up the hill toward the keep within minutes of Theiandar's reassurances. The first through the gate was the High King's general with Caityn's cousin and dear friend, Gavin, by his side.

Gavin was the son of her mother's brother and a guard in the High King's army. In fact, he had special placement in Theiandar's Royal Guard, being specially chosen for this position because he was from Taisce. Each subkingdom had one son in the High King's Royal Guard. While only eighteen, the same age as Caityn, he was also given this honor because he'd proved his strength was balanced by prudence and courage.

Caityn was proud of Gavin, and some of the anxiety melted at the sight of him sitting tall on his black steed. Surely if Gavin could travel to places unknown and defend her dear country, then she could meet her future in-laws with a brave and steady heart.

She took a slow, deep breath, determined to handle this introduction with grace. Theiandar must have sensed her resolve, because he wrapped his arm around her shoulders. The look of joy and anticipation at seeing his family today was reflected twofold in his eyes.

The rest of the travelers followed behind the High King and Queen. Caityn could only assume the young girl behind them was their daughter, her soon-to-be sister-in-law. There was no more time to prepare for the encounter. Attendants dashed forward to help the ladies and hold the mounts as the riders approached the base of the stairs.

Gavin jumped down first and quickly made his way to Princess Eliya. With swift movements, he reached up to offer his assistance in her descent. Bemused, Caityn watched him, knowing he was more of a flirt than gallant. After he received thanks from Eliya, Gavin bowed. He turned toward the steps where his eye caught Caityn's. He winked. She laughed at his antics and found herself relaxing. She waved in return before letting her own eyes follow Theiandar's movement. Instead, the High Queen of the Realms caught her attention.

She tried to keep smiling, but could only think that Theiandar was wrong. His mother, Queen Zoe, was impressive. Zoe was almost six feet tall, surely. Caityn was not considered short at five feet eight inches, yet she was sure she would feel inadequate in the High Queen's presence.

She stared long and hard and couldn't miss the look of love etched upon Queen Zoe's face while she embraced her son. It was beautiful and terrifying to see. Caityn mused it meant Zoe would love her as well, or she would hate Caityn for coming between her and her son. She suppressed the disconcerting thought by biting her tongue. Caityn found it difficult to make her stiff legs walk down the steps to greet her guests.

Her mother was already embracing her longtime friend, the High Queen. Caityn approached with trepidation. Ismene reached out her hand, taking Caityn's in her own, and said, "Zoe, may I introduce to you my daughter, Caityn. If I must share her with another mother, I can think of no other with whom I would rather do so than you."

Zoe's smile was bright, and instead of taking the hand Caityn extended to her, High Queen Zoe reached out to embrace her. "We won't be formal, dear girl. My men have told me all about you, and I am sure I must already love you, since I feel tears of joy close to escaping."

Caityn was surprised and relieved by the embrace. It took her only seconds to return it. When she did, it felt right and perfect. She smiled. "Thank you, Queen Zoe. My nerves have been getting the better of me this evening, and your welcome of me is refreshing. I, too, look forward to our familial union."

"Please, Caityn, call me Zoe. We'll not use such formality as family."

"Thank you, Zoe."

"Now." Zoe beckoned her daughter to come forward. Eliya had already been greeted by her brother, and now Caityn found herself dreading this new introduction. Eliya, while slow to move, obeyed her mother's call. "Caityn, I would like for you to meet my own daughter, Eliya. Eliya, this is Theiandar's bride-to-be, Caityn."

Sensing a tension here she wasn't sure what to do with, Caityn put out her hand in greeting. "Tis a pleasure to meet you, Eliya. Theian speaks highly of you, and I look forward to us becoming fast friends."

Eliya looked at Caityn's hand, reluctance evident in her very stance, before taking it in her own. She took obvious pains to coax the appropriate reply from her lips. "Thank you, Princess Caityn. The pleasure is mine."

* * *

Theiandar could see the introductions were already being made between his bride and his family. He didn't let it worry him too much when Gavin approached him and quietly asked to speak in private. Theiandar agreed, and the two men walked a few paces away from the ruckus.

"I'm sorry to interrupt your greetings, Sire, but, while most of the trip was uneventful, we did have one possible incident along the road. About three hours ago, we stopped for the midday meal, and the princess took a short stroll to the creek near the road. I happened to notice her departure from the group and followed her in order to assure her safety.

"But, while at the creek, I sensed a presence. I thought I saw movement, but couldn't quite place it. It was definitely not any animal I'm familiar with. I sent the princess back to the assembly and tried to follow whatever it was I'd seen. It moved through the underbrush and slunk away before I was able to track it. Your Highness, there was no trail. I'm sorry. I might have easily failed, and the princess could have been in real danger."

Theiandar placed his hand on his friend's shoulder. Even though he was barely five years older than Gavin, Theiandar felt a certain fatherly spirit toward him. "Don't be too hard on yourself, Gav. You did your best, and I'm grateful for your vigilant protection over my family. No harm has befallen any of the group, and I commend you for it." He smiled reassuringly. "Thank you for sharing this information, though, since we will need to set up a few extra watches over the course of the remaining days. In fact, I'd like you to organize them for me."

Gavin, eager to please the prince, replied with a salute. "Yes, Sire! It will be my honor. Thank you, Sire." Theiandar smiled and punched him in the shoulder.

"No, thank *you*. With you handling it, I'm freed up to be with my bride! Make sure you give yourself opportunity to come to tomorrow night's celebration, though. I think Caityn would be disappointed in me if I didn't ensure your presence for at least one dance."

Gavin grinned back. "No, Sire, I wouldn't miss it for anything."

"All right, soldier, you're dismissed."

Gavin did a smart turn on his heel before marching away toward the barracks.

Theiandar watched him go with a smile on his face, but he didn't miss the stealthy approach of someone from behind. He didn't know who it was at first, until the faint scent of sweet coconut wafted past his nose. He waited until the last moment then spun around, lifting his sister in his arms again. This time it was a huge bear hug.

"Ah, thought you could sneak up on me, did you?"

While the breath was being squeezed out of her, she gasped. "Oh, you big galoot! Let me down! You're squeezing the life out of me."

He smiled and loosened his grip without setting her down. "There, is that better, little one?"

Eliya's glower was only halfhearted. She loved this game they'd been playing since she was a wee toddler. She freed one of her hands and reached up to pinch his nose, which made Theiandar's mouth gape open. "I'm sixteen. And two can play at this game." The look she gave him was triumphant.

Theiandar set her down, and she released his nose but not before planting a kiss on his cheek. "I've missed you! Why did you have to come here so early? Isn't it the bride's job to plan the wedding? You could have waited and traveled with us. Then I wouldn't have had to put up with nosy guards." Her pert lips puckered and eyebrows lifted.

He could tell she was only half joking. Theiandar chucked her on the chin. "Now, now, little one, you know exactly why I came when I did. Besides, I would have been much nosier as your brother than any guard would presume to be with my Little Miss Pouty Face here."

She sucked in her lips and her glower returned, but her knew she couldn't stay mad at him. She responded by crossing her arms.

"I am not little."

Theiandar laughed out loud and hugged her again. "You, Eliya, will always be little to me." She rolled her eyes but smiled. He put his arm around her shoulder, and they strolled along to the keep's entrance.

* * *

Caityn entered with her mother and Queen Zoe. After seeing them to the guest chambers, she returned to the main entrance in search of Theiandar. She glimpsed him ambling up the steps with his sister wrapped in his strong arm. Her countenance fell a little.

Her reception by the king and queen had been more than cordial, but Eliya evinced her reticence toward friendship. Caityn could see how close a bond the siblings shared. She needed things to go well between herself and Eliya. With new boldness, she stepped from the shadows, a smile in place.

"Ah, there you two are! Your mother and father are settling in their chambers, and I would be pleased to show you to your room, Eliya."

Her courage was slightly shaken when Eliya replied, "Oh, no. Thank you, though. Theiandar can show me to my room." Caityn noted Eliya's adoration of her brother. "Besides, he and I have some catching up to do."

A slight frown creased Theiandar's brow, but he didn't respond. In the half-second of silence, Caityn was aware this would be much more difficult than she anticipated. "Of course, I understand completely. You're directly across the hall from your parents. Please make yourself at home. my lady, Idra, who is my cousin, is available to answer any questions you have about the castle or our prized Taisce."

Theiandar must have seen the look of disappointment cross her face because he chose that moment to interrupt. "No, Caityn, you really should show Eliya to her room to rest and prepare for the evening meal. I have some business to attend to right now. I will see you both at dinner."

He gave Eliya an almost stern look. "We will have plenty of time to catch up later." At this, he squeezed Eliya's hand and reached out to take Caityn's, which he kissed before meeting her eyes. Caityn smiled back.

Theiandar departed down a side hall. His hasty exit left the two young women alone. They looked at each other in awkward silence until Caityn gestured toward the interior stairway leading up to the guest rooms. There was only a slight hesitation before they both glided up the steps.

The stiffness of the moment grew heavy between them until Caityn could stand it no longer. She stopped and touched Eliya's arm. "Eliya, I think we've gotten off on the wrong foot. I'm not sure what is causing this tension between us, but I hope, truly, we can become friends. Your brother means a great deal to me, and because of him, so you all do.

"As you know . . . Of course you know." She shook her head in frustration at not finding the right words. "We'll soon be sisters. I've always wanted a sister." Caityn paused. "Please, can we try again, if not for me then for your brother's sake?"

Eliya's look was hard to read in the deepening shadows of the castle hall. "Fine. But I don't know you, and I don't particularly care to get to know you. I have plenty of friends and don't need another one. I'm only willing to try for Theiandar, not you."

Caityn was disappointed, but accepted it for the olive branch it was. "Thank you, Eliya. I'm sure you won't regret it. I know I won't." With a fake smile in place she led Eliya down the hall.

After seeing to the preparation of Eliya's bath and making sure she was settled in her room, Caityn excused herself. She stepped out into the hall and leaned heavily on the closed door. With her head bowed, she said a silent prayer. She raised her eyes, pushed off from the door feeling much older than eighteen, and retired to her room to prepare for dinner.

CHAPTER FIVE
Castle Taisce

Theiandar walked away from Caityn and Eliya with a feeling of disquiet. He couldn't quite tell what had gotten into Eliya, but she wasn't acting like herself. He only hoped she and Caityn would be able to work it out between the two of them. He wasn't at all sure he understood how the female mind worked.

As much as he loved his sister, there were still times when he was confounded by her. So far, Caityn had been easy. Every time he and his guard unit had made their rounds through Taisce in the last couple years, there had been opportunities to spend time with her.

She was beautiful to look at, but she was also enjoyable to be around. Caityn was lively, entertaining in conversation, and never stingy with her smile. He had also witnessed her kindness to her people and the generosity she shared with anyone in need. He'd had no occasion to see anything but goodness in her. However, being a wise soldier, he knew looks could be deceiving. If it wasn't for the fact that everyone who knew Caityn adored her, he would question her goodness, but as it was, there was no need.

He was wrapped up in his thoughts as he walked and almost bumped into his father. High King Dante was in quiet conversation with King Othniel.

"My apologies, Father, I didn't see you there! My mind was wandering." His sheepish grin gave away the fact that he'd been daydreaming.

Dante squeezed his son's shoulder. "Not to worry, my boy. Othniel and I were discussing the supposed sighting of something uncommon in the wood along the road. Your man . . . Gavin, is it?" Theiandar nodded. "He informed the general of it after our noon meal, and though there was no evidence to support it, I decided to take it seriously since you have such confidence in the young man."

Othniel spoke up. "Yes . . . a wise decision. My nephew also has my full confidence. Not to worry you, but I was telling your father of how before you arrived a week ago, two strange sightings occurred in the wood outside the castle wall.

"One of the incidents was when it was dark. A guard saw something moving in the shadow next to the sewer outlet, which is covered by a sturdy, locked grate. The other sighting was during the day, by one of our regular cattlemen from Nashua.

"His cows were behaving oddly, and there was a dark thing he couldn't describe just off in the grass next to the road. One of his boys said his cows tried to run several times, and his dog chased after something in the field. Eventually, the dog returned with a cut on its nose. Now my man, Geir, has added an extra lookout to be posted at night, and the gates are closed at dark."

"I've also asked Gavin to set up extra patrol guards around the castle. I'm sure he'll coordinate with Geir and have the castle secure at all times," Theiandar said.

"Very good. Thank you for your initiative. With the wedding upon us, there are many new faces in the castle and thus more people to protect. The extra guard is an advantage."

Dante agreed. "Yes, the people of the realms are here to celebrate this occasion, and we will make sure they are able to do so in safety!"

At this point, Theiandar felt his presence was no longer necessary. He excused himself and continued down the hall on his way to the barracks. Theiandar could have a room in the castle, but until the wedding, he chose to stay with his men.

It would be odd to have this change after years of inclusion in the brotherhood of soldiers. He was almost sorry to be losing it . . . almost. There was no denying that having Caityn sleeping next to him and holding her softness against him would be worth the loss of the barracks. Come to think of it, he didn't feel sorry about it at all.

* * *

For the umpteenth time that day, Eliya's guilt over her behavior crowded into her mind. She couldn't seem to change her attitude for any length of time. What on earth is wrong with me? She slunk lower in the warm bath water and let the heat relax her tight muscles.

Closing her eyes, Eliya promised herself, at the very least, she would try to be friendly to Caityn. Theiandar's behavior toward her hadn't really changed—not yet. It gave her some hope. She wanted him to forever be the close and special brother she'd always known.

Besides, it wasn't like her to be sulky and rude. Caityn hadn't done anything to deserve her censure. It was only right that Eliya at least try to be pleasant and kind. She recalled the incident with Keegan and tried to hold on to the feeling she got from apologizing to him. The realization occurred to her that she should probably apologize to Caityn as well, at some point anyway. *Then again*, she thought, *maybe if I just change my behavior toward her that will be enough.*

Eliya let her thoughts wander as the water warmed her from the outside in. Soon enough she would have to crawl out of the pleasantness of the tub and dress for dinner, where she would need to fulfill the promise she made to herself.

* * *

A soft knock sounded on Caityn's door. She called out a greeting, and upon seeing her mother she stood, offering a weak smile.

"Mother, what brings you here before dinner? Don't you still need to prepare?"

Ismene approached the vanity, gently forced Caityn back down on the seat and took over pinning her hair in place before answering.

"Yes. But I was on my way from visiting with Zoe, and I wanted to check in on you."

"Thank you, Mother. I'm well."

Ismene's hand cupped her daughter's cheek, "I know you better than that, my sweet. I noticed the tension coming from Eliya during your introduction, and I wanted you to know her mother did as well. Zoe tells me Eliya has been in a mood all day. She has always been discerning, and I believe her when she says Eliya is jealous of you."

"Jealous! Of me? Why?"

The confusion on her face must have amused her mother, because Ismene laughed.

"Caityn, don't forget, Theiandar is Eliya's only sibling. His age at her birth was far enough advanced that he is almost like a second father to her. She's jealous of his attachment to you, and she likely has fears about the marriage changing everything."

"But, Mama, he isn't that much older than me, and I'm only two years older than her. How can he be like a second father to her?"

"Well, you see, he was seven when she was born, and his parents felt it was important for him to be acquainted with his new sister almost right away. Soon after her birth, she was placed in his waiting arms. Like everyone else, he fell in love with her sweet face. He has adored her since then and treated her with special attention her whole life."

Caityn pondered what her mother said. "I think I see, but do you think it will ever get better between us? Eliya was dismissive of me earlier. Honestly, I'm afraid of offending her."

"Not to worry, dearest. She will come 'round. Just be yourself, and eventually she'll trust that you are a wonderful addition to her life, not someone to be feared. Don't take it personally if she seems rude. Zoe assures me this is not how she normally treats people. She feels Eliya needs time to adjust."

"I'll have to take your word for it, Mother. I trust you and Queen Zoe. She's already shown me kindness. I was grateful for her reception of me earlier and was literally weak with relief." Ismene hugged her then and left to prepare for dinner.

Caityn felt better after their conversation. She faced the mirror to finish her hair. She could have the chambermaid do it, but it was something she enjoyed doing herself. As she plaited the last braid and wrapped it around the others at the base of her neck, she nodded in approval. A little self-assurance seemed necessary.

"Caityn, everything is going to be fine. Theiandar loves you. His parents are already warm and welcoming to you. Eliya will come around soon enough." Closing her eyes, she said a quick prayer, too. "Great One, please help me be patient and gracious."

* * *

The night's dinner was an intimate affair and somewhat quiet as well. The traveling party was tired from their journey, and the rest were sensitive to their friends' laconic leanings.

The two royal families dined around one table. At each end of the table sat the two kings. The arrangement put Eliya almost directly across from Caityn, so she did her best to smile and make conversation with Theiandar's only sister. She did notice a positive difference in Eliya's behavior toward her, which was welcome. Perhaps Eliya had needed a bit of rest and to freshen up.

Dessert was winding down and Othniel used the time to quiz his daughter's betrothed.

"Theiandar, I am sure this has already been discussed amongst the important parties, but after the wedding, to where do you plan to abscond with my daughter?"

The sound of Theiandar clearing his throat echoed through the dining hall. "Well, sir, we'll journey to Marodan and take one of my father's lesser ships to Negeen, a tiny island off the coast."

"Ah, it has been a long time!" Othniel said. "You know, I once set my feet on Negeen. It is picturesque and will afford you a few adventures. If I remember rightly, there is a waterfall with a cave full of sparkling gems behind it."

Theiandar smiled across at Caityn. She beamed back, her cheeks touched by heat, as he replied to her father.

"If we have time, we'll surely have to explore, but I'll already be with the only jewel worth admiring." His eyes stayed fixed on hers. For Caityn, the rest of the table was forgotten.

King Dante interrupted the silence with a low whistle, and Caityn's gazed dropped to her hand in her lap, the heat of her face increasing tenfold.

The room seemed to hold its breath until Theiandar's good-natured laugh broke the silence.

Caityn finally looked up but happened to make eye contact with Eliya. Theian's younger sister was not smiling or laughing, and the earlier concern about their tenuous friendliness returned, but when Theiandar's smile entered her view, she was able to return it with little effort.

Caityn knew she was easy to get along with, but making close friends had never been easy for her. Knowing Eliya wasn't interested in friendship with her made it feel all the more daunting. It would have comforted Caityn knowing Theiandar was on her side, but this was his sister, not a stranger. At this point it was impossible to know exactly who he'd side with in the end.

Shortly after dessert was through, everyone retired for the night. Tomorrow was the last day to prepare for the wedding, and they were to have a grand celebration with all the dignitaries and people who had come to attend. It was to be a banquet followed by dancing and other festivities.

Caityn enjoyed celebrations, and this one would be even more special. She was walking on clouds as her gallant prince escorted her to her chamber.

Theiandar stopped in front of her door, his hand resting on the knob, but he didn't look at her as he spoke in hushed tones.

"Caity, if you'd had a choice, would you have picked me?"

She hadn't expected his question, especially not that one. She'd been told when she was thirteen she didn't have a choice, and after a short battle of will she'd accepted her fate on behalf of her people and all the realms.

The tension rolling off of him as he waited for her answer was palpable.

"What a thing to ask, Theian."

Caityn imagined she could feel the erratic rhythm of his heart from a foot away, and something induced her to close the gap.

He was facing the door, frozen like a statue, but she hugged him from the side and rested her upturned chin on the edge of his shoulder.

"Would I choose you? Yes, a thousand times, yes."

Caityn laughed when his whole body sagged with relief. He turned into her embrace and wrapped his arms around her.

"Really, Cait? Because I don't want you to say you would merely to avoid a confrontation or out of duty."

His stare was intense and had an unnerving effect on Caityn, but not in an unpleasant way. It was a sensation she couldn't quite place, one she almost enjoyed.

"Don't be ridiculous. I fell in love with you the first time I saw you. Well, the first time I remember seeing you. I wouldn't admit it to myself at the time, but I was smitten with you as Raz and dreaded the day I'd have to meet my betrothed." She laid her head against his chest. He was steady like his heartbeat. "I'm glad that day transpired like it did. I love you."

He reached up to touch her hair, and suddenly she felt a pin come loose. Her braids fell, scattering around her shoulders. She looked up at him, but the chastisement she'd almost begun died on her lips. She lost her senses in the obvious look of adoration he wore.

"I love you, too," he whispered.

She closed her eyes. Sheer contentment flooded her soul and desire for this man of hers tempted her to lean in. Her eyes opened, and with great reluctance she pressed her palms against his chest instead. Yearning for him warred with her better judgment.

"Goodnight, kind sir."

Theiandar caught her hand on his chest and pulled the inside of her wrist to his lips. "Only two more nights without you. I don't know if I can endure."

"I feel the same, but we must . . . and we will. We won't regret it." She had to repeat it all in her head.

Caityn loved that he held her hand in his while he opened the door. It felt right in every respect.

But once the door was ajar there was a cold rush of air and an eerie chill which swept over her, disrupting her elation. Everything was as she'd left it except the window. Oddly, it was unbolted and tapping in the slight breeze. After surveying the undisturbed room, she decided the chambermaid must have forgotten it open.

She shrugged off the sudden disquiet and offered her hand to Theiandar who gently kissed it. It was with impish pleasure she closed the door in his smitten face.

Caityn walked to the window, latched it, and settled at the vanity all the while scanning the shadows without knowing why, only sure something wasn't right.

She undid the braids Theiandar had unpinned and brushed out her hair. Caityn giggled as she recalled the silly look on his face, first at dessert and then again at her door. She knew what was to come—being married and wifely duties and all—because her mother had explained it to her in detail. Remembering those conversations made her blush again, but at the same time, she was in love with Theiandar. She wanted to please him. Her excitement grew with every passing touch and teasing him tonight had been fun.

A knock sounded at the door, interrupting her thoughts. Bimala entered. Caityn was surprised to see her old nursery maid. It wasn't a complete shock, though, because she did stop by from time to time. Like always, Caityn was happy to see Bimala and rose to embrace her.

"Bima! I'm happy you're here."

"My sweet little princess, how could I stay away? You have been in my care and in my heart since you were born. I only came to brush your hair for you one last time and tuck you in as I used to do each night. I miss my little princess at these moments, and soon you will be outside my reach." Bimala stroked Caityn's hair. "Oh, precious girl, I will miss you terribly." A tear slipped down her weathered cheek.

Caityn struggled to keep her own tears at bay due to the older woman's tender words. "Yes, please do my hair and tuck me in." She smiled at the thought. "You are like a second mother to me, Bima. I love you and will miss you, too."

Neither woman had more words to say as they moved to sit cross-legged on the bed.

After a time, Bimala said, "My princess, I lied a moment ago. I have one other reason for coming tonight. Would you do a favor for me when you are at High Castle?"

"Of course, Bimala, I would do almost anything for you." One couldn't mistake the smile in Caityn's voice. She knew she would attempt to do whatever her dear friend asked of her.

Bimala stopped brushing and pulled a small item from her pocket. She handed it to Caityn. While she examined it, Bimala picked up the brush again. The older woman brushed a few more strokes before weaving Caityn's hair into one long braid.

The princess knew Bimala would explain when she was ready. She waited patiently. After the braid was complete, Bimala came to sit in front of her on the bed and gestured at the object in Caityn's hand. "That belongs to my . . . belonged to my son."

Caityn remembered Bimala's son, Braden. He was three years older than Adair and had been in her father's army. He was married to Kendra, a girl from Nevin, and they had been stationed in the north country of Taisce. His unit protected the diamond mines at the base of the hills.

There had been an attack from the people of the Dark Lands, and Braden had been among the wounded. At the time, Kendra had taken a journey to Nevin to visit her family. She could not make it back to Taisce to say goodbye to her dying husband.

Because Kendra had no children or family in Taisce, she did not return for his burial. Even if she'd been able to afford the journey without him, she wouldn't have made it in time anyway. Bimala had been able to say good-bye to her son, but as Braden lay dying he asked her to give his wedding ring to his wife.

"It was a year ago when my sweet boy died, my little princess, and I have not been able to fulfill my promise. Please take the ring to Kendra. Nevin is not far from High Castle. Tis less than two days." The longing to have her son's life back was evident as she stared at the plain wedding band.

Caityn looked down at it, too. Because she loved Bimala, she knew, inconvenient or not, she would fulfill this meager request. "Of course I am happy to do this for you, Bimala."

Caityn took a leather hair strap from the vanity and put it through the ring, tying it around her neck. "For safekeeping."

Bimala's tears streamed down her cheeks while she nodded. It was obvious she was overwhelmed. Without a word, she gestured for Caityn to lie down. Bimala gently covered the princess and kissed her forehead.

"Goodnight, my gentle princess."

Her whisper was barely audible through her tears. Caityn's heart ached for her nursery maid as the older woman gave one more pained smile then slipped out the door.

CHAPTER SIX
A Celebration and a Curse

The next day, people buzzed and scurried all over the castle in preparation for that night's celebration and the next day's ceremony. Caityn was visited early by the dressmakers, checking her bridal gown and trousseau to ensure no more alterations were necessary.

She breakfasted with her parents and guests. After her hurried meal, she continued to work through the list of necessary work to be done, and she felt like a whirlwind dashing through the castle halls, giving orders, and answering questions.

As Caityn went from the kitchen back to her room to indulge in a short nap before the noon meal, she couldn't help but gaze at the family portraits lining the walls. Hundreds of years of family history stared back at her through haunting eyes. Some had eyes unable to conceal laughter; others were stern, and still others implied sorrow beyond sorrow. It was while contemplating one particularly sour-looking monarch that she quite literally bumped into Eliya.

"Oh! I beg your pardon, Eliya." Slight embarrassment permeated her laugh. "I should have been looking where I was walking."

Eliya looked vaguely disgruntled, but instead of a harsh reply, she said, "Tis well. I was woolgathering and not paying attention either."

Caityn thought she looked embarrassed at her own revelation. Eliya shook her head as if to rid it of any unpleasant thoughts.

"But our meeting is fortuitous, Caityn. I can't find your cousin. Would you tell me the best way to exit the castle walls? I feel a need for some fresh air and solitude. You must know High Castle is much larger. I really don't think we'd have noticed the crowds had the wedding been there instead."

She tried not to take offense at the last statement. Instead, Caityn focused on what Eliya had asked of her. "Of course, I would be glad to tell you how to get beyond the walls. In fact, if I had more time I'd take you myself."

"Oh, that won't be necessary."

"You should stop at the stables and ask for a groom to accompany you, though. Taisce is beautiful to explore, but there's danger outside our walls. The Dark Lands are not far north, and they have a tendency to raid our region looking to . . . pillage and plunder, you could say."

Eliya didn't appear to care and her tone was dismissive when she said, "I appreciate the concern. Which way do I go?"

Caityn didn't feel she had the right to insist the young woman take an escort.

"There's only the one gate in and out. You'll need to go out the front stairs. The stables are on the way down the hill, and the gate is just beyond there. Eliya, before you go, if I may suggest, the best place to walk is to the left and up the hill toward the mountains. There's a restful little waterfall over the rise. It isn't far."

Eliya halted mid-turn and gave a curt nod. "Thank you. See you tonight."

Caityn couldn't help but recognize Eliya's forced smile and stilted reply. She shook her head as her future sister-in-law floated with queenly grace down the hall.

Feelings of defeat and rejection warred with her stubbornness. She almost gave up the idea of a nap in order to follow Eliya. *Just to make sure she gets a groom and is safe.* Eventually, she decided retreat was the best option, knowing it wouldn't endear her to Eliya to follow where she wasn't wanted. She only hoped to win her over another day.

* * *

Caityn looked around at all the new faces and smiled as everyone sat down for dinner. There were many people she recognized, but the new ones outweighed them by a great deal. She was seated at the head table between Theiandar and her elder brother, Adair.

Looking between the two of them, she indulged in a masculine comparison. Both men were above average height and handsome. Adair looked much like herself in coloring, while Theiandar had dark hair with startling blue eyes. Theiandar's short waves of raven hair were unruly and tangled about his head in an attractive mess. His build was a bit more muscular than Adair, but not surprising since Theiandar was a soldier, while her brother had been more inclined toward the scholarly side of things after he'd completed his training with

Othniel's guard. Even though their features and coloring were nothing alike, they were much the same in character. Theiandar and Adair were both protective of their loved ones. They cared deeply for the Twelve Realms, were educated and honest—not to mention brave and strong.

Of course, Caityn herself was considered a beautiful young woman. While there had been times in her youth when she had cared more for her outer beauty than the inner, she had not stayed focused there long. Her own gentle heart and her upbringing had both played a part in forming her values. Her education as a princess had involved caring for the needs of her people, the people of Taisce, which proved to bring out the best in her.

While she sat there in the banquet hall, watching all the well-wishers enjoying the celebration, she overcome by untold emotion as she contemplated all her years here in Taisce with the people she loved.

Over the years, she'd helped in the little village school near the castle; learned the inner workings of every part of running a large home with many servants; she'd cared for the sick, elderly, and widowed; inspected harvests; taken food to the needy. Her life was full and happy here. She was humbled by this place, and her heart was softened by the love she'd received for all her duty had required of her.

Caityn knew she had much for which to be thankful. Sitting in the banquet hall, surrounded by laughter and feasting, she was overwhelmed with gratitude. Tears escaped, coursing down her cheeks, but she quickly wiped at her face to rid herself of the evidence.

* * *

Eliya was seated down the table from Theiandar and Caityn and didn't mind letting her disappointment show. She found herself situated between two unpleasant individuals. The first one was a dull woman. It had been like pulling teeth to even learn her name. And the other was a distant cousin of Caityn's, a bishop of some-such-or-other. He was overly forward through the entire meal. In fact, Eliya was certain he had imbibed far too much wine, and the intimacy of his hand resting on her knee was the last straw.

With practiced stealth, she removed her dagger from her secret skirt-pocket and jabbed at his hand. He cried out and quickly excused himself.

Eliya only hoped she hadn't injure him too badly and that he was intoxicated enough to forget how it had happened. It didn't stop her smile, though, at the thought of him waking up and wondering what trouble he'd gotten into the night before.

As she slid the lady's dagger back into the pocket of her dress, her hand brushed on the vial of potion the gnomish man at the waterfall had given her earlier in the afternoon. The young princess drew her hand back as if burned but quickly steeled her nerves before reaching for the bottle again. She squeezed it tight.

It still didn't sit well in Eliya's mind, what the strange old man had said, but she couldn't stop thinking about it. *What if what he said is true? Could it really be that Caityn is a liar, that she is unworthy of Theiandar? That she will be the ruin of the realms? And how does the little man know?*

At the time, Eliya hadn't promised him she would do it, but he did convince her to take the vial. He seemed so sure of himself, and he made it sound so simple. Besides, if she did what this stranger suggested, it wouldn't be terrible. She wasn't actually doing any physical harm. Right? He also seemed kind and compassionate, wanting to protect her brother from a terrible match and a broken heart, not to mention a disastrous union which was sure to tear the kingdom apart. *Why would he invent such a story anyway?*

She released the miniature bottle and reached for her glass. As she sipped, she noticed the dancing was about to begin. Eliya loved to dance. Until her thoughts had turned dismal, she'd been looking forward to it. Now, she watched as Theiandar led Caityn onto the dance floor.

Her knuckles whitened as she wrapped her fingers tight around her glass, and she scrutinized every look Caityn gave Theiandar. Eliya convinced herself that Caityn's sweet, innocent smile concealed something sinister.

Though her emerald green dress and half pinned up hair added to Caityn's appearance of innocence, Eliya was already rationalizing and convinced herself it was foolish to trust someone who seemed too good to be true. She noticed Theiandar's admiration for Caityn, and the jealousy she refused to acknowledge took full root. *Who does she think she is? She'd better not be hiding things from my brother or—*

Eliya jumped as a hand gently tapped her shoulder. She swung around, prepared to take out her ire on whoever had touched her. When she saw it was *him*, every angry feeling surged upon him.

"You! Stop sneaking up on me. You're lucky I restrained myself, because I almost threw this wine glass at you . . . and you would have deserved it, I might add."

Gavin's grin was lopsided. She wanted to wipe the idiotic look off his face.

He said, "I would expect nothing less. But I didn't sneak up to get a wine bath . . . or a tongue lashing." In gallant fashion he asked, "My lady, may I have the next dance with one of the loveliest women in the room?"

The bow of his head was almost imperceptible. His eyes never left her surprised face.

Pleasantly distracted from her previous thoughts, Eliya looked at his hand and slowly let a smile reach her eyes. "Why yes, I would be pleased to dance with you, sir. Of course, normally we'd require an introduction, but I think we're past formalities now, aren't we . . . um, Sir Gavin, wasn't it?"

To her eyes, he looked satisfied. She was also pleased she'd remembered his name from the afternoon before.

"I think you must be right, Princess. I apologize again for scaring you. Please accept this dance as my heartfelt regret and apology at having startled you . . . twice."

She reached up and took his hand. "While I find your apology hides a boast about your dancing skills within it, I'm willing to overlook any indiscretion since I do enjoy the pastime a great deal. You are forgiven, sir."

The stupid smile returned to his face, and she was promptly led out on the dance floor.

During the dance, Gavin started the requisite small talk. "How fairs your stay at Castle Taisce, Princess?"

"Well, it is crowded, but the area around the castle is lovely. Someday I'd love to explore it more."

They followed the complicated dance steps in and around the others. As Eliya twirled out of Gavin's arms, she passed Theiandar, who reciprocated her delighted smile.

When the dance sequence brought Eliya back to Gavin, he replied, "If you are here again, I would be honored to guide you. There are certainly more people than usual, but normally even the castle is a welcoming and restful place. I've spent many a childhood day exploring its halls and chambers."

The idea of this dashing soldier giving her a tour made her young heart skip a beat. During the course of the dance, Eliya only came in contact with Caityn once, and the unpleasant feeling that surged up was brief. She knew the reason, but it would be unthinkable to admit, even to herself, she was charmed by Sir Gavin. She was out of breath and wore a genuine smile by the end of the dance.

Theiandar approached before Gavin could lead her from the dance floor.

"Eliya, come dance with me, little sprite," Theiandar said.

Eliya released Gavin's arm so fast she almost forgot her manners. She remembered herself and curtsied to the young knight, and he returned the polite gesture with a bow to her retreating back while Theiandar grinned and waved his thanks.

As Eliya and Theiandar lined up for the dance, she happened to look over and see Gavin offering his hand to Caityn. She was troubled by the knowing look passed between them, the familiarity of their touch and movements as they danced. In her distraction, she missed the next steps.

"Eliya, are you well? Have you forgotten the steps? We can sit this dance out if you'd like."

"What, Theian? Oh! No, I'm fine," she said, her smile forced. "Please, let's continue."

* * *

Caityn laughed as Gavin regaled her with stories of his recent travels with her betrothed. His alignment of storytelling to dancing was perfect. Something horrifying or exciting was about to happen every time they separated during the dance. The suspense was exasperating and amusing to her, especially since he always came back with another silly ending.

At the end of the number they bowed to each other. The necklace Caityn had tucked in the bodice of her dress had come loose from its hiding place during the dance, and it hung between them when she bowed. Gavin noticed it as the candlelight glinted off the gold's shiny finish. He reached out in a familiar way and grasped it.

"What is this pretty thing around your neck?"

"Oh, 'tis nothing." She took it from his inquisitive fingers and slipped it back into the bodice of her gown. At the same time, she used her other hand to hold onto his now empty one.

His raised eyebrows displayed mock suspicion. "Nothing, you say? Then why do you hide a man's ring there?"

Caityn, recognizing Gavin's teasing and apparent curiosity, decided it would be for the best to explain it to him before he pestered her about it all night.

"Come out on the terrace with me. I need to cool off, and I'll gladly explain this ring to you."

Gavin bowed low over her hand which he still held. He then proceeded to tuck it through the crook of his arm.

"I obey your every command, my lady."

Caityn laughed again, her loveliness enhanced by merriment playing at the corners of her eyes.

The cousins walked to the railing. They stood in the cool, late spring air while she explained Bimala's request to him under the shimmering night sky.

* * *

Eliya observed Gavin and Caityn's exchange from a distance. She couldn't hear a word being said but couldn't mistake the closeness of their relationship. Livid, she watched them walk onto the terrace together, sure she'd just witnessed evidence of Caityn's beguilement and deceit with her own eyes.

Theiandar had escorted Eliya to the table to give her a chance to rest. While he danced with Queen Ismene, Eliya sat at the table, incensed over what she viewed as horrid deception. Not only had Caityn flirted openly with one of Theiandar's guardsmen, but the temptress was wearing his ring around her neck! *The lying betrayer! Oh! And to think I found him handsome and dashing!* A scowl screwed up her otherwise pretty face.

The doddering stranger had been right all along, and Eliya was the only one who could save her brother from marrying this deceiver. She knew she had to act without delay. She took a quick drink of wine to solidify her determination. Eliya pulled the tiny vial from her pocket and held it tightly in her hand. She sat there, refusing dances as she stared at Caityn promenading around the room, flirting with what seemed like countless men for the next two hours.

Finally, with the resolve of a mother bear, she approached Caityn with a spiked glass of wine and held it out to her. "Here, Caityn. You've been dancing a great deal, and you look parched. Drink this and I think you'll feel revived." Eliya held her breath.

Caityn considered the glass then smiled at Eliya. She took it from Eliya's outstretched hand with a look of gratitude. "Thank you, Eliya. I am thirsty." She tipped the glass back and drained its contents.

Eliya expelled a gush of air and took the glass back, nodding in reply to Caityn's thanks. Without a word, she headed back to the table as if in a trance. *Did I really do that? Did I really poison my brother's betrothed? The man said it was only a sleeping potion, but what do I really know of him other than what he told me? What if* . . . Eliya did not want to consider what she'd done. She went in search of her mother. When she found Queen Zoe, she begged leave to retire for the night.

"I'm sorry you are unwell, dear. Of course, you should go and get your rest. The wedding is tomorrow, and I'm sure you'll want to feel your best."

Her mother's embrace and well wishes were lost on Eliya, and she couldn't quite return the gesture. Guilt already seeped into her soul. She floated from the room in a daze. She couldn't bring herself to linger there and witness the effects of her handiwork.

* * *

A few minutes later, Caityn gripped the arm of her dance partner as she felt herself falling to the side.

"Highness, are you well?"

His concern was obvious, but his voice sounded far away. Woozy, she reached for her temple.

"Hmm? Oh . . . what?" She shook her head, trying to clear the cobwebs and steady her vision. "Yes. I think I am, but maybe I've had too much wine. Please help me to sit down for a moment."

"Certainly, Princess." He led her to a chair and, with great care, helped lower her to the seat.

Caityn tried to steady her eyes but was unable bring anything into focus.

* * *

Gavin happened to be standing alone, watching the dancers, and noticed Caityn with her hands covering her eyes. He also took in the look of concern on the young man's face. In a quick motion, he set his glass on a tray and approached the two. Gavin looked between the young man and the princess.

"May I be of service, Your Highness?"

He received a grateful look from the other man. To Gavin's eyes, Caityn seemed to be in a far off daze when she looked up. Her vision didn't quite focus, and it all felt off somehow.

"Oh Gav, is that you? I think I've had too . . . uh, too much wine. Could you p-please help m-m-me to my room?"

It was obvious to Gavin she needed to retire, and he caught the attention of Theiandar, motioning for him to continue what he was doing.

"Let Prince Theiandar know the princess is retiring and that I'm escorting her to her room," Gavin said to the young man Caityn had been dancing with who still hovered nearby.

The young man with whom she'd been dancing, nodded and made the trek over to where Theiandar stood in conversation among a group of the king's most trusted advisers.

Gavin helped Caityn stand, and with most of her weight resting on his arm, he led her from the great hall. "Let this be a lesson to you, dear cousin. There really is such a thing as 'too much of a good thing.'" He was joking but got no response as she clung to his arm.

She tripped on a rug, and it became quite clear to Gavin that they would never make it if he didn't intercede. He made a cursory glance up and down the empty hall before picking Caityn up and carrying her the rest of the way to her room. Her head rested against his shoulder, and her arms were flopped around his neck. "I'm s-sorry, Gav. I-I've never been d-drunk before. I feel awful. Mmm . . . so sl-sleepy." Her words became more and more slurred before her eyes closed.

The chambermaid was already waiting to turn down the covers and put out the lamp when Caityn and Gavin arrived. He wouldn't have to chase the maid down somewhere which was a relief. After depositing Caityn on the bed, he explained what the princess needed and left the girl to finish taking care of her charge.

* * *

Theiandar was concerned as he watched Gavin lead what looked like an inebriated Caityn from the great hall. He was too distracted to pay attention to what the chancellor was saying about possible war with the Crescent Cave Nation. He watched Kasen approach and focused on his body language. The young soldier bowed low.

"My Lord, I'm sorry to interrupt, but Princess Caityn was overtaxed and ready to retire. Sir Gavin wanted that I should tell you not to worry, and he would escort her to her chamber."

"Thank you, Kasen. I suggest you notify Queen Ismene. She may grow concerned over the princess's absence."

The soldier bowed again before walking away. Theiandar tried to return his mind to the older men's conversation but gave up, excusing himself to catch up with Gavin and Caityn.

He proceeded down the hall and stopped at the bottom of the stairs when he saw Gavin descending. "Is Cait all right?"

"Yes, Raz, sir. She's fine . . . I think. It would seem she was drunk." He shook his head with a look of confusion. "Tis strange, though, since Caity has never been one to drink much at all. She enjoys a little bit of wine, but I've never known her to be drunk on it."

"How strange. Maybe the excitement of tomorrow is making her nervous and causing her to lose track of how much she'd had to drink." Theiandar's remark was more of a question than a statement.

"At any rate, thank you for your care of her."

"Of course, Sire. Not only is she my cousin, she's my friend." They headed out to the barracks. "Caity and I grew up together, causing all kinds of trouble for her older brother, Adair. Of course, now their brother, Brennan, has taken on the role of impish younger sibling and performs the duty well!"

CHAPTER SEVEN

Midnight Visitor

The maid tucked the blanket around Caityn and extinguished the lamp. She shook her head and smiled ruefully at the sleeping princess. Even though Princess Caityn seemed dead to the world, there were still signs of life in her intermittent snores.

It had been a bear of a task to maneuver the princess into her night clothes. After considerable exertion and one last tuck of the covers, the main exited the chamber with an amused expression on her face.

The chamber, awash in the amber glow from the crackling fire, remained still for quite some time. He moved, a stealthy shadow emerging from the dark, hidden space behind the window curtain and slunk noiselessly across the cold stone floor and intricate rugs. The deeper darkness created by his grotesque shadow loomed large and foreboding. The intruder stopped next to the bed, climbed with great care onto the coverings, and looked down upon Caityn with an adoration he could not conceal. She slept on in a helpless stupor, while evil desires radiated from his dark presence, and knowing that no one was aware of his intrusion here caused a brief, triumphant laugh to escape his lips.

His slithery-smooth voice whispered into Caityn's ear. "Sweet Princess, I must thank you for being so beautiful, but mostly for your heart. Oh, I am beyond myself with excitement to obtain the beauty resting within! I could see it years ago, and now is the perfect moment to take it for myself. Your beauty upon beauty will be the best I have ever had and will surely bring me youth for one thousand years!" At this thought, the thing—this 'he'—clasped his hands together in blissful abandon, raising them over his head in a motion of praise.

He wrapped a lock of her unruly, soft hair around his crooked finger and brought it to his nose. He inhaled as though smelling the sweet fragrance of a rose. Then he drew the silken strands across his cheek, smirking as the satiny softness caressed his face.

"It was quite easy to convince that silly, jealous girl to administer the sleeping potion. Ha! Too easy, really! All it took was for a seed of doubt to be planted in her mind. Doubt is a powerful tool, my dear. Soon it took root in her heart. I am master of hearts, you know. Now, with a scant three weeks left before I can perform my ritual, I will have everything I need to own your heart, the very marrow of your being, and live fifteen more lifetimes!"

He released her hair with a flick of his wrist, and it landed across her face. With a crooked smile to match his crooked hands, he jumped from the bed and padded over to the satchel he'd left behind the curtain. The unnatural man slung it over his arm and went to sit by the fire. From the bag, he pulled a long, gold chain with an amulet shaped like a heart. It was half the size of a normal man's palm, and at the center of its intricate design was a minuscule glass chamber.

The chamber was empty, but the sinister man knew that after completing his task, it would be full of the crimson liquid of her true beauty. Experiencing the renewed knowledge of this left him elated and almost giddy. To steal this much beauty! It had been two hundred years since he'd last done it, but when he found her, this love she had in her heart, he knew it was worth the wait. He'd been right to choose this one, to remain in the shadows, anticipating the time when her love would deepen and mature into the purest possible form, as it was at this exact moment.

The anticipation of it caused him to fumble the amulet, but before it could touch the floor, he grasped it to his chest and sighed. "Clumsy, clumsy me! Be careful, dolt! Ha! I am talking to myself. You, Princess," he said as he approached the bed once again. "You will not remember any of this. In fact, your sleep is deathly deep, and you will remember nothing at all—not even the pain I will give to you as my gift in return for the one you give me this night."

He climbed up on the bed and straddled Caityn's hips. The little man stared down at her face. He couldn't help himself; he had to touch her. It wasn't enough to look at her. He allowed his fingers to slither over the curve of her forehead . . . along her eyebrows . . . down her nose . . . across her parted lips . . . over her smooth chin, until his physical memorization of her features ended at her throat.

His hands came to rest on her neck as though he would choke her, but instead he let go. Using both hands, he pressed the amulet down upon her chest. He grinned and all his jagged teeth shone bright in the dim light as a red glow emanated from the amulet's center. His whispered words were uttered from behind clenched teeth. He didn't flinch, even as the edges of the amulet burned into his palms and her chest like a branding iron.

Caityn never stirred, and after the ritual was complete, he gingerly placed the chain around his neck and crawled down from the bed. He shuffled back to the chair, pulled strips of cloth from his sack, and wrapped them around his seared hands. It was almost impossible to keep the hushed gasps from escaping his lips with each pass of the cloth. Still, it wasn't as bad as the first time he'd accomplished this task — a thousand years and many maidens ago.

He lifted the amulet in his throbbing fingers and admired the red glow.

Time stood still for him, and what seemed like no more than a few minutes in this position had actually been much more. The thief let his eyes roam to the window and noticed that soon the sun would rise. How did the time pass so quickly?

He wasted no more of it. It took effort to ignore the pain in his hands and sling his satchel on his back. Once he'd accomplished the simple task, though, he walked back to the bed. He looked at the peaceful, sleeping Caityn. "I thank you again, Princess, for I think I might have almost been too late. Another year later and that stupid prince would have ruined this beauty! He might have broken this love, and I certainly couldn't abide such a thing, now could I?"

His anger, brought on by thoughts of the High Prince, melted into a disturbing grin as he stared down at her. "Oh, he won't be likely to interfere now! I have your pure, sweet love, and its power is mine!" He hated her even as he thanked her, and then he slunk out the window the same way he'd come, climbing down the wall with spider-like ease.

* * *

Her mother's voice invaded her sleep. Caityn moaned and reached up to rub her eyes.

"Tis freezing in here Caityn. Your fire has gone cold. And what possessed you to leave your window open all night?" her mother said in a chiding tone. "I was worried when you didn't come to breakfast, so here I am."

Caityn heard the clink and tap of the window being shut and locked. She groaned in response to her mother's question and buried herself deeper under the covers.

"You have missed breakfast, and I was beginning to worry about you. Theiandar mentioned you not feeling well last night. Are you not well? Today is your wedding, my dear."

Another grunt was her only response. In truth, Caityn wasn't feeling like herself. She felt different and wanted to be left alone, but instead of giving a response she rolled over, turning her back on her mother.

With a sudden burst of chilly air, Ismene pulled back the covers, but it wasn't the cold which shocked her so much as the terrible scream from her mother and the hoarse question she asked.

"Who are you and what have you done with my daughter?"

Her attention gain, though unwilling to the end, Caityn answered with a question of her own, "What on earth could you possible mean, Mother? Tis me, of course, Caityn."

"You are not my daughter. Who are you?"

"Mother, have you lost your mind? I am your Caityn, your daughter."

As she crawled from the bed and moved toward the wardrobe, she passed the vanity. She stopped cold in her tracks. A scream much like the one Ismene had loosed escaped Caityn's unnaturally thin lips, and her now bony fingers gripped the edges of the vanity table. An old, wrinkled woman with long, dull gray hair stared back.

One of the strange hands—her hand—came up to touch her long, wiry hair. Then she touched the wrinkly, thin skin of her face and the wart on her nose before her repulsed stare traveled down to take in the age spots covering her arms.

With slow motion, Ismene turned Caityn to face her and really looked into her eyes. As they stared at each other in horror, a dawning realization spread across Ismene's face, and she knew. She knew this was truly her Caityn. Tears slipped down her mother's cheeks.

"Oh Caityn! My daughter! Oh dear me! How could this be? This is horrible! What has happened to you?"

Caityn thought her cry was not only full of horror and shock, but it carried a tinge of self-pity in it, too.

Caityn shuddered, too stunned to reply. It took a few hard swallows to clear her throat. "I only thought I'd had too much wine last night. That was all. Really, Mother. I don't know what this is!" A single tear slipped down her leathery cheek.

"Oh Caity, this is a great deal more than too much wine. This is some kind of treacherous sorcery. We have such scant magic in our world, but this is certainly something evil."

"Who's done this to me? How? What is to become of me?" Caityn collapsed onto the stool in front of the vanity. "I'm so ugly!"

"I don't know. I just don't know," Ismene said as she paced about the room. Minutes of frantic thought passed before she sat in a chair by the fire, staring at Caityn in horror. Without warning, she stood up. "I must talk with your father. We must postpone the wedding! And we need to find out what has happened." She stopped beside the vanity and took Caityn's frail hand. "I promise we will do everything we can to fix this."

"How, Mother? You don't even know what this . . . this is, do you?" she cried as she pointed to her aged, unfamiliar face.

"No, Caityn, you're right. I don't know, but surely anything that can be done can also be undone. Oh dear. Oh dear me. I will send Idra to help you dress, and she will stay with you while I get your father."

Caityn didn't reply. As her eyes darted from the mirror to the gnarled hands in her lap and back again, Ismene slipped from the room without her noticing.

Caityn walked to the full length mirror in the corner. She touched the burned place on her nightgown. It was only a second before she reached down, grasped the hem of her nightgown, and yanked it over her head. She stood there, stark naked, staring at her image in the mirror. The pure white of her nightgown stood in stark contrast to her disfigured body. She was appalled at the stranger before her. Everything sagged and drooped. Her skin was sallow and paper-thin, the bluish-purple veins visible beneath it as they tracked across her body. Her hand was drawn to the burn mark on her chest. Odd. There was no feeling of pain.

It was like this, some fifteen minutes later, when Idra found Caityn. The lady-in-waiting locked the door before she moved to the closet.

Idra must have already known what to expect, because she showed no emotion as she wrapped Caityn in her robe and led her to a chair by the fire. Caityn said nothing as Idra worked to rebuild the flames, nor did Idra.

Caityn shivered and let her despondent stare drift beyond the window, focused on nothing at all. She was confused. She felt normal—or at least she thought she did. Caityn didn't feel old in body or mind, but there was no doubt she looked it.

When the fire was rekindled, Idra looked at the princess. "Um . . . Caityn, your mother sent me to help you dress, and then I am to take you to your father's private meeting chambers. She asked us to be quick and discrete."

Caityn dipped her head in acknowledgment and continued to stare out the window, her dead eyes unfocused and unseeing.

CHAPTER EIGHT
Shock

Ismene explained to her husband what she'd witnessed in Caityn's room earlier. Othniel wasted no time. He sent for Theiandar and his parents to come join them. At the last minute, he decided to include Adair. He wanted his eldest to be fully apprised of the situation first hand.

Othniel watched his wife pace while she wrung her hands in trepidation. They did not have to wait long, though, because soon Adair arrived. They explained nothing. Within a few minutes Theiandar showed up, followed closely by his parents with Eliya in tow.

Othniel said, "Thank you all for coming. You may be guessing right now as to the purpose for calling you all together. It is because I must discuss with you something that has happened to my daughter." He cleared his throat and glanced at Theiandar to ascertain his response before continuing. "I have bad news. I think we must postpone the wedding or even possibly discontinue the alliance altogether."

He held up his hand to squelch any protests. "Now before you say anything, I'd like Ismene to explain to you the situation before Caityn arrives."

King Othniel gestured for everyone to sit down. He paid particular attention to Theiandar who couldn't mask the tension in his shoulders or the confusion written across his face. Dante said nothing when the prince chose to stay standing by the fireplace.

Again, Ismene recounted the events of the morning to a chorus of gasps and breathless denials. Other than this, there were no interruptions. Othniel watched each face as he took in their reactions, most of which he was sure mirrored his own, but one face in particular was ashen and downcast. It seemed almost out of place among all the looks of astonishment.

He was sure Idra and Caityn would arrive any time. When Ismene's explanations came to a close, he jumped up and said, "You see why I say we must postpone or cancel."

The air was weighty with silence. Othniel looked to Dante who stroked his beard, deep in thought.

Theiandar slammed his fist down on the mantle, rattling the candlesticks and pictures displayed there. As the clattering dissipated, they noticed the sniffling sound coming from the settee near the fireplace. Othniel looked to Eliya, sitting deathly still, tears streaming down her cheeks.

"Eliya, child, this is terrible news, but why do you cry like this, as though devastated?" he asked in a gentle, fatherly voice.

* * *

Eliya sat stock-still while Queen Ismene told the whole of what she'd witnessed, and her guilt was obvious. Now Caityn's father was showing her compassion, and all she could think about was her culpability. She wiped her eyes with the heels of her hands. King Othniel and the others were quiet but impatient while they waited for her reply. She knew the added guilt would be too much if she lied.

Taking a deep breath, she looked over Othniel's shoulder, her eyes pleading with her brother for forgiveness as she took in his look of confusion.

"She was deceiving you, Theiandar, even before the vows had been spoken. I saw it with my own eyes! She has his ring — Sir Gavin's — on a chain around her neck, and after they danced last night, I saw them go out on the terrace together, alone. It was awful. We had to stop you from making a mistake. We . . . I had to stop her from ruining your life and destroying our realms! But I didn't know this would happen! I swear I didn't know!"

She gulped in her next breath and buried her head in her hands. Her silent weeping turned into great, sobbing gasps for air.

"Eliya, how could you? How could you be so stupid? The ring she wears belongs to the dead son of her nursemaid. She wears it as a promise to return it to the dead son's wife!" He stopped when her head shot up and revealed her look of surprise. "Yes, she told me all about it. We're to be married, Eliya, whether you like it or not . . . and I love her."

"As far as Gavin is concerned, he's her cousin and one who grew up here with her. He's like a brother to her. Oh, Eliya, how could you? How could you be so stupid? There is no deceit here except your own."

Theiandar stopped. The pity melding with anger in his eyes was too much for her to bear and she moaned, weeping anew at this revelation. She jumped when his hand came to rest on her shoulder.

Through sobs she begged, "I'm so, so sorry! Please forgive me! Please! The little man . . . the man at the waterfall . . . he said it was only a sleeping potion. I don't understand. He seemed to know her so well. He said I should help you. Oh dear Almighty! What have I done? I didn't know this would happen! I swear, I didn't know." The tears continued to stream down her anguished face.

She let Theiandar hug her then.

Her father, High King Dante, said, "Othniel, in light of these circumstances we certainly must postpone the wedding until this can be better clarified. With that, there will be consequences for my daughter for her part. We must also send out a party to track down this man she mentioned. Everything possible shall be done." High King Dante sounded confident to his daughter, but Eliya's remorse was too great to be comforted by it.

"Thank you, Dante. This is all we can ask," Othniel responded with unpleasant gravity.

Being the only one facing the door, he crossed the room to where his aged daughter and Idra had entered without detection and stood a smidge inside the doorway. He looked Caityn in the eye and placed his arms around her stiff, skeletal body. "My daughter, I will do everything in my power to fix this," he whispered.

Eliya peeked around her brother and looked into the old woman's—Caityn's!—dead eyes. The haunted look was all it took to send her over the edge. Eliya fainted.

* * *

Theiandar's heart raced as he caught Eliya's limp body. He was unprepared for this—this what? Catastrophe? He felt Caityn behind him and heard Othniel whispering, but he couldn't make himself turn around right away. Everyone in the room was staring behind him, and the looks on their faces didn't bode well.

Finally, he released Eliya into their mother's arms and whispered a quick prayer for strength. He steeled himself for what he was sure would be a startling sight. Theiandar turned around and felt as though someone had punched him in the gut with a battering ram.

Othniel stepped out of Theiandar's way when he approached Caityn. The prince was hesitant and felt awkward as he took a moment to stare into her eyes.

"Are you really Caityn? This isn't some kind of sick joke, is it?"

He silently pleaded with this strange woman to contradict the story, to smile and laugh before telling him it was all in jest. Instead, she frowned up at him, and he knew in his heart that this was no tale.

"How dare you? I am not a joke. I am Caityn, daughter of King Othniel, Princess of Taisce. Heavens, but I'm already sick of answering that question."

Adair cleared his throat. Everyone looked at him expectantly.

Dante was the first to speak up. "What is it?"

"Well, Sire, I'm hesitant to say anything for fear I'm wrong, but I think I may know what has happened to my sister."

"Don't stop," Theiandar said, his voice taut with urgency. "What do you know?"

Adair hesitated again. "Well, at university in Conleth, I visited the Hall of Historic Records. Once, I read some ancient scrolls chronicling the strangest stories. Really, even looking at Caity now, I can't quite believe it."

Theiandar said, "Just tell us. Please."

Adair focused his gaze on Theiandar. "The stories told of someone called the Beauty Thief. They depicted a gnarled little man and a heart-shaped amulet he used to capture the beauty of young women. The amulet was said to have drained the source of beauty from their hearts—the love, the most pure love. It didn't rob them of their soul, but it might as well have."

"Adair, did the scrolls tell how to reverse it?" Theiandar eagerly entreated.

"I . . . I'm not sure. I don't really remember since I dismissed it all as an old fairy tale." He looked downcast. "I'm truly sorry I don't know more."

Theiandar looked around at the others. Eliya was recovering from her faint, and she looked up at him with abject apology written all over her face. Right then, he chose to forgive her for her part in it, knowing she had been a pawn, deceived and used by this menacing Beauty Thief. He looked back at the despondent Caityn and crossed the room again to stand before her. With gentle fingers, he touched her cheek just as he'd done a year before when their lives had been intertwined for good.

"Caityn, we will postpone the wedding, but only for a time. A few days ago I made you a promise, and I will keep it. I promise this now: we will find this thief and make him reverse the curse."

"Theiandar." She was emotionless as she stared at him. She pulled down the collar of her dress low enough to reveal the top of the burn mark on the thin skin of her chest. "What has been done, it is just as possible it cannot be undone, contrary to what my mother says. I feel I have no heart. Certainly there is none left for you." She let go of the dress and sighed heavily. "I look at all of you and think I should be more upset, but this is a lost cause. Tis likely too late, and I can't find it in me to care because it is an impossible task. I will not waste my breath. Now leave me alone."

He tried not to grimace at her words, but seeing her like this and hearing her utterance was enough to crush his hopes. A frown creased his brow.

Adair placed a hand on his shoulder. "All may not be lost, my friend." He took Caityn's withered hand. "Caity, there's more to the history record at Conleth. We need to find out what is in the rest of the scroll. I'm sure that if we do, we can unlock the answer to undoing this evil enchantment."

Theiandar felt a new spark of hope kindle in his chest. He grabbed Adair's shoulder in return and squeezed it to show his friend his appreciation, minimal though it was. "Then Adair, my friend, to Conleth we will go."

Caityn's father stepped forward, issuing commands. "Tis settled. Ismene, you and Queen Zoe must notify the household of the postponement. Dante, would you please perform the unpleasant duty of informing the guests? Adair and Theiandar, you will travel to Conleth to find out what we need to know. Dante and I will meet you at High Castle after you have retrieved the records. Adair, Theiandar, I think it best to have Caityn travel with you to Conleth in case something can be accomplished right away. In the meantime, I will organize a search party to locate this little man if he is still nearby."

"My entourage will start our journey back to High Castle immediately," King Dante said.

Idra, who had stood in silence behind Caityn, spoke up. "Your Highness, if it please the king, may I travel with Caityn in my regular duties?"

"Yes, Idra. Your presence would be most welcome. Thank you for your willingness to serve your princess," Othniel said.

"You're all crazy and this is pointless," Caityn interjected. "I am not going anywhere with anyone. What's the point, really? Who am I but an ugly old woman who cares nothing for any of you? Who am I to you? Tis such a waste of time and effort." An exasperated huff escaped her lips as her stooped body crumpled on to the couch Eliya and her mother had vacated just moments before.

Theiandar loved Caityn and was having a hard time reconciling what he saw before him—this ugly, grouchy crone—with the beautiful, gentle, kind, and sweet young woman with whom he'd fallen in love. The part of his heart belonging to her cried out for him to show her mercy and grace. It begged him from the depths of his soul not to be fooled by what his eyes saw but to look for the truth with his heart.

He closed his eyes and dug deep, trying to listen to the tiny inner voice. He chose to love the hag and fulfill his promise to his betrothed. He would do everything he could to save her heart, her love, the sweetest part of her soul, or he would die trying.

Theiandar opened his eyes, no longer lost in his introspection, to find himself alone with Caityn. As she stared blankly into the fireplace, he moved to sit next to her on the couch.

She stared at him, and for a brief moment he thought he saw his own Caityn in her eyes, desperately crying out to be freed, as though she'd been locked away in a prison. When she blinked, the image disappeared, replaced by dull despondency.

She spoke first. "This is pointless, Theiandar. I know I'm ugly, and there is nothing left in me to save. I feel the void and nothing else. I don't understand it, but what does it really matter anyway? You can be free of me. My parents won't hold you to your promise. Tis not worth it, so don't bother."

In the utterance of the last words, he thought he heard the same desperate cry for help in the tone of her voice, the one he'd seen in her eyes a minute before. "Caityn . . ." He looked at her and took a deep breath before placing his hands on her gaunt cheekbones, caressing them with his thumbs. "Cait, I am not fooled by what my eyes see. I'm not blind, either. I see your wrinkly, weathered skin. I see your crooked back and fingers. I see you are hurt or hurting. I'm not going to give up, though. I promised my love to you, and if it means searching the world to bring you back, then so be it. You may be lost, but you can be found." He stopped and as he lowered his hands, she shook her head again.

"Cait, I think I have loved you since I was eight years old. You were tiny and fragile, but you were brave. That courageous little girl needed my help but earned my deepest respect. I know she is not lost forever. We do have hope of restoration."

She looked at him without saying a word. He didn't know what to think, what to do. He ran his fingers through his hair. "My love for you is constant, and whatever this curse is that this monster has laid on you, I vow to undo it." Theiandar bent forward and placed a kiss on her forehead.

* * *

Nothing felt right to Caityn. It was all she knew for sure. *If I could decipher the purpose of that which has been removed maybe I'd be able to comprehend what's wrong with me. But there's just this empty space in my chest. Tis cold . . . black, like pure emptiness.* She shuddered. It was as if something more complicated than beauty had been taken. She was more apt to believe life itself had been robbed from her, but it was too difficult to contemplate any of it.

The only spark, something confusing, was when Theiandar's lips touched her forehead. What was it? Maybe he'd felt it, too, because after he did it there was a strange, peaceful look on his face.

Caityn's level of annoyance only grew when her father insisted she go along on the fool's errand. It proved pointless to refuse. Instead, she sat in the chair in her room while Idra packed some necessities for her. She resented the people who loved her and detested them for making her do something she didn't want to do. She cared not for any of them. Why make her go? She squeezed her temples to try clear her mind then puckered her lips in a scowl.

Oh, this is ridiculous! What on earth is the point? This will all be such a waste of time. I'm nothing but an ugly old hag. Who cares about me? Do I even care? I just want to lie down and hide under the blanket. I wish Idra would get out. She's so perfect and . . . and happy all the time. She has no worries or real responsibilities. I can't stand her. I hate her! I hate myself!

Then the strangest thought crowded into her mind, interrupting her internal ranting. It disrupted the depressed self-pity filling the void left by the absence of love. This aberration stirred up Theiandar's earlier words: his promises of love and devotion, his willingness to risk his own life to save her beauty and the marrow of her soul. This wisp of a thought stopped her cold in her mental tracks. Something changed.

CHAPTER NINE
The Journey Begins

After Caityn's necessities were packed, she solemnly followed a silent Idra from the room. They had both changed into clothing better suited for travel. Their dresses, while still high in quality, were in shades of muted browns and creams. They looked fairly nondescript and serviceable. But while Idra's dark hair and fair skin were enhanced by the less vibrant colors, Caityn looked even more washed out and pale. She tried not to grimace too much as she passed a mirror in the hall, sure it accentuated all the wrinkles around her mouth, on her forehead, and around her eyes.

They ambled down the hall, trailed by a manservant carrying their bags. Caityn was still thinking about her reflection in the mirror when she finally spoke up. "I really don't know why you agreed to go on this silly escapade, Idra. It will achieve nothing and will likely only rob you of your own beauty."

"Ah, you *do* care!" Idra was clearly teasing, but Caityn glared.

"You misunderstand my warning, is all," Caityn retorted.

At the top of the stairs, Idra placed a halting hand on Caityn's arm. "Caity, we've known each other a long time. You were such a sweet baby. I vaguely remember spending many afternoons with you in the playroom of this castle. I must have been all of four years old. I remember staring at your precious baby face and letting you wrap your tiny fingers around my own. I'm happy our mothers are sisters and that I have always known you. To be your lady-in-waiting has been a privilege, because it means spending time every day with my best friend. Now let's make this clear before we begin. This journey and our friendship mean a great deal to me, because I love you. I'll be here for you to the end, and we *will* succeed."

"You walk to your own death," Caityn mumbled, pressing her lips together.

Idra slid her fingers down the paper-thin skin of Caityn's arm to take her hand. She gave it a light squeeze before they started down the stairs.

When they emerged from the keep, it was to walk into a cacophony of noise and bustling activity. The horses and supplies for the various search parties as well as King Dante's group were being assembled. Men barked orders from every direction. Women hugged their men good-bye.

Caityn stopped and stared at the chaos. In her mind she pictured the waste of time it would turn out to be. Her life was over, and every day to follow would only be a pointless endeavor.

Theiandar bounded up the steps and took her hand in his to lead her down. She accepted his help, but something in her chest ached. The damaged skin over her heart itched. She absently scratched at it.

"My princess, we will be riding south as far as the river, and then we'll travel by boat to the docks near Conleth. It will save us at least two days. If you find yourself unable to cope with our pace, please speak up in order to allow us the ability to accommodate your needs."

Caityn pulled her hand from his when they reached the base of the stairs. She certainly didn't want to go, but she knew, regardless of how she looked, she was more than up to the rigors of travel. She didn't know why, but she did not want him to treat her like an invalid. Her reply dripped with misplaced scorn. "That won't be necessary."

He nodded at her, though the surprised expression on his face spoke volumes. Theiandar glanced at Idra before giving an almost imperceptible bow and turning to speak with the other men who were preparing to leave on their own missions.

"The nerve."

"What was that, my lady?" Idra asked.

"Nothing, Idra."

Caityn turned away. "Keep making those eyes at my prince. I see the way you look at him."

Caityn knew Idra hadn't heard her over all the noise around them, but she took smug satisfaction in knowing her words could have caused distress. After all, Idra was probably jealous of everything Caityn had at her disposal, including her prince.

* * *

Theiandar wasn't sure how this trip would go, let alone what they would find in Conleth. He only hoped whatever it was would really help to save Caityn. His gut reaction was to assume she was dying, like he was running out of time and watching her waste away. He feared the longer she stayed like this the more permanent it would become. He didn't dwell any longer on those fears, though, as he met with his father and Othniel. He came upon them laying out plans before they departed.

Othniel was saying, "We've always been friends, Dante. You've always treated me as an equal. I'm grateful for this, and I hope what has occurred here, at this most delicate time, doesn't ruin our friendship or cause strife in the realms."

"I see what you're implying, and I share your concern, Othniel. When word of this spreads across the kingdom, which it inevitably will, there will be many people ready to pronounce all sorts of lies against you or even myself. Some may even look to exploit what they will perceive as weakness. I cannot help but feel responsible for your daughter's and your current plight. I also have to consider my son. It grieves me that my daughter played a hand in bringing about this treachery. For my part, and that of my son, we will do everything we can to make this right," Dante said.

"I know you will. If it wasn't my own daughter I might be able to see this in a different light, but for now I am burning with anger. Princess Eliya was foolish and easily deceived, which is more than a little regrettable. I'm sure you'll seriously consider a proper order of discipline for her."

"Yes. She is already receiving some of it now. Her guilt is great, but whatever caused her to doubt in the way she did must still be dealt with. In the meantime, we will go west on the main road back to High Castle. I'll leave no stone unturned. You are going south to Nashua?"

"Yes. King Amerigo will welcome my search of his lands, ensuring his own people are safe. Geir will continue the search here in Taisce. There are two units headed north, toward the Dark Lands, as we speak," Othniel said. "Theiandar and his group will come south to the river crossing with me and take boats from the docks to make their way west to Conleth."

Theiandar could sense the tension between the two men. And then, after serious consideration, it dawned on him. If he wasn't successful in saving Caityn, it could cause a permanent rift in the kingdom. He prayed he was wrong.

"Father, King Othniel. I'm sorry to interrupt, but Geir gave a report. A young shepherd boy saw a stranger leaving the area around dawn. The person was heading south and west of the village. I'm going to send Sir Gavin and two other guards from my unit with you, Father, to act as extra scouts as well as protection."

"I welcome the extra eyes and swords. We have no idea how many are involved in this scheme, and we must stay vigilant. After you get the necessary information from the scrolls at Conleth, meet me at High Castle. We'll use carrier pigeons to take messages between there and Taisce," High King Dante said. "Now, 'tis time we all headed out. We are wasting precious daylight, and it is almost full noon."

Dante grasped arms with his longtime friend. Their eyes met for a minute, and it seemed as though they had come to an understanding. Next, the High King hugged his only son. Theiandar returned the embrace without a word, and then grasped the outstretched arm of King Othniel.

"Theiandar, I know my daughter is not who she was. I cannot expect you to marry an old woman, but I charge you to do everything you can to right this wrong. If you do this for me, I will never expect anything else from you in regard to my family."

Theiandar couldn't breathe. Othniel already sounded defeated, and he couldn't take the added weight of it right now. He needed reassurance that Caityn would be all right, that there was hope. He swallowed the lump in his throat and nodded. Othniel released his arm with a curt nod in return.

Theiandar's borrowed horse was behind him which made it quick work to mount up. From his position high atop his steed, he watched Othniel and Adair say their goodbyes to Ismene and Brennan. Caityn's fourteen-year-old brother, Brennan, looked confused, but he was putting on a brave face for his father as the king admonished him to keep watch over Taisce and take care of his mother.

They waved their good-byes and all rode out together, but at the trail leading south to the river, Theiandar's and Othniel's groups parted ways with Dante's. The High King's party continued down the road wending its way through Parlan en route to High Castle. Theiandar waved goodbye to his family, still resolute in his promise.

He could see his mother's confident smile as she waved back, but it was Eliya's look of dejection and misery that stayed with him as they headed toward the river. He wished he'd taken more time to tell her she was forgiven and that it really wasn't her fault. She'd just been a pawn in a man's evil scheme. Theiandar hoped it wouldn't be long before he'd be able to tell her what had happened was fixed and all was well. He wished someone would give him such assurances.

* * *

The next hour dragged by for Caityn. The village they were heading to at the river was south of Castle Taisce. It was where they would separate from Othniel's group which would be taking a ferry across the river to Nashua. The trip to the village was uneventful and mostly quiet. A few of the men carried on conversations about the weather, the planting season, new weapons they'd heard about, and various other things men find interesting. Caityn, however, had nothing to say to anyone and ignored Idra's attempt at conversation.

She was in no mood to entertain anyone. Frankly, from the looks she was getting, it seemed most of them didn't believe she was who she said she was anyway. In fact, of all the guards, only Gavin had looked remotely sympathetic toward her plight, and Theiandar had sent him off with that conniving sister of his.

It felt as though she didn't have a friend in the world, and maybe she really didn't anymore. Even if some were pretending now, eventually they would become tired of her and her problems. They would leave her, too. She was like a black hole, sucking the life out of anyone who stayed too close.

Her mind wandered along this dismal track for the entire ride to the river. They arrived and she didn't even notice. It was only when Theiandar's voice finally broke through her thoughts that she realized where they were.

"Let me help you down, Caityn. Here, take my hand."

Caityn automatically took his outstretched hand. She looked at him, confused, as he set her on the ground.

"Why are you doing this?"

He hesitated only a second. He must have known she wasn't referring to helping her dismount from the horse. His answer was frank. "Because I love you. You really don't know? I thought I made it clear at the castle. I love you, and I will get the real you back."

Caityn's eyebrows knit together, but she said nothing in reply, only stared at him. Eventually, he seemed to give up the mental battle. He bent down, kissed her forehead, and went on to help prepare for their travel by river.

Her nose itched and the same strange feeling returned to her chest. She reached up and scratched her nose until it burned. After a few minutes like this, Caityn walked over to the edge of the water.

Here the river wasn't really a river at all. It was more like a current-filled lake with a lonely island in the middle. Just west of here, the river narrowed again, and the currents picked up speed, but this spot seemed peaceful. It was calm except for the hustle and bustle of boats' crews and locals bartering for services.

Caityn watched her father as he made arrangements for their passage. Othniel and his men would cross by ferry barge to Nashua on the south bank. He was handsome and confident, which was certainly a winning combination. She'd been told she got her eyes from him and even her courage. Right now, though, she could definitely use a brave spirit. Fear crowded around the emptiness, expectant, waiting to dive into and fill up her barren heart.

Caityn stared at the water's edge, stepping closer to it until it lapped against the tips of her boots. The sudden temptation to step into the water and end it all fixed itself in her mind.

She followed the inclination, but a hand stopped her. In her confusion, she turned to see Idra, a stern look on her face.

"My lady, don't even think about it! I cannot believe that you, even in the state you're in, could be so selfish."

The chiding tone of Idra's voice made Caityn wince.

"I was thinking about nothing. I must have lost my balance. After all, look how old I am."

Idra's sad smile was her only response before she hugged Caityn tight. Still, Caityn couldn't bring herself to return the embrace.

"Daughter." Othniel approached the two women on the shore. "We are on our way now. Theiandar says your group will be ready shortly. After I'm done in Nashua I will come to High Castle. We are here for you, all of us, doing these things because we love you, my dear one."

It was obvious he was working to rein in his emotions. Instead of speaking further, he gave her an awkward embrace. It lasted only a moment before he was retreating the way he'd come.

She watched him and thought she should try to love him back, but she couldn't find it. Love was gone. *Does that leave me with just hate?* No, she didn't think this was the case, but if not love, then what else except hate? Oh how her head hurt!

Othniel had been right, though. Their boats were soon prepared, and with the few hours of daylight left, an unsettled Caityn and her group of protectors started out down the river toward Conleth.

Hours passed as they rowed. Dusk approached. They came to a calm area along the river near Parlan's outskirts, which were to the south, while the wilderness land of Taisce and Berne sat to the north. Theiandar motioned for all the boats to pull to the shore.

"We'll camp here for tonight and get an early start in the morning."

Theiandar commanded his men with the ease of one familiar with issuing orders. At the moment it annoyed Caityn. She knew he didn't take their obedience lightly. These men were more than soldiers; they were brothers, and for some reason it irritated her that they cared about listening to him.

CHAPTER TEN
Watch Your Step, Princess

Caityn woke the next morning to the sounds of men about camp. She stretched and every bone in her body cracked. It hurt but felt good at the same time. All she wanted to do was crawl into a soft bed and sleep her life away.

"Must you make such noise?" She complained to no one in particular.

"Oh good!" Idra said. "You're awake. I was beginning to think you'd sleep until someone carried you to the boat." Handing her a bowl of oatmeal, Idra smiled in response to Caityn's surly glare. "Eat up before it gets cold!"

Idra's pleasant voice and kind instruction only served to increase Caityn's annoyance. She grudgingly took the bowl, though, because she was rather hungry. She refused to say thank you.

Caityn frowned at Idra's back while she ate in silence. When she was through, she wandered toward the forest. Before she made it twenty feet from camp, someone called out to stop her.

"Caityn, wait!" It was Adair, jogging in her direction. "You know as well as I do how wandering in the forest alone isn't safe. With all the deer we have around here, there are sure to be mountain lions and even wolves."

"Adair, unless you plan on escorting me to go relieve myself, I suggest you wait here."

He laughed, a bit embarrassed. "Well, you should at least take this, then." He handed her a dagger. "I'll stay here. You call if you need help. Don't be long, because I'd hate to have to come looking for you!"

She couldn't help but roll her eyes as she moved off into the underbrush to find a private spot. As she entered the forest in the dim light of early morning, Caityn noticed the quiet and smelled the musty odors of dirt and moss. She touched a patch of moss growing on the bark of a tree. The green fluff was spongy and wet. Her hand dropped to her side. It was disconcerting that her senses no long afforded her the presence of physical appreciation.

The pine needles scattered here and there made a crunchy carpet beneath her feet, but the forest floor did not awaken her senses as it once had, either. She quickly finished her business and headed back out of the stillness of the woods. The difference was like night and day. Her senses, without realizing it, had been quieted by the forest. Now they were assaulted by the sounds of men talking and the rushing of the river's current.

From behind her, Adair spoke up, startling her. "Tis good you came out when you did. I was just about ready to come save you from the squirrels and raccoons."

"Last I knew, you were the one afraid of raccoons."

He exhaled in a whoosh, both surprised and disappointed. "It really is you, then. I mean, part of me was hoping this wasn't real, that you weren't really you but someone pretending to be you. But . . . you are you. No one else knows the shame of the raccoon incident except . . . . Only my sister would know, because you never told anyone." He stared at her for a moment, agonizing over the facts before relenting.

"I think I should be offended," she said, "but I'm beyond frustrated. Why is everyone dead set on me not being me?" She knew she looked different, but couldn't fathom their blindness. It really made no sense, but she couldn't explain the changes, even to herself.

"Caity, 'tis not only the way you look. Tis your very presence. You just *feel* different . . . cold and distant. I can't explain it, but 'tis as if your soul has changed."

She contemplated his words for a minute and then gave up the idea of wrapping her mind around the explanation. She didn't know what was different, but from the reactions of her companions, she knew Adair wasn't making it up.

"Sit here on this log while we finish loading the boats. One of us will come help you aboard." His tone was one of command. She sat but glared at him.

"Why does everyone think they can order me around? I'm not a baby anymore," she called to his retreating back.

* * *

"She's impossible to gauge," Adair said. He and Theiandar were together in the first of five boats carrying people and gear.

"Yes," Theiandar said, "I think she's scared, but she's also angry at everyone. Tis hard to tell. Maybe she isn't scared and really is full of anger." Neither man spoke for a time. "I'm afraid if she stays like this for too long it will become permanent. You really don't remember anything else from the scrolls?"

"Well, I've been trying to wrack my brain for more of the story, but the bits are all a jumble and pretty vague. I didn't pay enough attention to it. I was more interested in the dragon narratives from ages before that story. Who would have thought it could be real? Anyway, I'm pretty sure your concern isn't far off the mark. There is something about the amulet and its power that's niggling at the back of my mind, but there again, I can't remember. The scrolls will be helpful, though, I'm sure of it." Adair's reassurances did little to boost Theiandar's outlook.

The young High Prince looked out over the river at the sun sparkling on the surface. *How can this beauty remain and nothing else in the world be changed?* It seemed unfair that his love was the beauty stolen when all around him there was other beauty to be had. *How selfish I am! I feel torn in half for her, Almighty. I love her, and this pain, or whatever it is radiating from her, is striking my heart like an arrow.*

"Adair, we can't be too late. We *must* save her. Please tell me you understand?"

Adair smacked the water with his paddle. "My friend, I would follow you anywhere. For my sister, I would do anything. Yes, I understand you. Let's not be too late."

They picked up the lagging pace. The other boats followed suit. The feeling of urgency, as if the hourglass had already been transposed and was trickling grains of sand in rapid succession, was the incentive they needed to press forward.

* * *

Caityn was in the boat directly behind Theiandar's. She watched his strong arms paddle, and she allowed herself a moment of longing for those arms to surround her and hold her close, as if his embrace would fix the empty feeling consuming her from the inside. She didn't understand her feelings, and this strange desire was no different. *Why him? Why his embrace? He must mean something,* she thought, but the ache around her heart was drowning out everything else.

Instead of dwelling on the impossibility of understanding the tattered state of her emotions, Caityn took in her surroundings. She saw sparkling water, rocky shores, pine trees reaching to the sky, tall golden grass waving in the breeze, but nothing brought her any change. There was only emptiness. What was the point?

* * *

Caityn stood up and Sir Ahmad, who was behind her, steering the boat, jerked his paddle from the water. "Princess! What are you doing? Please, Highness, sit down before you fall out."

Theiandar, Adair, and the others turned at the commotion. Theiandar called out her name but not soon enough. She let herself fall backward out of the boat.

* * *

"Cait!"

Theiandar's heart skipped a beat, but his battle-trained mind jumped into readiness. In an instant, he was on his feet, dropping his sword and knife into the boat bottom. He dove into the fast flowing river.

They saw her matted gray hair surface down river, and Adair was the first to call out. "There! Theiandar, she's there!"

Theiandar swam in the direction Adair indicated, but he'd gone too far with the current. He pressed back against the forceful water and tried to focus on the strain of muscle against nature's force instead of the fear of losing Caityn forever.

She resurfaced behind him, gasping for air. He panicked and fought the current to reach her. He could hear Adair calling out orders, but he was too focused on what he'd seen to really listen. Theiandar dove down again. It was murky beneath the surface, and he couldn't see past his outstretched hands.

Theiandar had to come back up for air again. He had inhaled water, and his body was growing weak, losing the battle against the rush of the river. Just as desperation threatened to overwhelm him, he caught a glimpse of her hand above the water. It was a glimmer of hope in the darkest of hours.

Her hand didn't stay above the surface for long. *Her dress! Tis weighing her down!* He surged toward her last position, took a deep breath, and dove where he thought she'd disappeared. He searched the murky, churning waters, while hoping desperately to touch a part of her.

His lungs burned and he ached to take a breath. On the verge of giving up, Theiandar almost didn't believe it when his fingers touched on cloth. He fought the urge to take a breath. He pulled the weighted cloth up until he felt skin and grabbed on tight. Getting a hold on Caityn's waist, he pulled her up to the surface, but her dress was waterlogged. He had little time to shout for help before they were both dragged back under.

No! I will not let you die like this! He fought down the panic and pressed up to the surface again. He broke through. A hand shot out to grab his shirt collar, and more hands were there to take Caityn from his weary arms. Adair hauled him back into the boat, and while he gasped in the bottom, they rowed over to the shore.

As soon as the boats touched land, Theiandar jumped out and ran over to where the men had laid a motionless Caityn on the grassy shore.

"Cait!" No one said a word as he fell down on his knees and gathered her fragile, limp body against his chest. "Cait, wake up! Please be okay. I haven't forgotten." His words pierced the silence of the circle of men. "I can still see who you really are. Please, my love, wake up. I will save you from this curse. By my life, I will. Please, Great One!"

The remaining three boats arrived on shore and the passengers came to stand around Theiandar and Caityn.

Theiandar cradled her in his arms, stroking her pale cheek, not noticing the subtle changes to her aged complexion. When he was sure all hope was lost, without warning, her body shook as she was overcome by choking. Her eyes shot open, and water poured from her mouth. In his surprise, Theiandar leaned her upright. She pulled away from him, leaned on her hands, and vomited more water.

Spent from the whole ordeal, Caityn's arms gave way, and she sank to the ground in utter exhaustion. Theiandar's relief was intense. His own icy state and the audience surrounding them were forgotten. With gentle hands, he lifted her back into his arms, cradling her in his lap like a frail child.

Theiandar stroked her head, gray hair and all, and said, "Thank Almighty you're alive! I thought I'd lost you there for a minute."

She shivered. Even wrapped in his strong arms, it was clear she was chilled to the bone. The near-drowning was evident in her raspy voice. "How could you lose me? I'm already lost."

Theiandar didn't notice when everyone else moved away. He was too busy forming an exasperated retort to her obvious attitude of defeat.

"Things lost can be found. Is that why you jumped from the boat? To give up?"

She didn't answer. She refused to look at him, but her avoidance in itself was response enough.

"We *will* find answers. We *will* save you. I can't listen to any more doubts. I am not giving up and neither will you. Find that stubborn, confident, courageous girl I know is in there somewhere."

He kissed her forehead. "My love is still constant."

Her unrestrained shivering disrupted her movements as she reached up to scratch her chest. "I don't understand," she said.

He knew what she meant, that she didn't understand his love, but he was too tired to repeat himself.

"We need to get you out of these wet things and warm you up by a fire."

His head lifted to scan the area for the person he sought. He didn't have to look far, though, because Idra was standing a few feet away, wiping a stream of silent tears from her cheeks. He ignored her upset and spoke as if ordering a soldier.

"Lady Idra, help Caityn get out of this dress while I get some blankets. She's much too cold."

"Yes, Prince Theiandar." Idra's voice was still thick with tears, but she moved without delay to take charge of Caityn.

Theiandar was too tired to lift her after the ordeal, so he and Idra worked together to help Caityn stand. They had barely gotten her on her feet, Caityn's arm dangling over Idra's shoulder, her entire body leaning heavily on her lady-in-waiting, when Adair and two other soldiers approached, blankets in hand.

Adair handed the blankets to Theiandar and reached out for Caityn, shifting her weight to his own shoulder before lifting her up in his arms. Theiandar's gratitude was written all over his face. The two men who'd accompanied Adair took a good-sized blanket and held it up, their backs to the princess. Adair lowered her to the ground once again.

"Do you need help, Idra, or can you manage?"

"We'll do fine, Adair. Thank you."

Theiandar and Adair moved to the other side of the blanket to give the women privacy. Other than an occasional utterance from Caityn, it was quiet. Theiandar wondered if they might not need some help after all, but before he could inquire, Idra said they were done.

He and Adair wasted no time in circling back around. Adair lifted Caityn again, and Theiandar wrapped a blanket as tight around her as he could get it. The group moved over to the roaring fire.

Theiandar could feel the cold tightening his muscles, slowing his movements. There was a deep ache in his bones, and his wet clothes only added to his frigidness. After making sure Caityn was as comfortable as possible next to the fire, he grabbed the dry clothes Ahmad handed him and strode off into the trees.

* * *

The Beauty Thief stopped cold in his tracks. He'd made such good time and knew he was well ahead of any search parties. Surely there would be someone out asking questions. It wasn't as if he'd stolen the beauty of just any farm girl or peasant this time. No, he'd helped himself to some true, royal beauty, something hard to come by.

This beauty was strong and well cared for. They say the rich are never satisfied with their wealth, always wanting more. That must be part of why this princess's beauty was so pure and potent. She had everything she could possibly want; she should have been totally spoiled and selfish. Yet she was loving, content, and even generous.

Right then, though, he was worried. The glow of the amulet had dimmed and flickered, which could only mean one thing: the princess almost died! This would not do. *This* he could not have. She had to stay alive until after the transfer was complete, until after the total lunar eclipse was finished. After this one, another wouldn't occur for over a year. He was sure there was no love stronger or purer anywhere in the Twelve Realms. He had to keep this one safe.

After the eclipse it won't matter.

The greedy man stopped his forward journey and redirected his course south. There was a man who could help him obtain his objective. For a price, he could get this fellow to bring the Princess of Taisce to him for safekeeping until he was done with her. Mercenaries were easy enough to buy, and Larue was full of them, but this man was the only one worth choosing, as far as the Beauty Thief was concerned.

His only apprehension was over the extra time it would take to travel there. With three weeks until the eclipse and no telling what might happen to the princess, he decided to move forward with his plan. The beauty was far too priceless to him.

* * *

Adair sat next to Caityn in front of the fire. At first, he placed his arm around her to share his warmth. With time, though, she stopped shivering, and his presence and touch became more of a comfort.

"If I didn't know any better, I'd say a dip in the icy river agreed with you. My eyes must be deceiving me, but I thought there used to be a wart on your nose."

She glared at him while pushing his arm off her shoulder. "There is one, idiot. You must be blind is all."

"Oh, name calling are we? Well, while you're still grouchy, I dare say there really is no wart or mole or anything on your face. You look old, but for some reason you don't look as haggish to me." She reached out from under the blanket and smacked him on the chest.

"In all earnestness, I thought you were gone for good. All I could think was I'd failed to save you. I couldn't bear to lose my baby sister. It crossed my mind that I'd have to tell our parents. I suffered such relief when Theiandar pulled you up, I thought I was going to fall out myself."

Caityn wasn't listening. She rubbed her nose, and, sure enough, she didn't feel the wart anymore. She was distracted by the bizarreness of the change and didn't hear a word Adair said.

They sat in silence. Caityn glanced across the fire to see Idra approach Theiandar. He was dry now. She heard Idra talking to him in a low voice. "You were very brave back there, Your Highness."

"Thank you, but I really only did what anyone else in my position would have done."

"But you didn't have to do it. You nearly drowned trying to save her."

"True, but it changes nothing. I would do it again, for anyone."

"You're a good and brave man. Caityn would say the same, and she is lucky to have you." He bowed and continued the task of hanging up his wet clothes. Idra did the same with Caityn's things.

Jealousy reared up inside the princess like a rampaging bull. She was angry and confused. All her emotions were misplaced. The strongest feeling she could identify was anger. She fixated on it. Darkness descended upon the group, but Caityn didn't even notice. Like the blanket of night, she allowed her black, jealous anger to fall on the one person at whom she could direct it: Idra.

CHAPTER ELEVEN
No One is Perfect

"Here, Princess, let me help you down."

Gavin reached up to assist Eliya from her horse. She scowled at him, mostly out of guilt, as he gripped her waist and lowered her to the ground.

As he released her and stepped back, she bowed her head, her eyes focused on a patch of grass. She refused to look up at him. "You must hate me."

"What was that, Highness?"

"You must hate me. For what happened to Princess Caityn." She finally looked up as the words spilled from her mouth. "Tis all my fault. And all because I thought . . . ." Eliya looked away, covering her mouth.

"What? All because you thought she and I had a, ah . . . a thing?"

She nodded slowly, and he had the audacity to laugh. He looked around and then took her hand to lead her over to a spot away from the rest of the group.

Eliya's shock at his touch kept her from noticing the boldness of his familiarity in doing it. Her instinct told her to trust him, and she went along without a word. Gavin wiped debris off a rock and motioned for her to take a seat on it. She did so, and he lowered himself to the ground beside her.

"Now Princess, I want to be totally clear with you. What you did was wrong. There is no doubt. You let jealousy cloud your judgment. I'm sorry to be blunt, but please keep listening. We all make mistakes in one form or another. Yours happens to have hurt someone I care a great deal about. I do *not*, however, hate you."

"Really?" Timid hope sprung up inside her. Eliya didn't know why it mattered to her, but it did.

"Really, Highness. Raz, I mean Prince Theiandar, any time he's mentioned you, 'tis always been with love and pride in his voice. Based on how he blathers on about you, you're obviously a sweet girl, and whatever has come over you of late is not characteristic of who you really are."

"But I made some huge assumptions about Caityn . . . and about you. If only I hadn't gone to the waterfall, maybe none of this would have happened." Eliya wiped a stray tear from her eye.

"Maybe so, but there's no use dwelling on it now. And I'd guess Caityn and I didn't make it easy on you." Eliya could tell he was trying to clear the tears from her eyes with a dose of levity. "Raz told me everything that transpired in an effort to make sure I would be diligent in searching out the madman.

"But listen. Caity and I are close—as close as can be, really. We're first cousins, the same age, *and* I grew up near the castle. She and I spent a lot of time together. I'm a little embarrassed to admit it, but I used to have a crush on my cousin. Nothing ever would have come of it, of course, but she's beautiful, and not on the outside alone but through to the depths of her soul.

"She's smart, headstrong, and bossy as all get-out. Yet she's always had this attractive quality about her, this sense of right and wrong mixed with tenderness and compassion . . . and loyalty. She's a defender, you might say—one who protects and cares for those in need. I've always admired and loved her. You can probably see it in the way I look at her."

Gavin stopped for a minute. He looked to be contemplating his own words, as though he'd never admitted all that to himself before. When Eliya didn't speak up, he continued. "The year I turned sixteen and your brother came to choose a new recruit for his unit was the same year he found out who his betrothed would be. Caityn and Raz became good friends that season.

"Now, Princess, I didn't realize how jealous I could be until I saw your brother with Caityn. Keep in mind, though, I didn't know about her betrothal at the time. I got a mite cocky with Raz during training once. Let's just say he put me in my place."

He stopped to clear his throat. "Anyway, after a time, the jealousy faded. As I got to know your brother, my respect for him crowded out all the other, less attractive, emotions. It was actually a relief when I found out my cousin would be marrying the best man I knew. I hope when all this is over you can feel the same toward her."

He finished and stood, extending his hand to her. She hesitated before accepting the peace offering. "Do you really mean it, then? You don't hate me? Do you think she will?"

"No, I don't hate you and neither will Caityn. She's got a heart bigger than the Twelve Realms. Once this is over, I have no doubt you will be completely forgiven."

"You sound confident, Sir Gavin. I sincerely hope you're right. Thank you . . . and I'm sorry."

He smiled at her and deposited her next to the fire. Before walking away, he gave her a courtly bow. He turned his attention to fulfilling his evening duty of searching for any sign of Caityn's assailant. They still had no clues to lead them to the perpetrator. What kind of man or beast were they dealing with, who left no tracks or trail?

* * *

Idra was glad Caityn was all right. She doubled her efforts at breaking through the strange wall around her cousin's heart. As they ate their dinner by the fire that night, Idra recounted her memories from childhood. She hoped it would stir Caityn's feelings.

"Do you remember when we were younger, you were barely five at the time, and I had a terrible rash all over my body? Well, *I* do. I remember you were so worried about me. You sneaked into the kitchen and stole a tub of lard, almost as big as you, I might add. Do you remember? You slathered it all over me because you'd heard the cook say it was great at relieving dry, itchy skin on a cold winter's day. Ha! I'm not sure it even does that, but you were adorable. I couldn't say no. You are always thoughtful. You were, even then.

"And do you remember—"

Caityn put her hand up to cut off Idra's monologue.

"Idra, what are you trying to do here? Are you along to be a lady-in-waiting, or are you here for something more? Nevermind, don't answer. Just stop talking. I'm not in the mood."

Caityn stood and walked into the dark, away from Idra and

the warmth of the fire.

Idra sat, staring off into the dark. Fresh tears, weighted by confusion, slipped down her cheeks. It was getting harder to deal with this new Caityn. She was unkind and provoking, something Idra had never experienced from her friend.

She wiped her tears and bowed her head to pray. She was lost as to how to help Caityn but decided she would be a silent helper and love Caityn with her actions. That way, maybe neither of them would go insane.

***

Caityn wandered off into the dark. She didn't go far before she stumbled and fell. She grumbled and reached for her twisted ankle. It was one more injury to add to the bruises she'd collected during her watery incident.

A branch cracked nearby. Caityn jumped, peering into the darkness for the source of the sound. This far from the fire, it was pitch black, and she couldn't make out what—or who—it was until he spoke.

"Are you all right? Here, let me help you up."

"Ahmad? No. I think I will sit here a moment. You shouldn't skulk in the dark to scare people like that."

She couldn't see his face, but the smile in his voice was unmistakable when he replied.

"Oh, but 'tis my job, Your Highness. How better to protect those I guard than having the element of surprise on my side?"

"Touché."

"You know, this may sound unkind, but I'm thankful I'm here on this journey with you. I know your situation looks grim, but I feel as though this is where Almighty wants us. I have this sense of his plan and purpose. There's something to be discovered about him—and us—in all of this."

"Or you have spent too much time in the monasey in Nevin."

"Ah, Nevin. My home. No, my lady, I think not. I doubt any man could truly spend too much time learning of the Great One and finding himself covered by the overflowing cup of his grace and mercy."

"I don't wish to speak any more of this, Ahmad."

"My lady, I was given to understand you enjoy theological and philosophical discussion. My apologies if I've offended."

"No, I have no interest in what you're saying. It sounds like gibberish to my ears."

"Well, I think there is still hope that we can mend the void, and you will be bereft no longer. It will come. In the meantime, let me assist you back to camp. It grows late. We are starting out before the break of dawn, and we lost some time today."

Caityn bristled at the last remark. "No, I will take myself back." She stood and hobbled back to the fire.

"My apologies, Your Highness," Ahmad called out. He might have realized it had been unwise to add the last bit, but he couldn't take the reminder back now. She was still close enough to hear his regretful sigh, but she didn't bother to forgive his insensitivity.

CHAPTER TWELVE
Plans Change

The next morning came sooner than Caityn would have liked, but they were off and down the river before the sun even rose over the distant hills. She could see a mist circling over the chilly water in the morning's diffuse glow. The intermittent chirp of crickets carrying across the surface of the water should have been soothing, but it grated upon her nerves.

She found herself in the same boat as Theiandar today. Caityn was amenable to this arrangement but wasn't sure why it was better than any other. All she knew with certainty was there was something about him she couldn't resist, a strange and unfathomable connection. She couldn't even define the emotion attached to the sensation.

Instead of analyzing it further, she sat behind him, studying him as he rowed. She watched how his hair moved in the breeze, how it tickled at his neck and played with the collar of his shirt. She noticed how the shirt tightened over his arm muscles with each stroke of the paddle and how straight he sat in the seat, as though he were a mighty oak that no wind or storm could depose.

What is this feeling? Comfort? How strange to feel anything so light, she thought. Watching him row was comforting. *What should I do with this feeling?* She was surprised when the answer came immediately. *Hold on to it and don't let go!*

She was startled out of her thoughts by Adair's amused voice. "What do we have here? Could it be a smile on my sister's face?"

"What?" She wiped the remains of it from her face. "I don't know what you're talking about."

"It was nice, Caity. I haven't seen you smile since . . . . Well, I was just happy to see it. You're welcome to do it more. Smile, I mean."

Theiandar looked over his shoulder at her with a hopeful expression on his face. "I have to agree with Adair, Cait. Your smile has been too hard to come by." He stopped and looked more closely. "I find it strange, but your hair . . . . It doesn't look quite as gray today."

Caityn looked at him with a confused frown. None of this mattered or made sense to her. She froze in place when Theiandar reached back and touched the hair next to her face. The sensation of comfort flooded back into her consciousness again, and she didn't even notice the waning itchiness of her chest. Caught in the aftermath of Theiandar's gentle touch, a diminutive smile played at the corners of her thin lips.

* * *

They were nearing a modest waterfall in the river. Along the south shore, they saw more and more Parlanian people. Caityn reclined in the boat, watching the children of her neighboring realm fish along the banks. One young boy waved frantically, his grin boyish and happy.

The noon hour had almost arrived when they reached the rapids leading up to the waterfall. The boats pulled to the southern shore where everyone disembarked and stretched their cramped legs. The sweltering midday heat of summer had already begun, even though it was only the beginning of the season.

Theiandar wiped the dampness from his forehead. "All right, men, the slope of land here on this shore is more gradual next to the falls. We'll only remove the heaviest and most awkward gear from the boats in order to carry them down there, to the deeper water." He pointed downstream to a calm place a short distance from the base of the waterfall. "Cait, you and Idra stay put here on this rise where we can see you."

The men went straight to work, removing any heavy items from the boats and depositing them on the shore. The smallest boat which carried the food supplies and one rower was the lightest. They left all the food stuffs in it as four men carried it down the grassy, rock-strewn hill. Two more men hefted one of the now-lightened boats upon their shoulders and started down after them. Theiandar and Adair worked together to haul a third boat to the base of the waterfall.

While they were busy, Idra and Caityn sat on rocks near the top of the falls. Neither spoke as they stared from the water on one side of them, churning and misty, to the grassy fields on the other. The sun had risen to its highest point for the day, and the heat was becoming unpleasant. After less than half an hour, Caityn got up from the rock on which she was perched and walked toward the trees a short distance upstream.

Idra almost protested, but let the words die on her lips. Instead, she stood and followed Caityn. They stopped under the shady edge of the trees and leaned against the sturdy trunks.

Caityn broke the silence. "Do you see that?"

"See what, my lady?"

The princess pointed to the other shore, toward the dense underbrush of the dominating pine forest. "That. There! See the black thing moving there?"

Idra squinted and tried to make out the black thing Caityn spied in the dark of the forest. "I'm sorry. I can't see anything."

Caityn peered more purposefully. "I suppose 'tis possible I was seeing things, but 'tis odd, because I'm almost completely sure there was something—or someone—over there in the bushes. It felt as though someone was watching me."

"Well, if there was, they're gone now. The men seem to be done moving the boats and gear. We should probably go on down now," Idra said.

"Yes, I suppose you're right. Let's go." As they walked back toward the waterfall, Caityn made occasional glances across the river. When they reached the spot where they'd been sitting before, it was to encounter a rather concerned-looking Theiandar.

"I thought I told you to stay here," he said when they were close enough to hear him.

Caityn frowned and was about to speak up when Idra interjected. "Oh, I apologize, Highness. It was hot sitting in the sun, and we decided to go stand in the shade over there."

The prince took a cursory glance over Idra's shoulder. "Next time you decide to disobey an order, at least let someone know where you're going."

Caityn spoke before Idra could apologize. "We are not soldiers to be ordered about."

Theiandar looked back at her. At first his expression was stern, but then it softened. "There's a little of that stubborn girl I know. Well, 'tis good to see some fight back in you today. And I'm sorry for sounding harsh. I was worried something had happened to you."

He bowed and escorted the two women down the hill to the temporary camp where a meal awaited them. They anticipated an uneventful trip the rest of the way downstream. Adair explained they should be at the docks near Conleth by nightfall.

* * *

The thief knew he'd been given a gift. By altering his course to go south to Larue, he had inadvertently come across the best news he could get. The princess was no longer at the castle in Taisce! She was out here, in the open. It was almost certain they were on their way to High Castle.

If he made contact with the mercenaries soon enough, he could have her captured without a castle break-in. It would be much less hassle. Of course, it was possible the princess would make it to the castle before he had her abduction arranged. Once in the fortress of High Castle, it would prove much more difficult to accomplish.

He hid himself in the forest. He couldn't let the princess and her companion see him while he spied from his position on the other side of the river. Another change of plans occurred to him. When he was sure they hadn't made him out, he moved off to the west, in the direction in which he'd first started out on his journey.

The thief realized he must follow this group and see what their plans were. It was the best way to plot how to capture his prize. After he ascertained their strategy, he would make haste to recruit the manpower necessary to abscond with the prince's elderly companion.

* * *

Dark was closing in when the group arrived at the docks nearest Conleth's capital city. Here, there was a trading outpost which sported a tavern with one room to let. It was at this place they stopped for the night. Caityn and Idra were to share the only bed at the tavern, while the men made beds in the hay of the stable out back. One guard was stationed outside their room.

While the women were preparing for bed, a tray of food was brought for them to enjoy in peace and quiet. Meanwhile, the men were in the tavern enjoying a meal that didn't consist of their usual fare—dried bean soup with chunks of salted pork. The tavern actually had real meals such as hearty beef stew and slow-roasted pork.

Theiandar sat next to Adair. The two men reclined at a round table in the corner, watching the other men eat and laugh. Theiandar chewed a piece of bread and then drank some of the ale the barmaid had poured into his mug.

"This all feels unreal, Adair." Theiandar's companion was quiet. "I can't wrap my mind around the state of current events. Just a few days ago I was supposed to be getting married. Life was supposed to change in a good way."

"This is becoming a regular conversation for us, my friend," Adair said. "All joking aside, I hope the surreal quality of it proves to be a memory we can look back on and laugh. I can't imagine my sister staying like this. My parents will be brokenhearted for her and the future she's likely to have because of it. Besides, it wouldn't be fair to you to hold you to the betrothal. And you can't marry an old woman. Tis like she knows everything my sister would know, but she's not really my sister. No one, not even my father, expects you to fulfill the betrothal if Caity can't be saved from this curse."

"That's the thing, though. I made a promise to her. I promised I would be here for her and with her, no matter what. I promised myself I would always protect her. This has been an awful beginning to that promise. How can I give up on her when she needs me more than ever?"

Adair didn't reply.

"I can't give up, Adair. Not now, not ever. And if it means I live the rest of my life with the old woman who is the withered shell of the best part of me, then I think I have to do it. She's not someone I can cast aside, and I know she would do it for me if the roles were reversed. The only way I could leave her is if I died in this quest." Theiandar slammed the side of his fist down on the table. "I will save her! I must! Caityn is worth the risk."

Silence filled the space between them. The air grew oppressive. Adair took his time, but his response brought added courage to Theiandar. "I'm with you. She's my sister. We'll save Caity or die trying." His resolve was complete.

"Thank you for your help. I'm grateful to the Almighty, in his infinite wisdom, for placing you in that records room when and where he did. It gives me hope that if we find something in the scrolls at Conleth, we'll be able to do something to save her," Theiandar said.

* * *

The men did not notice their adversary hunched over at the table nearest them. He was sitting with a group of inebriated townsfolk who didn't seem to mind his presence.

He listened to every word the two princes spoke. Under his black hood, with his ale mug pulled up close to his face, he smiled. The thief reached into his cloak and grasped the glowing red amulet he kept hidden against his heart—his empty, cruel, and selfish heart.

He was pleased to know they kept a record of him through history, but he wasn't interested in stopping them from obtaining the scrolls. The evil little man doubted it would help them much anyway. The idea of his fame delighted him to no end, secreted though it must stay.

Waiting only a minute or two more, he slipped from the tavern and started his long journey south to Larue. He knew just the man to handle the situation. Devon Roache would do anything for the right price. *Maybe even kill a prince*, he contemplated with menacing delight.

* * *

Caityn rose from the table having expressed her lethargy and disinterest in the food. Her crooked fingers fumbled uselessly with the stays of her gown as she worked to undo them.

Idra rose from her seat and, without a word, went to work undoing Caityn's dress. Only two minutes passed before it was done. Idra hated the extra tension between them. No doubt, even her silence was an offense to her cousin.

Idra helped Caityn into her nightgown and covered the exhausted princess when she crawled into the bed. To Idra's surprise, Caityn reached out and grabbed her arm.

"Thank you." The brief sentence was halting. Caityn appeared as though she wanted to say more, but instead she released Idra's arm and rolled over.

"You're welcome, my lady," Idra said. "Um . . . my lady?" She hesitated, unsure if she should say anything else. Then she remembered her pledge not to speak out of turn but only do things to show her love for her friend. "Goodnight, Caityn."

CHAPTER THIRTEEN
Conleth

When Caityn and Idra were ready, they emerged from the tavern to find Theiandar and his men had already outfitted the group with a horse and a cart. The ramshackle place didn't have enough horses to rent to all of them. The ladies would ride in the cart with the supplies, and the men would march behind.

The one horse was hired for the half-day's journey to the actual town of Conleth. Their destination, the university, was located near the Hall of Historic Records, at the center of town.

"Theian, as soon as we arrive I'll need to head to the university," Adair said. "Master Collin, an old professor of mine, has the clout to get us in to the records without much hassle. The king would help, but this time of year he's likely en route to his summer chateau."

"Fine. Let's stop there before finding a place to stay."

Theiandar assisted Caityn and then Idra into the cart. Without an introduction, a woman approached the cart and spoke to Caityn. "Madam, I see you must be rich, for you travel with your beautiful daughter and under heavy guard."

"She's not my daughter," Caityn said.

"I beg your pardon, good mistress! Please forgive a silly woman her misunderstanding."

Caityn knew the woman paused in hopes of a word of acceptance for her apology, but none was forthcoming. The princess stared at her, impatience brewing below the surface.

The woman cleared her throat. "I am a woman in need, m'lady. You see, my family has no money at present. Our food is almost gone. I do not beg, though, m'lady. No, you see . . ." She held up two items for inspection. "You see, I have some valuable trinkets I'd like to sell, by which I can provide for my children."

She held up a lovely, iridescent scarf made of imported silk and an exotic quill pen crafted from a feather Caityn didn't recognize. It was long, and the colors were vibrant hues of blue, green, gold, and red.

The stranger was quick to continue. "These items do, in fact, belong to me. My late husband was a ship's first mate, and these are gifts he brought back to me from his distant travels." She looked at the items lovingly and then thrust them toward Caityn.

At first, Caityn didn't reply but stared at the scarf and feather. When Idra was on the verge of expressing their regret, Caityn's hand shot up to silence her.

"We will buy both from you, madam," Caityn said. "See that man there. He will pay you."

The woman looked. "Oh, why I recognize him! That is Prince Adair of Taisce. I didn't realize this was a royal party. Please forgive my forwardness, m'lady!"

"Nonsense. We are people like you, with our own needs. Besides, royalty a role we must play, like any other. It is not who we are as people. At least my mother, Queen Ismene, would likely say such a thing."

"Your *mother*, m'lady?" The woman voiced her question without thinking.

"Yes, my mother." Caityn recognized what the woman was implying. "Oh, I know why you look confused. Well, let me explain. I am Caityn, daughter of King Othniel of Taisce. It would seem I have been bestowed with a curse that has unnaturally aged me. In fact, it is the particular reason why we travel along this path. The ridiculous people with whom I travel seem to think they can uncover a remedy to what ails me. Tis a fool's errand, but they still drag me along anyway."

The woman was astonished, and it was obvious she didn't know what to say in response to the princess's diatribe. Idra took pity on her and directed the woman to see Prince Adair to receive payment for the items. She bowed and left their presence.

"You shouldn't have told her, my lady. Now word is sure to spread," Idra said. The rebuke was not lost on Caityn.

"What does it matter, Idra? Who has made you keeper of my life and choices? Word will get out eventually, and when this can't be undone, the whole world will speak of it. They will say, 'Oh that poor princess in the Twelve Realms! She had all her beauty dashed upon the rocks and was left as good as dead.'"

"Well, you haven't lost your flair for the dramatic!" Idra retorted.

"Why aren't you angry at me for speaking to you so?"

"Because I love you," Idra replied without even a bat of an eyelash. "You're my best friend, and you aren't fully yourself. There is much I can forgive."

They heard Theiandar call out, and the cart lurched forward. Adair walked up next to the slow-moving cart and held out the items the woman had sold to him. "Here, Caity. That woman back there said you told her I would purchase these items for you. I took her at her word, because it looked like she could use the money."

Caityn reached for the items. "That is correct, brother." She touched the silk fabric, rubbing its soft gauziness between her fingertips. Then she flung it up and wrapped it around her speckled gray hair.

They made their last stop an hour outside Conleth to eat a midday meal before completing the trip to the Twelve Realms' most prestigious university.

Theiandar helped Caityn out of the cart. Her body screamed in protest with every movement after a day spent in the cramped, jostling conveyance.

Adair said, "I'll find Master Collin while you get a place for us to stay tonight. I would suggest the Talking Ram, around the corner there. Tis large enough to accommodate our group, and 'tis clean."

"Thanks, Adair. After I get the ladies settled, I'll meet you back here," Theiandar said.

"Certainly. See you then." Adair bounded up the steps, disappearing through the massive stone building's ornate, arching doors. Caityn filled with jealousy seeing Theiandar's hand hold Idra's while assisting her from the cart.

His voice interrupted her concentration. "Ladies, let's head over to the Talking Ram. If at all possible, we want to leave for High Castle tomorrow at first light." He spoke to two of his men, Zaccur and Lieve. "Take these horses and the cart to a livery stable. Obtain fresh horses for everyone. We'll leave in the morning. Everything must be ready by tonight."

Zaccur said, "Yes, sir, I know the best stable in town. We'll get right on it."

The two headed off to complete their duties. Prince Theiandar held out his arms to the women, and Caityn took one, while Idra hesitated before accepting the other. It was as though they were just on a stroll down the street. Caityn almost felt normal for a moment—at least until she looked down at her hand wrapped around Theiandar's arm. Once her eyes settled on the thin, bony skin, she remembered that all was far from normal. A frown creased her brow. She reached up and touched the scarf covering her hair. *This is normal now. Nothing will ever change.*

Caityn worked at resigning herself to the gray hair, beak-like hook of her nose, dull pallor of her skin, ever-present frown lines, hunch in her back, gnarled fingers, and yellow fingernails—along with everything else. Was it even worth it to bother saving her? She didn't feel worthy. She felt ugly, tarnished beyond repair.

These thoughts still plagued her as they reached the inn. The sign hanging above the door was aged but cared for, with new paint depicting a strange ram standing on its hind legs, wearing a swashbuckling sort of hat with feather.

"This must be the place," Theiandar remarked. He released the ladies' arms and opened the door for them. The lighting in the common room was dim. What she saw consisted of a bar, tables, and, in the far corner, a check-in counter. It was plain but clean.

A short, round woman with wild curly hair stood behind the counter. She said, "Welcome to the Talkin' Ram. How might Yael be a-servin' ye?"

"Thank you," Theiandar said. "We'd like rooms to rent for the night. Five rooms to be exact. Can you accommodate us, Mistress Yael?"

"Yes, m'lord, we can be doin' it," she replied with a huge smile. "I ken from the quality clothin' ye be important guests. Calla will prepare rooms for ye." She looked over her shoulder and bellowed with a voice bigger than herself, "Calla, girl! Get out here this minute and get these purty ladies a room ready!"

A young girl, about ten years old and sporting the same wavy curls, came scurrying out from a back room with a harried look upon her face. "Yes'm!" she said as she skidded to a halt and curtsied. Before anyone could bat an eyelash, she bolted up a flight of stairs to the left of the counter.

Mistress Yael faced her guests with a proud smile stretched from ear to ear. "That be me own sweet bit of a gal. She's our pride 'n' joy, to her pa and me, that be! But, please, take a seat over there, m'ladies. It be a bit o'nothin' to get the room fixed up for ye."

Theiandar escorted the women to a nearby table and pulled out their chairs for them before heading back to the counter to make the rest of the sleeping arrangements. Soon, Calla bustled back down the stairs, prepared to lead Caityn and Idra to their room.

His hand was gentle when he reached out to take Caityn's elbow. "Princess, I'll be back shortly. You ladies please stay in the room and rest. I'll have Mistress Yael send some tea up for you and prepare baths." He looked into her eyes to make sure she was listening. She gave a stunted nod before they followed Calla up the stairs.

"I'll be right on it for ye, m'lord. No mistakin', ye be in the right place for a good bit o' pamperin'!"

Yael had spoken before he could even ask. Theiandar ignored the eavesdropping and gave his thanks before heading out to inform the men of the arrangements. He planned to send some of them back to the inn to watch over the ladies. His impatience and growing anxiety were obvious to everyone present.

* * *

It had been eight months since he and his men had passed through Conleth on their regular travels, but the town looked the same. This was one of the few kingdoms in the Twelve Realms with no castle to speak of, although it really didn't need one because of its close proximity to High Castle, only a day away.

The realm they now inhabited was named for this city, Conleth. The ruler of this area lived in a home built with white stone and beautiful columns, all having been floated down the river from the distant hills of Taisce, where brilliant white quartzomite rock was found in abundance. It was an impressive mansion and would certainly withstand the test of time. Theiandar could see the king's grand courtyard from the steps of the university. The school stood exactly opposite the home and was a perfect counterpart, having been constructed in a grand style as well, but with gray stone and beautiful stained glass windows.

The prince stood with his men who'd stayed at the university to wait for Adair. He wondered what was taking his friend such a long time. Finally, Adair emerged from the arched doorway with a muscular, blond-haired man in tow. Master Collin looked nothing like Theiandar imagined an esteemed professor should look, but the smile on the man's face was welcoming.

Adair made introductions. Theiandar said, "Thank you for meeting with us, Master Collin."

"Of course, Your Highness. Tis my pleasure to be of service. The men who have been assigned the job of protecting the Historic Records here in Conleth do take their job seriously, and even though you are the High King's son, they have strict orders to keep everyone out unless they have special permission. I am happy to come along and ensure your easy access of the records." He bowed to the prince.

"Besides," Collin said, clapping Adair on the shoulder, "this young man was one of my best pupils until he completed his studies last year. I'm sorry to hear of your plight, though. I hope you find what you need."

The group headed next door to the Hall of Historic Records. While also made of stone, it was fairly unspectacular by comparison. The walls were gray but had no arching doors, no stained glass or remarkable stonework. The double door through which they entered led into a massive foyer. The floors were bare and the room was fairly dark. It took Theiandar's eyes a moment to adjust.

The guards waited outside while Adair and Theiandar stood just inside the door. Master Collin strode over to a desk near the rear of the room. His footsteps echoed in the considerable, empty space. Sitting behind the oak desk was a pale, bent, old man without a smile line to be found.

The unhappy man glared up at Collin. From where Theiandar stood, he could not hear what was being said between the two of them, but the professor became quite animated, pointing at Adair and Theiandar before gesturing at the man sitting behind the desk.

"That's Gerhardt, the keykeeper," Adair informed Theiandar. "He's a grumpy old man, but I don't think he'll cause any problems. He likes to pretend he wields all the power around here."

Gerhardt finally stood, and after a moment more of what looked like arguing, the two men walked over to the door. The keykeeper continued to frown as Collin made the introductions.

"Your Highness, this is Gerhardt, the master of the keys. He will allow you access to the records room of ancient folklore. Gerhardt, you know Prince Adair of Taisce, of course, but this is Prince Theiandar, High Prince of the Realms."

Gerhardt knew his place and made a bow before he answered.

"Only Prince Adair may enter, Collin. You know the records rooms must be kept free of contaminants. Prince Adair is aware of the protocols. He can do the search, but Prince Theiandar must wait out here. I'm sorry."

Adair and Collin were about to protest when Theiandar spoke up. "I understand your concern, Gerhardt. We will honor this rule. The history of our people is deeply important to me, as it is to you, and I wouldn't risk its security unless absolutely necessary. Prince Adair is familiar with the records and can likely locate what we need without my help."

Gerhardt's only response was a slight bow of his head.

"Adair, you set to work looking, and I will come back to check on you in two hours," Theiandar said. "I'll go check in with the men and make sure things are totally prepared for tomorrow's journey. I think we'll hire a carriage to take your sister the rest of the way to High Castle. She seemed worn and tired when I left them at the inn."

"Very good, Theiandar. Instead of you coming back here, though, I'll just meet you at the inn by ten tonight, at the latest," Adair offered.

Theiandar thought for a moment.. "That will be fine. See you tonight."

Theiandar and the professor exited the building, leaving Adair to tackle the work of locating the right scrolls.

"I wouldn't worry too much, Your Highness," Master Collin said.

"What's that?"

"I wouldn't worry about Adair finding the scrolls. He's got a great head for memorizing dates and locations. He'll find them in no time."

"Ah, yes. Thanks, Professor."

"Anytime, My Prince. Now I will leave you to your business," Collin said.

They parted ways at the steps of the university, and Theiandar strode in the direction of the livery.

CHAPTER FOURTEEN
Unmerited Rancor

Adair followed Gerhardt down a long, dark hallway. There were two burning sconces along the hall to illuminate the path, but they left most of the hallway in darkness. They stopped in front of a door bearing a simple sign: Ancient Folklore.

Gerhardt went to work finding the correct key. His search was slow while he grumbled and mumbled about inconvenient tasks. Adair tried to ignore him, knowing what the old keykeeper could be like when plans were changed. If Adair planned on staying until he found what he was looking for, Gerhardt would have to stay as well.

While the older man continued to look for the key, a door they'd passed creaked open, and a young man stepped into the shadowy hallway. He locked the door behind him and sauntered toward Adair and the keykeeper.

"Gerhardt, what on earth is going on down there?" the young man asked.

Gerhardt looked up as he located the correct key, *almost* smiling at his success. "Ah, is it you, young Simon?"

"Yes, 'tis me. What's going on?" Simon stopped beside Adair.

"Hello, Simon. We've not met for quite some time. When did you start working at the Hall of Historic Records?"

Simon peered up at the guest. Adair watched the recognition pass across his face. Simon's annoyed expression turned to a glare. His eye sockets were black holes beneath his bushy eyebrows, most likely because he was almost six inches shorter than Prince Adair. He had no idea what to think of Simon's reaction.

"Adair. I can't say 'tis a pleasure to see you here. If you must know, I was employed here three months ago. The headmaster at the university decided that if I couldn't continue my education, the least they could do was find me a job which could lead to my being able to do so in the future."

The prince was taken aback by Simon's venomous reply, but his royal training brought out the diplomat in him every time. "I'm sorry to hear of your financial distress, Simon. I hope soon you'll be able to complete your degree."

Simon nearly managed to keep the jealousy from showing on his face, but Adair caught it.

"Soon, I hope. What are you doing here?"

"I have some research to do. Tis imperative I complete it as quickly as possible. Gerhardt was just letting me into the room I need. I'll likely be here until late. I should go now and get to work."

Adair couldn't miss the grumpy look on Gerhardt's typically gloomy face.

"Yes, which means I have to stay late as well. I can't say I'm happy about it. I had plans for this night and now they're ruined," the surly keykeeper said.

"You go on home," Simon interjected. I'll see to Prince Adair's supervision."

Gerhardt looked surprised but didn't wait for him to change his mind. "If you're sure, I'm off. Good-bye, lads." He scurried down the hall into the darkness, leaving the two young men to face each other.

Adair cleared his throat to ease the uncomfortable silence.

Simon squinted at him in the dark. Without looking down, he flipped his keys to the one for the Ancient Folklore door. He inserted it in the lock and twisted. The latch clunked and the door was free to swing wide. He gave a grand, obviously mocking, gesture for Adair to precede him into the room. Wary of Simon's presence, Adair hesitated before stepping through the open door.

The assistant keykeeper followed. Using a narrow taper from the hall's sconce, he lit the other candles inside the room. The candlesticks were sitting on the desk just inside the room. He returned the sconce's light to its place and reentered the dusty-smelling space.

"That's all right, Simon, you can go back to whatever you were doing before. I'll be a while and don't want to unnecessarily waste your time," Adair said.

"Oh, I don't have any great plans. What exactly are you looking to find?"

Adair didn't want Simon to stay; there was something about his behavior that was peculiar, but Adair couldn't place his finger on it. With no excuse handy, he told the truth. "I'm looking for an old tale of someone called the Beauty Thief. I need to find all the information pertaining to the legends about him."

Simon sat down on the edge of the desk while he thought about Adair's description. "It doesn't sound at all familiar, but I can probably help you locate it. What's the significance?"

Adair hesitated, not sure he wanted to tell Simon the reason for wanting those scrolls. "Tis just some research I need for a project of mine, that's all." It really was something he was working on, mentally reassuring himself to justify the lie.

Simon lit another candle and held it high. The unwarranted hatred reflected in his eyes sent a shiver down Adair's spine. Before he could question him, though, Simon turned away into the sinister blackness of the scroll-filled room and walked down one of the aisles. Adair shook off the eerie feeling. He decided to follow Simon, since he couldn't remember where they'd been when he found the scrolls the last time he was here.

"Around what time period are we talking here? Was this tale pre-Anno Domini or post-Anno Domini? Because if the date is pre-Anno, you'll have to start looking over there." Simon pointed to the other side of the room.

Adair said, "No, I believe it was post-Anno, but not by much. It was probably a few hundred years after, I think."

"Well," Simon said, stopping in front of a stand of yellowed scrolls, "I suggest we start here."

"You don't have to help, Simon. I'm capable of looking through and caring for the scrolls."

"Oh no, Your Highness." He wasn't facing Adair, but the prince could hear the sneer coloring Simon's tone. "We couldn't have your princely self working in such tedium alone. Surely you should have a servant here doing this for you."

Not knowing what to think of Simon's behavior, he replied, "I'm perfectly capable of doing the work myself. But, if you insist..."

Adair picked up a scroll and unrolled it enough to read the first few lines as Simon did the same nearby. Finding the scroll to be a bit too early, Adair moved to the next section. He hoped, now for multiple reasons, it wouldn't take long to find the ones he needed.

***

Simon gritted his teeth as he opened scroll after scroll. Of all the people to walk into the Hall of Historic Records, it had to be Prince Adair, the person he hated the most. Adair was top of the class, rich, esteemed—*royal*—and had everything in the world he could possibly want. He didn't have to work for anything. Everything was handed to him on a silver platter, while Simon was stuck here in this musty, dark, completely boring cave, hidden away as though he was one of these useless, old relics. It was demeaning to have to work here among the rotting past.

He wasn't sure what Adair wanted with the scrolls, but if he found them first, maybe he could make them disappear before the prince could get a look at them. Adair was a pompous royal brat, after all, and what did he need some old stories for? *Probably to impress his friends with a scary tale for bedtime. What an imbecile*, he thought.

"Wasn't there some event happening this week at your home, *Prince*?"

From ten feet away, his head bowed over another scroll, Adair replied, "Yes, but there was a change of plans. The event has been postponed for now but will likely happen before too long."

"It was something big, I thought." Simon paused with a scroll halfway unrolled. "Oh, right. Your sister was getting married. What happened? Prince Theiandar find she wasn't pretty enough? Have to renegotiate on the particulars before he'll marry her?" His joke was cruel, but he had no idea how close to the mark it fell.

Without an ounce of hesitation, Adair dropped the scroll and marched over to stand in front of Simon. Simon looked up at him with laughter in his eyes, as though everyone should get the joke and appreciate it. Adair snatched the front of his shirt and pulled him close.

"Don't ever talk about my sister like that again or so help me . . . ." Adair stopped short and released Simon's shirtfront.

Simon watched Adair's jaw clench tight. He let his own anger build to barely-contained rage. "Or what, *Your Highness*? Will you have me beaten and thrown in a dungeon somewhere? I don't think you'd actually sully your own hands to do anything, Your High and Mightiness."

"Tis one thing to insult me, Simon, but another thing altogether when you drag my sister's good name through the mud. You will take it back, or we'll be forced to duel."

Seeing how Adair was deadly serious, Simon decided to relent for the time being. His rage could be better spent elsewhere. "Of course. I apologize for speaking poorly of your sister. I'm sure she's better than you."

Simon glared at Adair's retreating back and let himself hate the pompous prince a little more. He went back to opening scrolls, intent upon thwarting the rich ruler's search.

Another thirty minutes of silence and searching went by. Simon had lost interest in actually looking for what Adair wanted. He pulled one more scroll out of its cubbyhole and read.

"What have we here?" he muttered.

His interest was piqued. It talked of an amulet used to steal the beauty of young women and gave it to the owner of the amulet as renewed life force. The stories said one could live forever if in possession of the magic of the amulet. Simon's eyes widened as he read the scroll's accounts, and the legend captured his imagination.

He looked over at Adair to see if he'd noticed, but the stupid prince was still searching halfway across the room and hadn't observed Simon's intent reading. Simon picked up the next scroll and found contained in it the second half of the narrative.

With both parts in hand, he decided to exact a bit of revenge on the prince. He looked at his candelabra, its four tapers burning bright, and unrolled the scrolls.

"Prince Adair, I think I've found something!"

Adair hurried across the room. Simon didn't hesitate to follow through on his plan. He pretended to trip and swung the ancient scrolls over the top of the candles. The dry, old paper ignited immediately, and he dropped them to the ground.

"Oh no! How clumsy of me." Simon feigned upset, and he didn't care if the prince recognized it or not.

In a panic, Adair pushed Simon aside and lunged for the papers.

How dare he lay his hands on me! Without a second thought, all the jealous anger and rage inside Simon burst forth. He pulled the dagger from his belt and stepped behind the kneeling prince. With complete control, in utter hatred, he plunged the dagger into Adair's back, not once, but twice.

The prince had no idea what hit him, but he struggled to his feet. Adair grabbed his own knife and swung at Simon in an attempt to squelch a second attack. The knife sliced across Simon's cheek, and his scream of pain echoed through the room as he fled into the hallway.

CHAPTER FIFTEEN
The Blow's Affliction

Theiandar paced the floor of the inn's tavern. He checked the time on the mantle clock again. It was fifteen minutes after ten and still no Adair. This wasn't like him at all. They'd been friends a long time, and Theiandar knew Adair liked promptness. He slapped the mantle of the impressive fireplace and addressed his men who were seated at tables nearby.

"Zaccur, Lieve, Jarl, Daray—you men stay here. The rest of you come with me. We're going to the records building to see what's keeping Adair."

Theiandar led the men to the building but stopped short when he saw the front door ajar. That seemed uncharacteristic of the older man, Gerhardt, he'd met earlier. He motioned his men to approach with caution and crept to the door. With a slow, methodical pressure, he opened it. The foyer was dark and appeared empty. After his eyes adjusted to the darkness, he led the others in farther. There was only one lit hallway. That was where he headed.

The light from the wall sconces must have been at its end; the darkness was consuming almost every last vestige of illumination. What caught Theiandar's eye was the bright light emanating from the room at the end of the hall. Every step was made with caution. When they'd gone halfway down the hall, he stopped, standing in the darkness between sconces.

"Hello? Who's here? Is anyone here?" Theiandar called out.

Silence was followed by a low moan. Theiandar's instincts kicked in, and he sprinted down the hall and around the desk by the door. "Hello? Where are you?" No one responded to his urgent queries.

Theiandar's heightened senses took in everything around him, including the smell of old, decaying paper and burning candle wax. He blocked out everything but the task at hand and ran toward the light near the back of the scroll-filled room. He burst around the corner and stopped cold in his tracks.

"Adair!" He dropped to the floor next to his injured friend. "Adair, can you hear me?"

Theiandar tried to ignore the blood everywhere while he took a quick look at the wounds. Gently, he rolled Adair onto his side and checked to be sure his friend was still breathing. "Wake up, Adair! Come on, my friend."

The other men gathered. Hanif, the blue-eyed baby of the bunch, pushed his way to the front. "What's happened, Raz?"

"He's been stabbed in the back." Theiandar pulled off his shirt and tore it into ragged strips. He pressed some to the wound on Adair's back. With Hanif's help, he wrapped the rest of the cloth around Adair's body to hold the temporary bandage in place.

"Hanif, help me lift him. We'll take him back to the inn and try to determine how bad these stab wounds are. Florian, you and Rance go get the local sheriff. Bring him to the inn. Parker, you, Silas, and Wade sweep the rest of the building. See if the assailant is still within the Hall. We need to find out who did this and now!"

It took two men to lift Adair, but because of the location of his wounds, they decided hoisting Adair onto Theiandar's shoulder would put the least pressure on his injuries. Ahmad stepped up to help Hanif and Theiandar. The three of them tried to be careful. Theiandar staggered a bit under his friend's weight but got his footing. As they tottered from the room and down the hallway, Theiandar remembered the scrolls.

"Ahmad, go back. Get those scrolls. They were on the floor next to Adair."

"Yes, Sire!" Ahmad sprinted back down the hall.

* * *

Adair was regaining consciousness when they arrived at the inn. He moaned low. Theiandar struggled under Adair's weight as he carried him up the stairs to the room. Mistress Yael and her husband went to work, hustling and bustling about in order to get water and clean cloth.

Theiandar and Hanif laid Adair on the bed, but it still caused him to cry out in pain when his back touched the bedcovers.

"Take it easy, my friend," Theiandar said as they rolled Adair onto his stomach. "It would seem you have an enemy in town."

Adair groaned. "How bad?" His eyes were closed and teeth gritted.

With adept movements, Theiandar removed the temporary bandage and cut away Adair's damaged shirt. Using great care, he picked the remnants from the edges of the wounds. Adair winced but made no sound.

Mistress Yael showed up at the door. Her awkward halt reminded Theiandar of his bare chest. He grabbed his jacket from the chair by the fire and threw it on.

"My apologies, Mistress."

She shook her head. "Nothing I haven't seen before, Sire." She entered, carrying a bowl of warm water and fresh pieces of cloth to clean the wounds.

The punctures were both high, obviously executed by someone who didn't know what he was doing. But regardless of the perpetrator's knowledge, the knife had pierced deep and done its job, causing Adair to lose a lot of blood. One wound appeared to be close to vital organs, but it was hard for Theiandar to tell.

He addressed himself to the hovering Mistress Yael. "Is there a physician close by who could be of assistance?"

"I already sent me good husband, Efrem, to get 'm, Prince. Will he live, Sire?"

Theiandar looked from her to Adair and back before answering. "Yes, Mistress Yael, I think he will, but I'm no expert. We'll let the doctor give final say."

Before he'd even finished speaking, the proprietor and the doctor strode into the room. They'd had to shimmy past Theiandar's men, who were hovering in the hall outside the room. The doctor shuffled over, and Theiandar moved out of his way.

After a moment and a few pokes to the wounds, eliciting more groans from the semiconscious Adair, the doctor said, "Well, it isn't good. He's lost quite a bit of blood, from the looks of it. But he appears strong and healthy otherwise, Sire. He'll not die today, I think. We'll sew him up, and I'll apply a poultice and clean bandages.

"You must be careful not to reopen the wounds. The one is extremely close to his lung. Another inch and he'd have suffocated to death from drowning in his own blood."

"Thank you, doctor. We'll see to it," Theiandar replied.

As the doctor located a needle and thread in his bag, the innkeeper and his wife stepped out into the crowded hall with Theiandar. "Thank you for your hospitality. As soon as the sheriff arrives, please send him up. We need his assistance to get to the bottom of this," Theiandar said.

"O' course, Your Majesty," Efrem said with a bow. His wife followed suit, and they scooted down the hall.

Theiandar stepped back into the room and settled on the edge of the bed where Adair could see him. The doctor had given Adair a swig of something. It seemed to have made him unintelligible but took away the pain. He lay there, relaxed as a cat.

"Adair, can you tell me who did this to you?" Theiandar asked.

"Yeah, it was . . . a man I was at university with . . ."

"Where was the man who was with you earlier? Gerhardt. He wasn't there when we arrived tonight."

"Huh? Oh, no, he went . . . uh . . . Simon stayed," Adair mumbled.

"What, Adair? Focus! *Who* was there? Who stabbed you?"

"It was Simon. Don't know why . . ." Adair closed his eyes.

"He won't be of much more use to you, Sire. That medicine I gave him is strong stuff. Makes suturing up big fellas a whole lot easier!"

"I see. Thank you, Doctor—"

"Oh, you can just call me Doc Eko. Thank you kindly. I'm about done here, young Prince. Make sure these bandages get changed and the wounds get washed out every day. We don't want an infection finding its way in. No, we surely don't."

"Yes. Thank you again." Theiandar pulled a weighty gold piece from his pocket and handed it to the doctor.

"Well, here's more than I get paid in six months of house calls!" the doctor said with a hearty smile. "Thank you, Your Majesty. Thank you kindly."

"You're welcome. I would pay you more if I had it to spare. You've done us a kind service tonight. Good night, sir," Theiandar said.

"Good night to you, also. And don't forget to tend to those wounds."

Doc Eko kept jabbering to no one in particular as he made his way back down the hall. It was nearly empty now, as Theiandar's men had gone back to the tavern to await the sheriff's arrival. Only Daray remained behind to guard the ladies' door.

Theiandar waited in the chair next to Adair's bed for Rance and Florian to return with the local authorities. In less than five minutes, Efrem marched in, followed by the sheriff.

"Now what's this I hear about a stabbing?" the sheriff asked.

"Sheriff, I'm Prince Theiandar. My injured friend here is Prince Adair of Taisce. He was stabbed twice in the back by a man called Simon; he was a student at university with the prince. Are you familiar with any of the students there?"

"I can't say I am, but I do know a Simon. He's been in trouble before, but not over stabbing anybody." The sheriff sighed. "He's a bit of a troublemaker when he drinks, but nothing like this, I'd say."

"I'm under the impression this Simon may work at the Hall of Historic Records."

"Yes, I think 'tis the same man. He's a local fellow. I'll have a couple of my men head over to his house and ask some questions while I inspect the records building."

Adair raised his hand off the bed and whispered, "Wait."

Theiandar said, "Sheriff, he's come to again." Theiandar leaned over the injured man. "What is it, Adair?"

"I think . . . I cut him . . . his cheek. I'm not sure." Adair closed his eyes and drifted off again.

"Our culprit should have a cut on his cheek, if that helps," Theiandar said, noticing the impatience of the sheriff to be off.

"I'll come speak with you first thing in the morning." The sheriff left without further questions.

"Hanif, you and Florian take shifts guarding the princess tonight," Theiandar said to the men who'd remained hidden in the corner. "We'll be leaving in the morning, as soon as we've talked to the sheriff. Go now and relieve Daray of his post by their door. Florian, you can take second watch, but first go inform the other men of our plans. Everyone requires rest before we leave in the morning. I'll stay awake to keep an eye on Prince Adair."

As the two men left the room to fulfill his orders, Theiandar walked back over to Adair. He removed the injured prince's boots and covered him with an extra blanket he found in the wardrobe.

He then wandered over to the window and leaned against the frame, staring out into the dark street below. He wondered where Adair's attacker was at that precise moment. His upset over finding his friend wounded was slowly evolving into anger. So much mischief accompanied them on this journey! Theiandar wasn't sure how long he stood there, but the flickering candlelight brought him back to the present.

He threw a log on the dying fire and sat next to the bed. Whatever was going to happen during the night, someone should be close by. Theiandar crossed his arms over his broad chest and rested his feet on the post of the footboard. The warmth of the quiet room lulled him into a place of physical relaxation. He closed his eyes. *Surely a little catnap couldn't hurt,* he thought.

CHAPTER SIXTEEN
Truth in a Story

A faint knocking startled Theiandar from his dubious rest. He shook his head to clear the cobwebs and opened the door. Idra stood wrapped in a frayed, blue blanket. He looked past her shoulder, down the empty hall, to see young Hanif, slumped in a straight-backed chair against the wall.

"Let him sleep, Highness. We have all endured a difficult journey thus far, and I'm sure if anything comes along, he'll pop awake quick enough."

He continued to hesitate in the doorway.

Idra added, "She'll be fine for tonight. And besides, I won't be long. I wanted to ask about what happened earlier."

Theiandar gave half a nod and opened the door wide for her to enter, leaving it open a crack as was the custom in such circumstances. Theiandar offered Idra a seat close to the fireplace.

"Is something wrong with Adair?" she asked, her voice soft and hesitant, while her eyes were trained on her cousin's awkward position across the bed. "I peeked out the door earlier because we heard the commotion, but no one paid any attention to me at the time. I decided to wait until I was sure Caityn was resting and then come find out."

"Yes, Lady Idra. There's been an incident. Adair was attacked tonight at the Hall of Historic Records. He said it was a man named Simon—someone he knew from university. He was stabbed twice in the back. What a coward this Simon is!" He promptly regretted the outburst, in part for letting his emotions get the better of him and also for the shock displayed on Idra's face. "The sheriff is out looking for him now and will report back in the morning. I only hope they catch the man, because if I find him, well . . . ."

Idra stared at the still form of her cousin. "How serious are the stab wounds? Will he be all right?" She sat forward, rigid in the chair.

"He'll be fine after he heals."

"It seemed like the doctor came and went quickly." She stood and walked over to the bed. "How can he sleep so well?"

"The doctor gave him a strong sedative. It will likely have him out most of the night."

Idra reached out from under the blanket clutched between her delicate fingers and stroked Adair's flaxen locks. "I don't have any brothers, Prince Theiandar, but Adair and Gavin are as close as a girl could get to having real ones." She paused for a moment, her eyes never straying from her cousin's motionless form.

"It strikes me, Sire, Caity would be distraught over this if she were herself, but in her current state, well, I don't know what to think." Tears pooled in her eyes and glinted in the flickering firelight. "She wasn't even interested in knowing what was going on. She just said, 'They found out there's nothing to be done.' Then she finished eating her dinner without another word. I can see the faint evidence of struggle in her, and I'm certain she must be afraid, but 'tis spewing out of her as petulance, anger, and depression. After dinner she watched out the window for a while. The only thing she asked—ordered—was for me to help her undress for bed. It didn't take long for her to fall asleep, either." Idra stopped rambling and looked up. "I feel powerless. I want to help her, but 'tis like she's not even really in there, you know?"

He nodded for lack of words outside a commiseration of frustration. The feeling of defeat welled up again, and his weary mind attempted to squelch it. "I know how you feel. Adair and I agreed it is probable we're working within a limited time frame in our quest to save her, but he couldn't remember enough to help us. The scrolls were—" He jumped up from the chair. "The scrolls! Lady Idra, stay with Adair while I go to Sir Ahmad. He picked up some scrolls from the floor of the records room. I need to know what they say."

"Of course, Your Highness, please hurry. The sooner we know, the sooner we can help Caity. I'll look after Adair. Please, go!"

Theiandar left the room, closing the door quietly behind him. He woke Hanif, who apologized profusely for falling asleep.

"I'll overlook it this time, Hanif, but in the future, you must always stay vigilant. I have to find Ahmad to get a look at the scrolls that were with Adair. Lady Idra is in with the prince. Pay attention to both doors."

"Yes, Sire. Again, Raz, I'm sorry for nodding off. I can't believe I did it!" Hanif said, still rubbing sleep from his eyes.

"Just don't let it happen again, my friend."

Theiandar strode down the hall toward the room to which Ahmad had retired. When he knocked on the door, Ahmad answered it right away. There was still a light burning on the table. There, spread out on the wood surface, were the scorched scrolls. It was obvious parts were missing, but from where Theiandar stood, they seemed mostly intact. The two men approached the table.

"Were you already reading through them, Ahmad? Did you find anything helpful?" Theiandar couldn't contain his eagerness.

"Well, Sire, I did start reading through them. I thought it was a way I could help, but I've not found much. This first one is charred, and there's quite a bit of it missing. I was able to confirm things we already know. Such as here, for instance," he said, his finger hovering over a spot on the first scroll. "It talks of the Beauty Thief being a slightly-built man. It does say he ages as the life force he gains from the stolen beauty—or love, as it seems—begins to wane. It depends on how much time has passed since he last stole some, I think. Well, possibly. Unfortunately, that part was seriously burned.

"And here it talks of an amulet's power to take the beauty. The amulet houses the love from the girl's heart. By some power, it causes not only the loss of love but the loss of her outer beauty. That explains why Princess Caityn looks like an old woman. I think I figured out this burnt part here."

Theiandar listened, intent on every word.

Ahmad said, "Although 'tis not fully clear, I was able to piece this together. If she is touched by love, it should reverse portions of the amulet's curse. I hesitate to say it, but the reversal has a limited window of time. Raz, we only have until the total eclipse. Now, there's a word missing here, but I'm fairly certain it must be a lunar eclipse. They happen anywhere from a couple times a year to once every few years. Here's the issue: there happens to be one coming up in two weeks."

"How do you know this?"

"The disciplers at the monasey taught us how to read the stars and the moon's orbit. I didn't even think about the eclipse, but this reminded me of it. A total lunar eclipse will take a while. It can glow red, which also makes me think this is, in fact, a lunar eclipse we're talking about." Ahmad pointed at another section of scroll. "See? It says the love which is drained from the victim is held in the center of the amulet, and 'tis like a glowing, red liquid."

"So you're saying if we don't stop this scoundrel before the lunar eclipse, the curse is irreversible?" Theiandar slammed his fist down on the table and swore. "We don't have much time! Did you find anything else? How to stop this Beauty Thief? What was the part about a touch?" Theiandar's urgency was reignited.

"I haven't gotten to the second scroll yet, Raz. Maybe there's something there."

They both reached out for the second piece of charred paper. Adair had saved the scrolls from becoming completely useless. Theiandar let Ahmad take the scroll and lay it out on the table between them.

Ahmad read through it for a few minutes, trying to decipher the missing parts, while Theiandar read over his shoulder. Most of it was narrative, telling the stories of people who'd been victims of the Beauty Thief, but important information, such as the significance of the eclipse, popped up every now and then. Finally, after what felt like forever, Ahmad tapped his finger on the paper.

"Aha! It says her heart cannot be fully restored unless the amulet is placed on her chest before the total lunar eclipse is complete."

"Then we have to find this pernicious thief and get the amulet," Theiandar said.

"Yes, but where is he?"

"Keep reading, Ahmad. Does it say anything else about how he receives the love? Or how it turns into a source of life for him? You mentioned it, but I wasn't clear on what you meant."

"I'm not sure. It said the love becomes a life force for him and allows him to extend his existence almost indefinitely. Tis akin to a serum for perpetual youth. I'll keep reading and see what else I can decipher."

Theiandar picked up the first scroll and studied it, searching for anything speaking of the touch of love Ahmad had mentioned. He came to a story of a young woman who had her beauty and love stolen from her, but the love of her husband restored her outer beauty. His devotion could only reach part of her heart to restore some emotions. He could not bring back her essential love, the compassion for which she'd been known before the thief took it from her. The girl in the story had her youth, but she forever lost joy, hope, and compassion from her life.

It was a sad story, but Theiandar soaked up what he could. It didn't say it was impossible, and Theiandar knew he loved Caityn. He could help restore her outer beauty. As long as they got the amulet before the eclipse, it was possible to restore to her the inner beauty which mattered most. This was substantial. Now they had to figure out where they could find the Beauty Thief himself and how to get the amulet from him.

"Have you found anything yet, my friend?" Theiandar asked.

"Actually, I think I have. This particular story speaks of someone tracking the thief—a very difficult task by all accounts—to the Saddle Ridge Mountains. It mentions Ophira's Peak. There's a cave where he performs his last ritual to imbue himself with the stolen love's life force. However, the story before this says the amulet cannot only be pressed back onto the heart of the victim to restore it." He paused, gaining the resolve to share the news. "Raz, the amulet must be placed over her heart, and an arrow with a tip made from rubinthynium has to be shot into the center of the amulet. Tis the only way to release and restore the beauty."

Theiandar rested his elbow on the table and rubbed his eyes with thumb and forefinger while he pondered. It was dangerous, yes, but he was confident it was possible.

"I think we have what we need from the scrolls. In the morning you will return them to the Hall for safekeeping. After we meet with the sheriff to square up this other situation, we'll leave for High Castle. I must speak with my father. We've got to find out where to get this rubinthynium stone, too. In the meantime, get some sleep. We have another long day ahead of us, and I will need your quick mind."

"Yes, Highness, I'll return the scrolls on the morrow. Sleep well," Ahmad said.

Theiandar crept back down the hall and was surprised to see Florian outside the princess's door. He hadn't realized how much time had passed, but half the night was gone. When he opened his door, he found Idra asleep in the chair she'd pulled up next to the bed, her hand resting on Adair's. He gave her shoulder a slight shake. She sat up and yawned.

"Oh, I must have dozed off. I'm sorry, Your Highness. Did you find what you were looking for?" The lethargic rubbing of her eyes didn't mask her hopefulness.

"Yes, I think we did, but we can do nothing tonight. I'll explain in the morning. For now you need to go find your rest."

"That's wonderful. What must we do?"

"In the morning, my lady."

"Of course, Highness." Idra stood and floated out the door as if a specter of the night instead of a drowsy lady-in-waiting. "Good night."

He watched her walk down the hall. Florian opened the door for her with a bow and returned to his station. Theiandar closed his door and checked on Adair, whose breathing was shallow but steady. He removed his jacket, boots, and weapons and lay on the other bed, exhausted but unable to sleep.

His mind was spinning with all the new information. He reminded himself that his touch was vital to restoring at least part of Caityn's beauty. It was clear she needed to stay with him, which meant she'd have to go along with him to find the rubinthynium, whatever kind of stone it was.

This was one thing he could do for her. He wasn't as powerless as he thought. Theiandar couldn't wait for morning to come when he would be able to touch Caityn. His thoughts wound down as the night sky gradually lost its depth of darkness. He slept.

CHAPTER SEVENTEEN
To Forgive or Not to Forgive

The road was dark and uninhabited at this time of night. The crooked little man in the black cloak pressed his stolen mount in a continued gallop toward his destination at Larue.

He was sure the sum of money he carried in his satchel would be enough to buy Roache's services, but he knew he'd also have to sweeten the deal with an offering of human flesh. This particular mercenary enjoyed the lucrative exploits of the slave trade.

The thief doubted Roache would care to keep the shriveled, old princess, which didn't harm the Beauty Thief's own intentions for her. Her companion, on the other hand, would be easy enough to capture and would make a delightful prize for the man.

"If only I could steal the beauty of more than one lovely at a time," he muttered.

That girl with the princess is a pretty little thing as well. If she is willing to travel with someone who's been touched by the amulet, then she must have goodness and beauty in her heart. Ah well. There is nothing to be done in that regard. At least I can still use her in trade.

He sat up straight in the saddle of the horse he'd stolen the night before from a quaint farmhouse near the river in Conleth. His mind wandered to a curious notion: What was in those scrolls the princes were set on finding? Surely there was nothing in them which could prove harmful to the beauty he carried close to his heart.

The idea did leave him agitated, which caused him to push the horse harder in order to make it to Larue as fast as possible. He needed the princess under his own watchful care to ensure no one and nothing got in his way.

* * *

With a groan, Theiandar rolled himself off the soft bed at the Talking Ram Inn. He yawned, running his fingers through his matted hair before stretching tall. He checked Adair's vital signs, which he found to be satisfactory. Adair was not resting as peacefully as he'd been the night before, however, as evidenced by the moans he uttered more often than not.

Theiandar dug in his satchel for a clean shirt. He threw it on and yanked on his boots. It only took a minute to get his sword and dagger in place. Upon entering the hall, he found Parker had replaced Florian at some point. He grew concerned about the hour.

"Parker, where's Florian?"

"Raz, sir, I was up and offered to spell him."

"Thank you, Parker. Have the mistress send breakfast up to the ladies and get some for yourself as well. After I talk with the sheriff, we'll be leaving for High Castle."

Theiandar continued down the hall to Ahmad's room. He didn't bother knocking on the door but entered unceremoniously. Ahmad and the other guards were still sound asleep. Theiandar cleared his throat, which brought the three of them to attention, ready to pounce on whoever or whatever had interrupted their much-needed rest.

Theiandar allowed himself a brief laugh. "Good morning, men. Prepare yourselves and wake the others. We need to leave. Zaccur, go watch over Prince Adair. Change his bandages with clean ones. Ahmad can ask the mistress to bring up a plate for you. I'm going to speak with the sheriff about what happened last night, and then we want to be gone within the hour. You need to dress and eat quickly."

While he was still speaking, they were busy getting on their gear. He could see they were almost ready, and so headed downstairs to see if the sheriff had arrived. When he came into the common room, he found Parker and the sheriff deep in conversation.

"My Prince, I have bad news," the sheriff said as Theiandar approached the pair.

"Please, let's sit down, and we can eat while you tell it to me."

"No food for me, thank you," the sheriff said. They took their seats. "I'll get right to it, as I can see you're in a hurry."

Six of Theiandar's men came tromping down the stairs. A few sat down to eat. The rest hurried out the door to the livery.

"As I was saying, Sire, I have bad news. It must have been the same Simon. We went to his home on the outskirts of town. His mother answered the door, and she was not pleased to see us. Of course, that could be because we have been there before.

"The problem is, she said her son is gone. He came home with a cut on his face and ran off into the night with a satchel of belongings and some money. She was livid and said whoever caused her son to run away probably deserved whatever they got.

"I've sent men out to track him down. I also informed the guardsmen at the mansion of what has transpired, and I'm sure they'll join the search." The sheriff stood, obviously done with his report.

"Thank you for your diligence. I want this man caught and brought before the duodenacort. He's fortunate he's not better with a knife, because he almost killed Prince Adair," Theiandar stated.

The sheriff bowed and exited. When Theiandar was finished with his breakfast, he went back upstairs to check on Caityn. His knock was answered by a muffled call to enter. The first thing Theiandar noticed was the food on the table, scarcely touched. Caityn sat on the bed, brushing her hair.

Theiandar stopped cold in his tracks when he saw it, unable to believe his eyes. Her hair! Most of the gray had disappeared! He hurried to her and reached out to touch the soft, multicolored strands.

"Tis odd, is it not?" she asked.

He studied her. "Yes, it is, but then we found something in the scrolls last night at least hinting at this possibility. I guess I didn't believe it until this definitive moment."

Without waiting for her to offer, he sat next to her on the bed and reached up to caress her cheek. "It said love's touch could reverse some of the effects of the amulet, but until now I didn't realize it was happening. Now I can clearly see that you are changing." He smiled at her.

"I don't feel different, Theiandar," she replied while tipping her head away from his touch. "I still feel empty . . .

and here in my chest is an ever present ache. Idra said I should be upset about what happened to Adair, but something is missing. I know he's my brother, but I cannot fathom what she says I don't have: compassion." Caityn glared at the back of Idra's head while the lady-in-waiting packed their few belongings.

Theiandar picked up Caityn's frail hand and stared down at it, nestled in his own strong one. "I fear you are powerless. It will take my love to restore yours, and I will gladly give it all since it was always yours. But we don't have much time, Cait. I promise, with Almighty's help, we will find this man and get your love back. The beauty from within, your love and compassion, will be returned to its rightful place." He lifted her hand to his lips and kissed it then took the brush to finish her hair.

Caityn looked confused but didn't stop him. He twined her hair into one long braid.

"I didn't know you knew how to braid hair," she said.

"Well, I've done my share of braids for Eliya."

At the mention of Eliya, Caityn froze. When Theiandar finished the braid, she turned to face him. "This is her fault. I will never forgive her!"

Theiandar frowned and shook his head at her vehemence. "Don't say it, Cait. That is not you speaking. I know you. You would never hold on to condemnation. Please, even now, don't say it."

The scowl on her face softened to a frown, and her shoulders drooped in defeat. "I know, but I can't help it. I can't feel like I should. There are no words in me to describe this. I'm lost, Theiandar. There is no hope, and I don't know who to blame. If she hadn't given me a sleeping potion none of this would have happened."

"Maybe and maybe not. It seems this Beauty Thief has been doing this for a long time, and he's a master of deception. Please try to forgive Eliya. She was used, just as you have been. I'm sure she's devastated by all this. She'll not forget what her jealousy led her to do."

For the first time, Caityn's absentminded scratching episodes were not lost on Theiandar as he watched her tear at her thigh. Instead of agreeing to forgive Eliya, she asked a strange question. "Will you hold me?"

Without another word, his arms wrapped around Caityn. She melted against his chest, clinging to his shirtfront as tears streamed down her gently wrinkled face. He didn't understand her tears, but hoped they were a good sign. Idra chose that moment to pick up the bags she'd finished repacking and slip out the door.

After a few minutes holding the princess like this, Theiandar placed his hands on her shoulders, holding her out in front of him. "Tis time I escorted you down to the carriage. Adair is seriously injured, and he'll be in the carriage with you. I know you're having a difficult time caring as you once did, but please look after him on the ride. The wounds need to be protected. Can you do this for me?"

She nodded and picked up her scarf. After running her hands along its silkiness, she wrapped it around her head again, and Theiandar escorted her down the stairs to the common room, where Mistress Yael waited.

"Your Majesties! I'm awful sorry for your troubles, but may ye go with him who is on high," she said while offering a basket of fresh bread, cheese, and fruit to Theiandar.

"Thank you, Mistress Yael, for your hospitality and all the care you've shown to my friend, Prince Adair. Here is something extra for your trouble," he said.

Her eyes grew wide as she stared at the gold piece he placed in her hand. As she bowed her head in thanks, Theiandar offered his arm to Caityn, and they walked out the front door. Idra was already in the carriage when they arrived. She looked exhausted but smiled at Caityn when she climbed in.

"I'll be back with Adair in a few minutes," Theiandar said. "We'll be leaving shortly. I want to make it to High Castle before dark."

"Yes, Your Highness," Idra said.

Caityn said nothing and ignored them, looking out the window.

***

After he'd been gone for a minute or two Idra spoke. "Eventually you'll have to talk to me, Caity. You've been silent with me all morning, and when I told you about Adair, you didn't even pretend to care."

"That's because I *don't* care, Idra. I know you think I should, but I can't force it. I thought I made myself clear already. I can feel something right now, though what I suffer under is unpleasant. Tis disgust and distrust. I do not trust you."

Idra couldn't hide her hurt. "But why? What have I done to lose your trust?"

"Tis simple. You're taking advantage of the situation in order to steal Theiandar. That's the only reason you came along on this disaster of a trip. And I can't say I blame you. He's certainly a handsome man. But to do it now, in front of my very nose? You're cruelty in this even I can feel."

Idra listened in stunned silence. Anger built in her heart. "How dare you! I would never do such a thing! I can't believe you would even accuse me of it!" She raised her eyebrows in an attempt to loosen the angry glower from her face. "Caityn Ovlander, your heart may be damaged, but your mind is not. You know you can trust me. Oooh, I'm too angry right now to be kind. Let's go back to not talking."

"Fine by me," Caityn replied, moving her gaze to the window.

It was upon this silent scene that Theiandar and Zaccur arrived, hefting a pained-looking Adair upon their shoulders. It was a tedious and delicate process to get Adair into the carriage.

"Idra, could you please switch to the other side? Then, we can lay him down over there. I'm not sure how else to fit him in and not rupture his stitches."

She moved to sit next to Caityn, who shot her a piercing glance which Idra did her best to ignore.

Theiandar settled Adair on the bench and pulled a blanket from under the seat to cover him. The invalid prince whispered his thanks, his eyes closed tight.

As Theiandar backed out of the carriage and closed the door, Idra exhaled her frustration and sank to the floor next to Adair.

"Hello, cousin. I'm here." She stroked his hair.

Idra sat up on her knees long enough to wave good-bye to the kind family who owned the Talking Ram before she settled herself into a cramped position on the floor to keep watch over Adair. It was after more than an hour that she finally broke the silence.

"Caity, I'm sorry for losing my temper with you, but what you said wasn't true. But I shouldn't have reacted the way I did. I promised my love and friendship to you, and 'tis still yours. I know you're not yourself, but what you said hurt. Please let's not fight anymore."

Idra stared up at Caityn whose piercing stare revealed nothing. She didn't reply right away, and Idra had almost given up hope of hearing any reconciliation from her cousin when Caityn said, "You're right, Idra, my mind does know you wouldn't do what I accused you of, but my heart is black, and I can't find my way out of the depths."

"Caity." Adair's raspy voice broke through their fog of hurt. "We made this journey to help rescue you out of the all-consuming darkness. I, Theiandar, Idra, and a host of others are here because we know you and love you. Everything will work out." He closed his eyes as the recent dose of medicine lulled him to sleep.

No one spoke again for quite a while. The carriage jumped and bumped down the road, softened and rutted by the late spring rains. There was nothing to say, really, that hadn't already been said. Even though Caityn hadn't come straight out and apologized, she'd admitted she'd wronged her friend. It was good enough for Idra.

CHAPTER EIGHTEEN
Weariness

They'd been on the road for three and a half days, riding hard. Gavin could see Queen Zoe, Princess Eliya, and the ladies-in-waiting were bone-tired. He wished they'd been left back at Castle Taisce instead of dragging them along on this urgent journey. Gavin was aware King Dante wanted to keep his family close in order to protect them. And while he understood the desire, it was difficult to watch the women endure the grueling pace to which they were subjected.

They were hardy travelers who didn't constantly complain about the pace or the lack of rest. On occasion, he heard Eliya grumbling to her mother about her aches and pains, but for the most part, she'd been much less snippy on this trip than the last. It was probably due to the fact that she still felt guilty about what she'd done.

Gavin directed his mind back to the task at hand. He squatted down to take a look at the crossroads they'd come upon. Less than half a day's travel remained to reach High Castle, but here the road crossed one coming south from

Conleth and Berne. It was a seldom used path employed for the purpose of trade between Berne and the southern realms.

It wasn't the season for trade right now, which made it odd to see horse tracks heading south from the intersecting trail. The tracks were at least half a day old now, but the oddest part was how obvious it was the horse that left them had been at full gallop.

No one lived near this crossing. The tracks weren't likely left by someone out for a pleasure ride. He couldn't decide why it bothered him, though. Gavin stored the information in his mind as they remounted and continued on their journey.

From behind him, he heard Princess Eliya's exasperated sigh.

"Mother, I know we're almost there, but I wish there was some way we could be transported in an instant. Then I wouldn't have to ride any more. My bottom is terribly sore. I don't think I'll be able to sit down again for a week!"

King Dante laughed out loud but made no reply to Eliya's comment, and Gavin found himself trying to stifle a laugh as well. Without looking, Gavin could tell Queen Zoe was smiling when she replied.

"Now daughter, it is unbecoming of a lady to complain about her . . . posterior in public. I certainly hope no one else heard you." It was evident everyone within earshot had heard the comment.

Gavin took a peek back in time to see Eliya frantically looking around, embarrassment coloring her otherwise clear cheeks. She caught his eye and scowled, but she didn't disappoint him, because her expression was quick to transform into a sheepish smile. She shrugged. He returned the smile and, unable to resist, winked.

* * *

When they stopped for a third break six hours after starting their journey, Caityn wasted no time. She flung open the door and jumped down without waiting for assistance, leaving Idra alone to care for Adair.

I'm sorry, Idra," Adair said. "I know you need to get out and stretch, too. Please help me sit up first."

"There's nothing to apologize for, silly." She reached out in an attempt to help him. "Tis no fault of your own you've been hurt or that your sister is not herself. We both know she would never leave you if her heart were intact."

They did not speak while they worked together to prop Adair into a sitting position. The effort had spent all his energy and he sat hunched over in pain. "You're a good friend and cousin, Idra. I guess I needed a reminder, since I'm missing my real sister . . . the one who actually cares."

"Me, too, Adair. Let's hope and pray she can be saved in time."

"Go on," he said. "Get some fresh air for us both."

Idra climbed out through the open door. She made a startled gasp to find Theiandar standing beside the carriage.

"My apologies, Lady Idra, I didn't mean to alarm you. I only wish to check on Adair. I saw Cait get out and thought you could use a hand with him," he said as he peered into the carriage. "Apparently that's not the case at all." Theiandar directed his attention to Adair. "How are you feeling, my friend?"

"I could be better, but Idra and Caityn have been watching over me. I can't complain."

"The stitches are holding," Idra said. "If all goes well, he won't need fresh bandages until we arrive at the castle tonight." She bowed and went to join Caityn.

"Good," Theiandar said. "Adair, do you need anything?"

"No, I'm well—or as well as can be expected. Though I feel like an infant. I don't think the wounds are excessive, but it will be a few days before I feel up to moving about much."

"You lost a lot of blood, my friend. Go easy on yourself. We'll be here another ten minutes, and then we'll be leaving. We're within three hours of High Castle. It will be dark when we get there, but it will be good to arrive. I'm sure the castle physician will have something he can give you for the pain, which I see is making you sweat."

Adair lifted his arm in an awkward arc and wiped his brow. "What, this? Oh, that's nothing. Tis hot in this carriage. Forget about me. Idra told me you'd gotten the scrolls and found something in them, but she didn't know the details. What did you find?"

"I plan on telling everyone when we meet with my father at High Castle. If you're up to it, you'll hear all the details then. In case you haven't noticed, Caityn is regaining some of her outer beauty. Look over there." Adair strained to see his sister through the carriage window.

"Her hair is covered by the scarf, but much of the gray is lost and near to her natural color. You can see her skin; 'tis lost many of the wrinkles, and the wart is gone. She says the burn mark on her chest is almost completely healed, though 'tis going to leave a scar. The age spots are fading, too."

"That's fantastic, Theiandar! What's causing the changes?"

"Tis love's touch. There's a catch, though. It won't restore her inner beauty, the real her. The beauty of her soul can only be taken from the amulet by a rubinthynium arrow, but I don't know what rubinthynium is, exactly."

"Hmm, neither do I, but someone must. The biggest problem, then, is getting the amulet."

"We don't know where the little man is, but we do have an idea where he's going. We'll need to formulate a plan to get the amulet from him once we find him. We'll discuss this more at the castle, though. Tis almost time for us to head out."

Idra was the first to return to the carriage. Theiandar helped her up before joining Caityn beside the road. "My lady, may I?" He held out his hand for hers.

She studied his hand before setting her own within his. He could see she was in a foul mood, but he let his thumb caress the top of her hand as he held it. "Caity, look at me, please." She did so, her expression blank. "Tell me what's bothering you."

She hesitated before she answered. "I'm useless. I know I should be helping Idra with Adair, but I can't make myself care. I can't look at him with anything other than pity. Tis the best I can do, and it doesn't seem right."

"That's actually good news, Cait."

"Good? Why?"

"Because it means you're feeling things again. It means your heart is not as empty as you thought. Pity is an emotion, but not what a truly loving heart would feel. But I'm pleased you notice the difference."

She scrunched her eyebrows together in concentrated thought. "I don't know if I understand you, Theian. I suppose I will have to take your word for it."

"Yes, you will." He smiled at her and led her back to the carriage, stopping in front of the open door to kiss her hand. He quickly pressed it to his heart before lifting her up and in.

"This last part of the journey will be at a fast clip and will get us there in about three hours," Theiandar said before closing the carriage door. "If you need anything, let Jarl or Hanif know."

Then he mounted his black stallion and raised his arm for his men to follow as he led them to his home at High Castle.

* * *

He'd traveled with few breaks. The Beauty Thief had gone two nights without sleep and only stopped for one short nap the day before. His body was worn, and the exhaustion was enough to make him fall from the horse, but he held on. Larue was not far now. He had important plans to fulfill.

He now rode his second stolen horse for this mad dash. The first one had fallen dead the day before. This one was foamy and limping. It refused to go any faster than a canter.

Since he was almost there, he decided to let the horse take its own pace. He didn't want to waste time getting another one. Besides, the little man knew he could walk the final distance just as quickly as the horse was moving, but he also knew he'd be less conspicuous on horseback. Once he was close to the city, he could walk without being noticed in the multitude of people.

He checked to make sure no one else was on the road around him. When he was sure he was alone, he reached down and pulled out the amulet, glowing red even in the daylight. It was beautiful to his eyes. His fingers stroked the golden casing. He brought the heart to his lips and gently kissed it.

"Soon you will be mine in entirety. Oh, I have waited for such love for far too long. She was a jewel among common quartz, a priceless gem, and now the beauty she encased has been placed in my hands. The shell of the girl will be cast away, and the precious pearl inside will be mine. I will have what is most vital: the heart! Love is a language spoken through the ages. My ages will be many, many, many more."

He heard horses approaching from behind, kissed the amulet again, and tucked the necklace back in his shirt as four soldiers from Larue surrounded him.

"Sir, you've ridden that beast too hard. She will keel over at any time. You should let her rest," a man said. He was wearing full leather with a bow and arrows across his back.

"Ah, you are right, sir. Certainly you are right," replied the little man while hiding his face behind his hood. Thinking quickly, he tried to come up with a believable story. "Unfortunately, I am on an urgent errand for my master, and I cannot possibly delay."

"What could possibly require such urgency?" asked another, similarly garbed, man.

"His daughter is terribly ill. The physician said the medicine she needs, it can only be found at Larue's capitol. My master has sent me. I must hurry, because her life hangs in the balance."

"Ah, that is a concern," said the first man. "Then we shall be honored to escort you to the city. Tis not much farther."

He did his best to convince them to leave. "Oh, no, I don't want to keep you from your duties, sir. I assure you, I am fine and can make it without escort. Please don't let me keep you."

"Tis no trouble at all. We're actually on leave tonight and heading into the city. I don't recognize you. From what home and master do you travel?"

The equivocating thief was becoming agitated, but he continued with his lie, "Oh, it is not a home of Larue, explaining why the horse is worn, sir. I come from a great distance." He paused as he tried to think of some place with which to appease them. "Berne, in fact, from where you have gotten your splendid leather garments, I'm sure."

The leader of the group replied, "Yes, actually, we did. They have fine leather in Berne. Larue is a great trading realm. We make sure you Bernians get good quality items in return. Our gemstone trading and foreign goods are worthy."

"Oh yes, very worthy, sir." The little man was having a hard time keeping up the ruse, but he was relieved he'd successfully distracted the soldier.

They continued down the road until they reached the first livery on their path. It wasn't hard for the little man to convince them to be on their way. He assured them he'd be able to get what he needed without incident.

After parting ways, he dropped the horse's reins in the street and slinked off behind the buildings to take a less noticeable path to a tavern where he could contact Roache's people. He grinned. His escape from the simpleminded soldiers was unpleasant but easy. He could have killed them, but this way he'd avoided leaving a trail or expending precious energy.

Soon he would have his assurance of success. He needed the princess in his clutches, just for a while, and after the eclipse, her future would not concern him. He took little pleasure in killing, but if it came down to it, he would not hesitate, especially if it meant protecting his life source, the beauty of body and pure heart.

CHAPTER NINETEEN
Arrival at High Castle

They'd arrived at the castle just before dark. While everyone else was getting settled, Gavin paced the barracks floor like a caged animal. He was exhausted and anxious at the same time. He knew Raz and his fellow guards were a day's ride away in Conleth. Gavin was tempted to hop on a horse and find out what the news was of Caityn's situation.

He frowned at the thought of Caityn, and he was repulsed by what this coveter of life had done to his sweet cousin. He could kick himself for not having been more diligent at Taisce. If they'd done a better job, there was no way this evil man could have gotten anywhere near the castle, let alone Princesses Caityn or Eliya.

He continued to pace, making some of the other soldiers either nervous or amused. Finally, Captain Saar asked the question haunting all their minds.

"Gavin, why are you back so soon? What happened at Taisce?"

"The whole of it is a long story, and I'm not sure I'm at liberty to repeat all the details. I can tell you only this, the wedding has been postponed until further notice."

Raising his hands to stave off more questions, he said, "The High Prince is fine, as is the rest of the royal family. I'm sure High King Dante will inform you of anything you need to know beyond."

As Gavin ended his speech, a commotion could be heard at the gate tower outside. The men filed from the barracks in time to see the massive gates swing to a close.

"What's all this about?" Captain Saar yelled up to the gatekeeper.

"Prince Theiandar will arrive shortly with his group. Prince Adair of Taisce has been injured. Sir Lieve rode ahead to make sure we were ready for their arrival and to get a physician to meet them at the keep."

Gavin, upon hearing the news, dashed around the back of the barracks and toward the physician's home, hoping to meet up with Lieve. He arrived in time to see Lieve and the doctor exiting the humble house built near the castle wall.

"Lieve!" he called, out of breath. Lieve turned to see who'd called his name. His smile was bright when he saw Gavin.

"Well, you've arrived already! I'm surprised you've arrived in such haste from Taisce. How did you manage it, Gavin, especially with ladies in your party?"

"Our queen and her ladies are capable. But that's no surprise; we in the Twelve Realms are full of mettle." He grinned wide. "But they're exhausted and sought out a well-deserved rest immediately upon arrival. It was tough travel for everyone. It looks like we got here in time, though. What's happened to my cousin, the prince?"

"He was attacked by someone at the Hall of Historic Records, stabbed twice in the back. Unfortunately, one of the wounds broke open about an hour ago, and he's bleeding a good deal. The doctor here is needed right away. That being said, let's be on our way."

The two guards and good doctor headed toward the keep. Silas and Rance met them as they sprinted up the steps. With growing anxiety, they watched the arrival of Prince Theiandar and his group. Gavin greeted the High Prince at the bottom of the stairs.

"Your Highness, we only just arrived a short time ago. Before Lieve showed up, I was contemplating riding out to Conleth to meet you."

"I appreciate the thought, Gavin. We came as quickly as possible. It turns out I have good news and bad news, but time is of the essence. I need to hold a meeting tonight with our guard and one more of my father's guard units. Then 'tis imperative we get some rest and a fresh start first thing in the morning," Theiandar explained.

"I can arrange the guard, Your Highness."

"Thank you, and you are forgetting, tis Raz to you," Theiandar said as he slapped Gavin on the back. "Let's meet in my father's planning room in one hour. I want to ensure the ladies are settled and Adair is taken care of."

"May I see them before I go, sir?"

"Of course, Gavin."

They looked toward the carriage to find two men assisting Adair as the women waited nearby. Gavin scanned the group, but his eyes stopped on Caityn's face. It was totally changed again! All the age spots had disappeared, and her skin, while still slightly wrinkled, was clear. She looked younger than she had only days ago. The transformation was astonishing.

Theiandar caught his arm. "Don't let appearances fool you, my friend. While the outside is improved, her inner beauty is missing. She is not the same woman . . . yet. I'll explain later."

The joy Gavin had felt upon seeing her diminished somewhat. He walked over to Adair who was being carried into the castle.

"Well, cousin, it looks as though you're not as popular as I thought! How are you feeling?"

Adair's smile was pained and did nothing to improve his pale face, but he said, "Admit it. You always wanted to be just like me. I'm well enough. The doctor will have this all fixed up in no time. I'm relieved to see you. Please help watch out for my sister."

Gavin nodded as Adair was toted away. He waved then approached Caityn and Idra, giving both a quick hug. While Idra returned the embrace with familial affection, Caityn stood stiff in the circle of his arms. He said, "I'm sorry Adair was hurt. I'm sure he'll be fine, though."

"Well, maybe if you'd been there, he wouldn't have gotten hurt in the first place," Caityn said out of nowhere, without even looking at him.

He was too surprised to say anything, but Idra spoke up. "Caityn, you know there is nothing Gavin could have done to prevent what happened to Adair. That was uncalled for! Apologize."

Caityn looked at her with a stunned expression. "Idra is my conscience, apparently. Please forgive my outburst."

Gavin didn't know what to think. "Caity, I'm happy to see the changes in your appearance, but I'm sorry you must endure this. I swear we'll do everything we can to help fix it. I'm sorry I wasn't able to stop this man from gaining access to you and Princess Eliya. I still don't know how he slipped through our guard."

"I'm sure you don't want to hear my thoughts on the matter, Gavin. We are tired, and I have nothing else to say on the matter," Caityn said, dismissing him with the tone of her voice.

"Yes, Gavin, excuse us please. We'll see you in the morning. It looks like we'll be traveling more to find something called rubinthynium and to locate the man who did this awful thing to our Caity," Idra explained.

"Rubinthynium? Isn't it an old word for ruby? I'll ask around, but I'm almost certain that's what it is. If so, I'm sure someone knows where we can get it," Gavin said.

As the women headed inside, Gavin returned to the barracks to gather the men Raz had asked to join him. Within a short amount of time the two guard units were ready and marched back to the castle to meet in the king's planning room.

* * *

The chambermaid led the princess and her cousin up two flights of stairs and down various hallways to a spacious, yet cozy, suite of rooms. Caityn's room was luxurious, with a colorful bedspread and matching furniture. The crackling fire offered warmth and comfort to the huge room.

The chambermaid looked at her questioningly, obviously not sure who she was; Caityn was in no mood to explain it. As she dismissed the girl with a wave, Caityn caught sight of her hand and stopped to inspect it. *Could it be?* Her skin looked supple, having lost the aged appearance it had only a day ago. She turned it over and admired the silky smoothness. Caityn carried the candelabra to the vanity and sat down in front of the mirror. She slid the scarf from her head.

It was the first time she'd looked in a mirror since leaving Castle Taisce, and the transformation was surprising. She'd listened when Theiandar told her about how love's touch could restore her outer appearance, but she hadn't really *heard* what he'd been telling her. It had all sounded quite ridiculous. If it was love that could change a person, then he must love her, but what did it mean? She didn't know love anymore.

She let the confusion simmer while she pulled her braid around front and removed the leather strap holding it in place. Slowly, she unwound her tresses, still a little gray and a darker shade of brown than before. She saw a slight recovery to her looks but was empty, barren of anything except self-loathing.

Loathing. Well, at least I feel something, she thought. In fact, she hated herself. She liked what she saw in the mirror, the improvement to her looks, but she knew she was not herself inside her heart. This girl she looked at, while recovering on the outside, was still an ugly, wretched thing on the inside, devoid of what really mattered; she didn't know what mattered anymore. There was only a vague sense of what once was.

Her musing was interrupted when Idra entered the room unannounced.

"My lady, servants are bringing water for the tub now. I've come to help you prepare for a bath. I'm having them bring your favorite scent of vanilla to freshen your water."

"Idra, shouldn't you be bathing yourself?" Caityn asked, still staring at her reflection.

"I will after I have you all taken care of. You'll just have to live with my stink for a while longer."

"Idra, go. I'm capable of bathing without assistance, although . . . help me undo my stays before you go."

"If that's what you want, my lady."

"Idra, what is this 'my lady' business? You have never called me that in private before, and, frankly, 'tis getting on my nerves. We're cousins, and you say we are friends, so just stop!"

Idra flinched at Caityn's scolding. "Fine, Caity. I've been having a hard time with what's happened to you. I feel like you're pushing me away. I don't know what to call you anymore. I'm frustrated, too. I'm doing my best to stick with you, but every time I think we've gotten closer again, you get all prickly and mean. This is hard."

Caityn scowled at her. "Yes, it is hard, but I'm the one who's the most affected here. If you don't like me the way I am, leave me be and stop following me around. I don't need you."

Idra could take no more of it. "I am done with this pouty nonsense, Caityn! I made a promise to stay by your side, and I'm bound to keep it, but I will not put up with your poor treatment of me anymore. Undo your own stays," she said and marched out the door.

Caityn was surprised by the outburst. She watched Idra leave. She returned to the vanity bench, self-hatred brewing deep within her, and cried for how she'd treated her dearest—

and perhaps only—friend. *Who am I? Who is this awful person who doesn't care about anyone?* She knew one thing: having lost her love had created a hole in her too deep to fill, and there was nothing she could do to fix it. She needed help.

The servants delivered the bathwater. Caityn directed them to fill the tub and when they had exited, she struggled out of her clothing. She padded across the cold stone floor to sink into the tub filled with the sweet, vanilla-scented water.

As she lay in the water, her hair floating around her half-submerged face, she thought about the memories Idra mentioned a few days before. The girl Idra described was obviously someone else, some long-lost memory Caityn could only see from the outside and not feel within herself. *What am I now? Why go on in this world if I am forever fighting this darkness in me?*

She sank below the surface and stared up through the water at the darkness above. It would be easy enough to let go, to suck the sweet water into her lungs and end the misery, but the memory of Theiandar pulling her from the river and the look of joy on his face when she awoke from her near-death experience gave her pause.

She sat up in the tub and wiped the water from her eyes, strands of hair plastered across her face, neck, and shoulders. The rest floated on the water's surface. In that moment, with that memory, a tiny spark of hope flared in the darkness. Perhaps her heart could be healed after all. It was only a spark, but it had surely happened.

After drying off and slipping into her nightgown, Caityn wrapped herself in a blanket and tiptoed next door to Idra's room. She found her friend sitting on the bed, brushing out her own damp hair. Upon seeing Caityn at her door, Idra stood, her movements stilted and uncertain.

Fortunately, Caityn didn't leave her in suspense for long. "I'm sorry, Idra. I keep saying it, but I don't know who I am or how to be the person you remember. I think I must want to, but I can't find it in me. Trust me when I say I keep searching, but she's missing, long gone."

Idra put down her brush and ran over to Caityn, throwing her arms around her shoulders. Idra squeezed her tight, tears coursing down her cheeks. For the first time in a long while, Caityn responded by returning the embrace. They stood like this until Idra had to pull back to wipe her nose.

"I forgive you, Caity, I do, and I'm sorry, too. Even though I was angry, I never should have spoken in anger to you. Can you forgive me?"

"I wish I could, Idra, but without love, what is forgiveness but empty words?"

"Then I have a heart full of enough forgiveness for us both," Idra replied. "We will do this. We'll find your love and bring you back to life." Idra hugged Caityn again.

They looked into each other's eyes, and Caityn tried to return the smile Idra beamed at her. It wouldn't come. She settled on a nod instead.

"Good night, Idra." She paused, her hand on the doorknob. "And Idra, thanks for not giving up on me." The words spilled out in a muddle. She opened the door and slipped out without waiting for a response.

CHAPTER TWENTY
Paramount Unity

"Thank you all for gathering with such haste," Theiandar said to the men who were seated around his father's planning table. While many war plans were made around this table, it signified much more. Here, the unity of the kingdom was the primary focus. Though the Twelve Realms existed separately, in truth, they were ruled as one.

"Father, I'm glad to see you're already here. We need your insight and wisdom in the decisions we're about to make."

"I am at your disposal, Theiandar," King Dante replied.

Theiandar acknowledged his father and began his report. "Men, I will start by informing you that Prince Adair, while seriously injured, is not at death's door. He will recover. He'll just need time."

The men were silent. Theiandar knew the group appreciated this news, but it was not why they were called to the meeting. They waited for their orders without disrupting.

"This brings me to why we are here. As you know, I was to marry Princess Caityn four days ago, but she was attacked by a malicious man the night before our wedding. She is uninjured, but she is not herself in mind or body."

He glanced around at the wide variety of responses—from comprehension, to astonishment, to confusion. "Basically, this man who is called the Beauty Thief has stolen the love from the princess's heart. In effect, she has lost the ability to love or feel emotions. If you see her, do not be shocked, because he robbed her of her outer beauty as well."

"How can this be?" asked one of the other unit's guards.

"We, too, were in shock when we found out, but it is true. This is some evil force, and it has been at work for centuries. Our histories recorded it as legend. Thanks to Prince Adair, we were able to locate the records chronicling the acts of the Beauty Thief, but they are incomplete. I believe we have all the essential information. We need only figure out what to do with it.

"Captain Saar, I need your unit to head to the Saddle Ridge Mountains. Locate a specific mountain called Ophira's Peak. There should be a cave where the thief performs his ritual to complete the transfer of beauty to life force for himself. I am giving you eight days to get there and find it, and then meet me in Wyeth. This will, I hope, leave us enough time to find him and take back what he stole," Theiandar said.

"Yes, Sire. What does this man look like?" Saar asked.

"Unfortunately, all we know is he is a smallish man, and as the beauty he's already taken begins to fade, his body ages. He will likely look old. Tis clear he's an expert at covering his tracks. Keep a sharp eye out. He wears a necklace with an amulet we must get back from him in order to restore Princess Caityn's true beauty."

"That being said, Sire, how will we obtain the amulet from his person?" Hanif asked.

"Your question is one for which I'm open to answers. Does anyone have any suggestions?"

You could hear a pin drop in this silence that followed. Ahmad cleared his throat. "I have an idea, but it means traveling to Nevin. The monks there have learned of a poison, when applied to a blowdart, capable of knocking the victim unconscious for almost half an hour. They are the only ones I'm aware of who know how to make this serum. It would be a simple way to immobilize him and get the amulet without risking its damage or loss."

"That's a worthy idea, Ahmad. Thank you. Does anyone else have an idea?" Theiandar inquired.

No one spoke up, but a few men were heard mumbling about killing the sorry excuse for a man.

"Tis settled. Ahmad, you and two men are to go to Nevin and procure this sleeping serum and the requisite darts. The other issue we have is clear; time is running out. We only have until the total lunar eclipse to find the thief, get the amulet, and restore the princess. If her beauty is not restored before the eclipse is completed, the princess, as we know her, will be lost forever."

The gravity of Theiandar's words settled over the men like a thick, wet blanket. The seriousness of the situation could not be overstated. Marriages between royals in the kingdoms, especially those of future high kings, were seen as unity seals. If Theiandar did not marry Princess Caityn, it could cause a breach in the long-held wholeness of the kingdom. As it was, there would be whispers and gossip across the realms.

Theiandar evaluated their responses. "We cannot be divided, men. The final element we need to save Princess Caityn is an arrow made of rubinthynium. I don't know what it is, but I was hoping one of you might."

"I know what it is, Son," Dante said. He'd sat in silence through the entire discourse. "Tis the ancient name for ruby. But they are difficult to come by in the Twelve Realms. We do have some here at High Castle, but they're not large enough. I think the only place you might find the size of ruby you would need would be in Larue, at the trader's market."

Theiandar's sharp exhale was the only sound in the room. He closed his eyes and steeled his nerve. This meant more travel and more precious time, but what choice did he have? He had to have a ruby in order to save his betrothed. She was more valuable to him than his own life, but how could he possibly do this in time? He stroked his chin as he thought through the dilemma.

"Sire? If I may interject," Gavin said. "From here, the trip will take two days each way. But if you return via Nevin and take the back trail to Wyeth, the one between here and Glass Lake, you should be able to meet Captain Saar's unit in seven days."

"Thank you for calculating it, Sir Gavin. What do you think, Father? I have to keep Caityn with me at all times because . . ." Standing in front of the soldiers made the intimate details of this curse fall awkwardly from his lips. "As strange as it sounds, my love for her is restoring her outer beauty and can even help repair part of her heart. It cannot touch on actual love, the true love of her soul."

The king considered this information before replying. "It will be hard riding for Caityn and her lady-in-waiting. You need to ask them if they are up for it, but I think it best you go, either way. If her love cannot know full restoration, then what is the use of outer beauty?"

Everyone knew it was a rhetorical question. Theiandar let it sink in. This was much more important than making a princess pretty again. This was about restoring life and protecting the realms from corruption.

The group discussed a few more details then broke up to find rest before traveling on the morrow. The high prince did not move in the same direction as his men. Theiandar knew he needed to speak with Caityn before he retired to the barracks.

King Dante stopped his son in the hall. "Theian, I'm sorry you must do this thing. If there was a way to avoid the task, I would take it. The kingdom must be protected at all costs, but your happiness matters to me as well. If you cannot restore the princess, we will find a way to break the betrothal. I feel the kingdom can withstand a blow such as this could be."

"I appreciate your support, Father, but aside from the betrothal, I made my own promises to Caityn."

"Son, as the heir to this kingdom, your life is not your own to do with as you choose. Now hear me out. I know you love her. And while your commitment is commendable, you owe much more to this kingdom and the people who will follow you."

Theiandar backed away from his father. "I know who I am, Father. I haven't forgotten my place. But I will not abandon Caityn, one of the very people I live to protect, in order to spare my own life."

He didn't wait for his father to reply. He was too angry to listen anyway. It took him the entire walk to the guest room wing to calm down.

He stood outside Caityn's door and took a deep, calming breath. He knocked. There was no answer, but then he heard her door click and crack open a bit. It was dark in the room, except for a muted orange glow from the fireplace.

"I apologize for waking you, Cait. I needed to discuss something with you."

"I wasn't asleep."

He gestured toward the room and she motioned him inside where he crossed the room to stand by the glowing embers of the fire. Out of habit, she left the door ajar before settling in a chair before him.

He stood rigid, unable to forget his father's recent words. She watched him with some impatience evident even in the shadows until gathered his thoughts and sat on the edge of the chair opposite hers.

"Cait, I need to go to Larue and find a ruby big enough to make an arrowhead. I'm sending Ahmad to Nevin with a minor contingent of men. They will procure a sleeping serum and darts to use on the Beauty Thief. The plan is to use it in order to safely remove the amulet from his possession. I think it best you go to Nevin with Ahmad. You will wait there for us, and we will travel to Wyeth together. There, we will have a master arrow artisan craft the arrow we need to pierce the amulet."

Caityn's hand shot up to her neck. "I still have the necklace with the ring I promised Bimala I would give to her daughter-in-law. I didn't see the point in taking it off."

He smiled. The change in subject didn't faze him. He hunkered down in front of her, took her hands, and kissed them one at a time. He looked into her eyes.

"I love you, Cait. I love you so much, I would do anything for you—even die for you—though I know you don't love me back at this moment. My love is overflowing. I would pour it all out for you."

"Oh Theian!" She sounded exasperated. "I wish you wouldn't say that. It makes me uncomfortable. It means nothing to me. I can see you mean it, but I don't understand it."

"You don't have to understand now. When this is over—when your love is restored—I will tell you again, and you will understand. You are my bride, the one I love. My gift to you is that my love will never fade or change."

He stood and kissed her forehead. "Good night, sweet Princess. Tomorrow will come early."

* * *

The little man took a room in the tavern where he'd met with Roache's man earlier in the day. The next morning there would be a meeting with the intimidating leader—not that he found the man frightening, but many did.

In reality, he could think of no one who truly intimidated him. He knew more about deceit, protection, scheming, and strategy than any man alive. Of course, it was helpful to have lived for twenty lifetimes already and traveled to all corners of the world gaining knowledge and riches.

His lust for the theft of beauty, though, always brought him back here, to the Twelve Realms. It was the only place where love could be stolen and transferred. He knew the land well and could travel with stealth wherever he needed to go.

This night he decided to sleep in comfort. If someone were to recognize him, they might share information about his activities. He did not foresee any trouble in this regard, since Prince Theiandar was far away. He had to assume their next stop would be High Castle. Negotiating a contract with Roache to kidnap the princess was imperative.

The sinister man lay on the bed, admiring the amulet, first stroking it against his cheek and then staring into its depths. The glow seemed to have diminished, even in this dark room, but he paid it no mind. He chose to assume his aging body was losing some of its sharpness.

He could have stolen the beauty at any time, when his last life hadn't worn thin, but he knew this one would be perfect if he let it simmer, as he liked to call it. The princess! Ah, the princess. Yes, she is mine. Her life and body given to prolong mine forever. I will use her for my own ends, and it will be exquisite, he thought in the pit of his soul—the black hole that sucked the life from his victims and was never sated. His greed and desires were overwhelming, and he certainly enjoyed feeding them. Caityn's life would satisfy him for a thousand years—much more than any other before. It was worth the wait, he assured himself.

With these twisted thoughts coursing through his head, the Beauty Thief fell asleep. He dreamed of burning the princess's chest again and of flying in the sky, through the starry night. It was a pleasant dream until he was stabbed through the heart by the prince, at which point he woke with sweat on his brow. He stayed awake the rest of the night, anxiety crowding in on him. Morning could not come soon enough.

* * *

Caityn was awakened the next morning by Idra throwing open the curtains. She covered her eyes and groaned at the thought of getting out from under the warm, welcoming covers, but Idra would have none of it. She pulled the blankets off Caityn and leaned over her.

"Rise and shine, sleepy head."

When Caityn's eyes cracked open, she saw an expression of awe on Idra's face. "The oldness, Caity, 'tis gone! You look like you again!" Idra pulled the still half-sleeping Caityn off the bed and over to the mirror.

Caityn leaned in close to the mirror and touched her youthful-looking reflection. It felt more familiar than anything had all week. A half-smile transformed her lips.

Five days they'd been on this crazy whirlwind of a trip, and in the span of days she'd barely seen herself. Today she looked like the real Caityn, as if the old hag had been a nightmare. She knew it wasn't a dream, though. It was all real; her empty heart was a relentless reminder. The smile faded away before she sat down on the vanity bench.

"Oh Caity, I know 'tis only a start, but this is good! It'll take at least another week before this curse can be lifted, but Prince Theiandar is doing his utmost. There's only one way to save you, and he will do it. His love is true, and strong, and pure. I've seen it. Please don't give up now when there's still a great deal left to do."

Caityn closed her eyes and took a deep breath before looking at herself in the mirror again. Although the looking glass showed only a fleeting image, her reflection proved love was not without purpose. Love could change her. Theiandar's love had changed her outward appearance. Love's passionate determination could look past the outside and work to change the inside, too.

Was this hope? She stared at her likeness in the mirror and said, "Caityn, you can do this. You may not feel love, but you can see it with your eyes. You know it is real."

She wanted to give up. Caityn wanted nothing more than to stay in this room and forget the world existed. But there was this infinitesimal voice at the back of her mind reminding her of who she once was. She shook her head, her beautiful hair falling in tangles around her shoulders.

"No. I will not give up. What everyone is doing for me is done out of love. If love includes diligence, then I am loved. If love includes hard work and sacrifice, then I am loved. If love is patient, then I am loved. If love forgives and is honest, then this must be love they have for me."

"Wonderful, Caity!" Idra said. She stood behind Caityn and squeezed her shoulders. Idra brushed out Caityn's lovely, soft hair before helping her dress for the journey.

"By the way," Caityn said as Idra retrieved her dress from the wardrobe, "Theiandar is going to take some men to Larue to find a ruby while we will travel with Ahmad to Nevin. We must wait there for him. It appears there is some kind of sleeping potion the monks have to knock the thief out long enough to take the amulet from him."

"Sounds like a fine plan. Is there more?"

"We then head to Wyeth to have the arrow crafted. He didn't share the rest with me. I can only assume it has to do with locating the man."

"You must be correct. Well, now you're dressed, we should make our way to breakfast. Before I came in, I noticed the men were almost done preparing for travel. We have a perfect view of the courtyard from our windows," Idra explained.

Caityn assumed she would see Eliya at breakfast. An unpleasant feeling gnawed at her stomach at the thought of it. Was it fear? Was it hate? She couldn't say, but Eliya was the last person with whom Caityn wanted to speak.

Caityn's apprehension had built up over the ten minutes it took to get to the dining room, but to her relief, she found Eliya was not present. It was only the king and queen with a few other people she didn't recognize.

At first she was confused by the king and queen's surprised reaction to her appearance until she remembered the last time they'd seen her she was in the physical state of the curse. This new change must have caught them by surprise.

"Caityn, my dear, Theiandar told us of the transformation, but he didn't say you were completely restored. I'm happy for this," High Queen Zoe said.

Caityn watched the queen approach. She stood in awkward silence as Zoe captured both her hands.

"Tis not complete. Outer beauty, to be sure, but my heart is still a black hole." She frowned. "I don't know how else to describe this lack within me, Queen Zoe. Vagueness must suffice."

"There's nothing to excuse, Caityn dear. You didn't ask for this. We don't understand this hardship now, but maybe someday it will all make sense. Now, do sit and eat. I believe you must be famished."

During breakfast, King Dante was inattentive, but he shared the details of what he'd learned earlier in the morning regarding Caityn's father, King Othniel. "I received news by carrier pigeon about your father's trip to Nashua. While it is good the people have not suffered under the appearance of this Beauty Thief, it is disconcerting to know we have not found any trace of him by river or by road. I'm sorry I cannot report any good news." He stopped to take a bite. Caityn said nothing in reply.

"I sent a reply to your father, assuring him we have a plan in place. I told him of Adair's injury. I'm not sure if he will travel here or not, but you must continue with the plan we made last night, regardless."

"I'm well aware, Your Highness," she replied.

As they were finishing their breakfast, Eliya happened into the room. Caityn froze, her spoon midway to her mouth. Eliya halted in the doorway; her indecision was obvious.

"Come Idra, I am finished. There is a long journey before us."

Eliya looked frantic, but no amount of remorse from the young princess could melt the ice of Caityn's soul.

"I'm so, so sorry!" she exclaimed as Caityn approached the doorway. "Please forgive me for all the misery I've caused you!"

Caityn's response was cool. "There is nothing you can say to wipe it away, Eliya. I have no forgiveness in me and no love, thanks to you." She walked out, her shoulder nudging Eliya's as she passed. Eliya stood by, the pallor of her skin her only response.

* * *

Idra looked apologetically at Eliya. "Please don't be hurt, Princess. Caityn is not herself. If your brother is successful, then you will know her full forgiveness. She is not one to hold a grudge, and I know she desperately wanted your friendship before this happened."

Eliya let a tear slip down her cheek and nodded, unable to make eye contact. Idra understood, and with surprising boldness, she reached out to squeeze Eliya's hand before following Caityn out the door.

When Idra arrived at the main entrance, Caityn was standing in the shadows near the door, peering out through the opening. "I know you're hurting, Caity, and I know you can't find it in you to forgive, but don't despair. We will keep our faith and hope for you."

It warmed Idra's heart when Caityn, arms crossed protectively over her chest, turned from where she leaned and shared one of the faint smiles she'd conjured as of late. If Caity could smile then there was hope. Surely there was hope yet.

* * *

Eliya remained in the doorway, tears streaming down her cheeks. The room before her was quiet. She couldn't see anything through the haze, but she could feel every eye in the room staring at her. Even though tears clouded her vision, Eliya knew her parents were looking at her with compassion, or pity, or both. Knowing it was thus only increased her anguish. It was a painful weight on her shoulders, what she had done. She couldn't stand charity and ran blindly from the room.

CHAPTER TWENTY-ONE
Rubinthynium

Gavin checked his saddle and the bags on his horse. He noticed Caityn and Idra as they emerged from the dark entryway. It was as night and day, the change in Caityn's appearance. He couldn't help but stop and stare. She really was beautiful, and if he wasn't her cousin, he'd vie for her hand. It was a good thing Theiandar loved her the way he did. Gavin wouldn't put up with anything but the best for his cousin.

He walked around his horse, running his hand along the steed's flank and approached the women. Gavin lifted each woman's hand to his lips and kissed it. "You are a lovely sight this morning, fair cousins. I only wish I could gaze on your beauty all day."

"You, sir, are a chronic flirt if there ever was one," Idra said. He grinned and shrugged. "What are the plans for travel?"

"Well, Idra, since the two of you will be going with Sir Ahmad, Prince Theiandar has increased the guard to six men. You'll go directly there. Ahmad has a letter for King Trygg asking him to provide you shelter while in Nevin. Ahmad and two men will travel the extra few miles to the monasey without you.

"The rest of us are heading to Larue to locate a ruby large enough for an arrowhead. Daray seems to think he knows just the trader to get it from. While it can be a dangerous area, it shouldn't be too difficult to obtain what we need. We'll meet you at Nevin in three-days' time."

"Be careful, cousin," Idra said. "I've heard the stories about the gem traders of Larue. It makes me shudder to think of the ruthlessness invading our kingdom by means of trade. I wish it could somehow be stopped."

"I know, Idra. I certainly agree, but right now we're focused on Caityn's need. We'll have to be quick and careful. I'm grateful for your concern." He smiled, hoping to reassure Idra, though there were no guarantees for their safety or the success of their mission. He bowed to the ladies and moved off to finish preparing for the journey.

* * *

As Gavin walked away, Theiandar approached, taking in Caityn's physical restoration as he strolled in their direction. He greeted Idra, but only had eyes for Caityn. It was amazing to him how such a remarkable transformation had come about so quickly.

Caityn was lovely to look upon. He still desired her. It was apparent she didn't understand or return his yearnings, but he chose to overlook it for now.

He didn't reach out to touch her, even though his arms ached to hold her. His words were meant to reassure her—or perhaps himself. "The physical beauty of all people fades away, but the inner beauty can always remain. Lovely Cait, 'tis encouraging to see you look this way, but what I desire most is your inner beauty."

The urge to touch her was intense. He lifted her chin, wanting her to look him in the eye. "I see you for who you really are. I haven't forgotten the beauty of your love and depth of your soul." He caressed her jawline with his thumb. "This evil man thinks he can steal the most precious part of you, but remember I am on your side. I will fight for your love and give you all of my own."

He wrapped his arms around her, holding his breath as he awaited her reaction. The tentative touch of her hands on his back was all he needed. "I love you," he whispered into her hair before letting her go.

As Theiandar helped Caityn mount her mare, his hand lingered on her waist. He slowly backed away, his eyes focused on hers, memorizing her, as he called for the others to mount up.

* * *

She stared at him, longing to feel for him whatever it was he felt for her. She knew she should—that once she had. The emotions had been robbed from her, and unless they could find the amulet . . . . *Lord help us*, she thought, though the desperate plea to the Almighty caught her off guard.

Caityn watched Theiandar mount his horse with strength and ease. He was a natural leader. When he ordered them to move out, the soldiers followed without question, but she couldn't muster even an inkling of regard for him.

The castle folk had come to watch the procession, and many called out to them with love and support.

"Caityn, look up at the window there," Idra said. "Adair. He can't come with us, but he's waving good-bye. I talked to him early this morning, and he said he'll be praying for our journey." In absentminded obedience, she waved good-bye to Adair, but she didn't care one way or the other about his coming along.

An hour into the journey, they arrived at a crossroad. From there, half the group would head west, toward Nevin, and the other would continue on the main road south to Larue, the trading capitol of the Twelve Realms.

Theiandar stopped his group and whistled for the other to stop as well. "Remember, we will meet you in three-days' time. Get what we need, and on the morning of the fourth day, meet us at the entrance to the back trail to Wyeth. We'll move as quickly as we can. If we're not there, start without us and we'll catch up."

Ahmad confirmed his understanding of the plan with a curt nod.

Before they started moving again, Theiandar jumped down. He strode to Caityn's horse, reached up, and lifted her from the saddle. Only her surprise kept her from protesting. Without a word, Theiandar bent his head and tenderly kissed Caityn's lips. Her eyes never closed. She stared at him, her breath caught in her throat. Theiandar looked as surprised by his actions as she did, as he brushed his thumb over her brow. Then, with great reluctance, he helped her remount.

The travelers were silent, turning a blind eye to what they'd witnessed. Caityn was relieved they paid no attention. The feel of it had left her dazed. She didn't even notice the others leaving in the opposite direction.

They traveled all day without much talk amongst the group. That night, as they sat around the fire, Jarl and Parker regaled the ladies with stories of their youthful adventures in the northern realms before being recruited to Prince Theiandar's guard.

Caityn found herself amused, much to the delight of her companions. Idra couldn't help herself and hugged Caityn from time to time. Caityn didn't reciprocate, but she accepted it for what it was: a loving gesture of hope. And though she felt anything but hopeful, Caityn could see its effects on the faces of the people in her company. *It must be nice*, she thought with some regret.

* * *

Theiandar's desperation grew with each passing mile. It was taking too long to travel to Larue, but what else could he do? Even his father, the High King of the Twelve Realms, didn't have a ruby large enough to make an arrowhead. He found himself praying they would find what they needed and quickly. He begged for Caityn's life to be protected and saved. He could quite easily lose his own life trying to save hers, but he was willing to try. After all, he knew one who loves will sacrifice himself for another.

Their pace was quick, and no one interrupted Theiandar's brooding. They were well aware of the urgency of their quest. At the pace they were traveling, they could make it to Larue City by midmorning of the next day.

The hours dragged by, and as night came upon them, they made camp near the road. Instead of sitting by the fire with the others, Theiandar tended his horse, speaking to him as thunder rumbled in the distance.

"Well, my friend, we went far today. You worked hard. Here's a little treat for you." Theiandar held out a sugar cube, and the horse made no effort to check what was offered by his master's hand before taking it from him. It made Theiandar smile. "We're good friends, aren't we? You trust me a great deal. I'm certainly glad I thought to send you home with my father when I left Taisce. You're a good horse. I trust you to carry me far, old friend. Caityn trusts me, and I can't let her down. Tomorrow we'll find a ruby, and then we must ride harder still. Are you up for it?"

As if in reply, the horse nosed Theiandar on the forehead.

"I knew you were," he said. "Good night."

The next morning they were up before the dawn and back on the trail after a quick breakfast of stale bread and beef jerky. With tensions mounting, they rode in silence. Four hours would put them on the outskirts of Larue City and decidedly closer to finding what they needed.

***

"How much farther to the castle?" Caityn complained. "I'm tired of waking up dirty, and now we're soaked through."

"I'm sorry, Princess. We'll arrive at Nevins's stronghold in less than two hours," Ahmad replied.

"You don't have to apologize, Ahmad. I'm complaining." After a minute of silence, she asked, "What is Nevin like?"

Ahmad smiled and said, "Oh, 'tis a splendid place to grow up, Highness. Most of the countryside is dominated by orchards of different kinds of fruit trees. There are vineyards at the base of the Saddle Ridge Mountains, below Glass Lake."

"It sounds like you're homesick, Ahmad," Florian teased. "Do you miss your mother?"

Ahmad laughed. "If your mother was anything like mine, you'd miss her, too!"

"Maybe 'tis not his mother," Hanif said, "but a sweetheart from his village he pines after since leaving to become a High Castle guard."

"Oh no. That can't be, Hanif, because I saw his sweetheart and she is nothing to pine after. Oh, wait . . . no. She was his milk cow. Never mind," Jarl kidded.

Everyone laughed at Jarl's joke. Ahmad shook his head with a smile fixed in place. "Laugh now, but you never joke about a man's milk cow."

His remark brought another peel of laughter as they continued on in this companionable way. It helped to take their minds off the misery of traveling in clothes soaked through from the rain.

When they rounded a bend in the road, they could see the castle in the distance, standing tall. Two flags flew from each turret: the gray and red flag of the kingdom of Nevin, and the masterful dove flag of the Twelve Realms.

They made their way straight to the castle, and when they reached the gate, a man stepped out through the opening. Ahmad jumped down from his horse and ran at the man as though to tackle him.

"Father! Yours is a splendid face to see upon entering a city," Ahmad said as he wrapped his father in a bear of a hug, love and pride shining in his eyes.

"Son, you always have a kind word to say. I've missed you, lad, and your mother will be happy to see you. But what is your business here? You were only here some three months ago. We did not expect to see you for at least another."

"We have urgent, official business here in Nevin before we travel to Wyeth. In fact, we need to gain entrance to the castle in order to meet with King Trygg right away."

Caityn dismounted unassisted and marched over to the two men. "Father, this is Princess Caityn of Taisce." Ahmad's father's eyebrows rose in surprise. "Princess, this man is my father, Axel. He is the keeper of the king's gate."

Bowing low, Axel said, "It is my pleasure to meet the bride of High Prince Theiandar."

"You'll excuse me for not returning the sentiment," she said without a hint of emotion.

Perplexed, Axel looked to his son for explanation.

"She has been cursed by an evil man who stole her beauty. While her outer beauty has been restored, she has no love in her heart; her inner beauty has been stolen. It seems she cannot feel much in the way of pleasure, or joy, or hope, or compassion. We must capture the Beauty Thief and take back the amulet which houses her inner beauty before the total lunar eclipse is complete."

His father said nothing but hugged his son again before sending them on their way to see the king.

Caityn walked next to Ahmad, the reins in hand as she led her mare into the castle. "I didn't really picture you having a family, Ahmad."

He laughed. "I suppose 'tis because you've only ever seen me as a soldier with the unit. But, yes, I do have a family and a wonderful one, to be sure!"

He grinned at her, but his smile faded. "Your family is wonderful, too, Princess. They love you. Until now, you've been sheltered and protected from all harm and given more love than your heart could hold." His brow furrowed. He could see what he said wasn't helping. "I feel that I say the wrong thing to you. I'm sorry for it."

She looked at him as they stepped lightly along the muddy path. "I'm sure what you said was well and true. I was distracted. I haven't lost my memories of my family, but I can't feel them. Tis strange to remember things but not grasp their meaning. I think feelings—especially love, it would seem—direct much of our lives . . . maybe."

"I think there is truth in what you say. But remember, love is not just a feeling, although it is a strong one. It is also a choice we make—a difficult one sometimes, but a worthy one all the same. For example, Prince Theiandar, while his feelings for you are strong and help drive him to save your heart, his quest is not led by them. He chooses to embody his love by acting in spite of what his eyes see. He is willing to die to save your life. Love is powerful," he said with a contemplative edge to his voice.

"I'll think on your words, Sir Ahmad. I am seeing love acted out by others. Though I can't feel it, perhaps I can still do it."

"Very good, Your Highness! That's a step in the right direction."

As they approached the entrance to the keep, a woman dressed all in black stepped out to greet them. While her appearance spoke mourning, her smile beamed with hearty welcome, and her words echoed the same.

"Welcome! Welcome to King Trygg's home! I am Mistress Sarah, keeper of the keys. His Highness is in his private chambers at this time, but as knights of the realms you are welcome." She bowed to Caityn and Idra, who had been assisted from her horse and stood beside her cousin. "And you, young maids, I can see, are to be highly esteemed guests. But, oh my! Look at you, all soaked through! Please, do come in and warm yourselves by the fire while I order rooms prepared and tea served."

"Thank you, Mistress Sarah," Ahmad said. "Also, would you please deliver this letter to the king? It is a missive from High King Dante about our presence here."

Taking the sealed paper in hand, she replied, "But of course!" She led the travelers into a long room with two massive fireplaces and directed them to the closest one.

Mistress Sarah made it her personal mission to get them settled by the fire. She sent a young maid after the tea and another to make two rooms ready for the ladies. Ahmad and the other guards moved close to stand next to the fire.

"That should help you dry out, dear ladies. Tea will be here soon. It will help to warm your bones." She curtsied and hurried off to deliver the letter to the king.

* * *

In a hasty move, the Beauty Thief tucked the amulet away while he sat in morbid anticipation watching Roache and his men approach. He'd received a message at dawn saying the "trader" would meet him in Bella's Theater at ten o'clock in the morning.

The theater was always empty at the specified time of day. It would be a quiet, inconspicuous place to conduct business. The hours dragged by until the meeting-hour, but he waited patiently, knowing once this meeting was finished, he'd be able to ensure his prize would be protected until such a time as the girl was no longer needed.

Roache sauntered from the door to the dark corner where the little man sat. He lowered his tall, sturdy frame onto a chair opposite the thief. Two of his men did the same. Roache wore a look that spoke of his desires in ways the Beauty Thief knew well. While he could read the mercenary and knew he was the best choice for such a job, he still disliked Roache and his business.

"Welcome, Roache. Thank you for meeting me this morning." The little man oozed artificial obeisance.

"I'm in no mood for pleasantries, Nox. What do you want?" Roache's reply sounded curt, but he had a false smile plastered in place.

"Yes, of course. We'll get right to business. I have a delicate matter with which I would like assistance. My time is short, and my conquest is . . . well, shall we say, under royal guard." Nox smiled at his allusion. "I need a woman apprehended and brought to me."

"It will cost you a pretty penny, especially if she is guarded by who you say," Roache replied.

Nox nodded, pulled the bag of gold coins from his inner pocket, and, in slow motion, set it on the table between them. The man to Roache's left opened it and peered inside before handing it to him. Roache weighed it in his hand.

"I think you will need to supply two of these if we are to do business. Unless you have more, the answer is no."

Roache made to leave, but the thief stuck out a hand to stop him. "There is more, my friend. It will be satisfactory, I'm sure!" He waited for Roache to settle back in his seat before speaking again. "This guard has not only my object, but one for you as well. She is young and lovely, strong, and worth at least one of these bags of gold. She is yours when you get me what I need."

Roache narrowed his eyes. "What do you need this acquisition for, Nox?"

"Tis best you not know, but it is important that you let no harm befall her."

"And what do you expect me to do with the other one?" Roache asked.

"Whatever you decide; it is entirely up to your discretion, sir. The old one is the only one I need; the young one is yours. Bring the old woman to Ophira's Peak in the Saddle Ridge Mountains, and your work will be complete. You will have the gold and the girl for any purpose you desire."

Roache's eyes sparkled while he listened. He stroked his dark mustache and goatee as he contemplated the proposal, weighing the difficulty of it against the payment he would receive. Suddenly, he slapped the table. "I like it! I'll do it, Little Man! Give Voss a map to your peak, and we'll provide the woman you need."

"Wonderful!" Nox said, clapping his hands in delight. "The gold will be yours when you deliver the old woman to me." He stuck out his hand to shake on the deal, but Roache chose not to return the gesture.

"You must deliver her to me within ten days' time. Less, if possible. She must be unharmed. She is in the presence of Prince Theiandar himself. It will be difficult, but nothing you and your men can't handle, I'm sure. They are likely on their way to or already at High Castle."

"Fine. Is there anything else we should know about this acquisition?"

Nox grinned and shook his head. "No, the rest will be up to me." He rested his hand upon the hidden amulet.

Roache stood from the table. He and all but Voss left Bella's while Nox drew up a map. When complete, Voss took the hasty map and placed it in the inner pocket of his jacket.

Nox sat back and watched him leave, a smile displayed on his face. The anticipation of events to come gave him goose bumps. He rubbed the raised flesh of his arm and shivered with unspent desire. This was going to be good, so good. He couldn't wait to finish it. The moon may have its own schedule, but time had been on Nox's side for a long while. What on earth could make this special eclipse different?

CHAPTER TWENTY-TWO
Beauty Comes with Age

Roache and eight of his goons gathered in the back room of his fine goods shop. They could hear his saleswoman haggling over gemstones with a customer. Rayna was a master at convincing people to spend more than was necessary, and Roache made sure she was compensated for her troubles.

Voss spread the map out on the table. Roache could see High Castle was not too far out of the way on the trail to this place, Ophira's Peak. Nox had marked out a path leading to a strange, gnarled tree to serve as a meeting place. It all seemed straightforward enough. They discussed the possible need for an extra horse and the weapons required to abduct a person found with the guard unit of High Prince Theiandar, some of the most well-trained soldiers in the entire Twelve Realms.

Before they had finished, Rayna peeked her shimmery, gray head in the door. "I'm sorry to bother you, Master Riggs." She drew out the fake name, the one he used in his "regular" business dealings, with a long hiss, like a snake hidden in the bushes. "But this man out here is asking for a ruby of exceptional size. I showed him our largest, and he is not satisfied. He says he's willing to pay a pretty penny."

Roache's eyes lit up at the thought of the money they could get from this man, whoever he was. He straightened his jacket and smoothed back his dark hair before following Rayna out. He came up short upon seeing one of the high king's men at the counter but didn't miss a beat before transforming himself into a pleasant man of business. He walked to the counter, exuding confidence and a false air of humility.

"Sir, I understand you are interested in our fine rubies, but you are looking for something weightier. I am sorry, but this is the most substantial ruby we have here."

The knight's exasperation was palpable. "Well then, we will have to continue our search elsewhere. Thank you for your time," he said. He turned to go.

Roache's hand shot across the counter and grasped the young man's arm. The soldier looked down with a frown before meeting the store owner's eyes. Roache let go immediately, apologizing for the inappropriate touch.

"I only said we do not have any *here*, sir! But if you will come with me, I can show you to our more prized gemstones. They must be protected because of their great worth, of course. I pray you'll understand."

The brunette knight held up his hands and formed a circle the size of a small apricot. "Do you have one about this big around? It doesn't have to be thick."

Roache's eyes lit up as he agreed, fighting hard to hide his growing voracity. Just the thought of how much money a ruby like that was worth made his mouth water. Today was turning out to be an excellent day. "Yes! In fact, I have some of even greater size, if you prefer. Please, come with me." He motioned for the guardsman to follow him behind the counter.

"Thank you, but first I need to notify my commander. After that, we can finish conducting our business. I can be back in five minutes. Is this acceptable?"

"But of course, sir! We will wait for you right here." Roache's cordial offer was accompanied by a surreptitious wiping of the drool from the edge of his mustache.

As the door banged to a close behind him, Roache called Rayna to the counter. "Wait right here for him to return and then bring him into the back room. I have good news to share with the men. Our other job just got a lot easier. Plus, we'll be making more money from the idiot prince and his guard than we thought!"

He hurried into the back room where the others were waiting for further orders. "Men, our plans have changed. It looks like we will not need to go to High Castle after all. The prince has landed in our laps, it would seem. Fate is on our side today! Zaide, I want you to follow the prince when he leaves here. Find out everything you can about who is with him, where they are staying, where they are going, and what their plans are. You know the drill. The rest of you prepare items for travel and plenty of weapons. The prince has a unit of twelve men, thirteen including himself. There are ten of us. We'll be hard-pressed in battle, if it comes to that."

They left and Roache prepared the room for their visitor, cleaning up items which might appear suspicious. In less than five minutes, Rayna escorted the same young guardsman, Prince Theiandar, and another man into the back room.

"Your Highness, I didn't realize I would be graced by your presence," he said with a bow. "Sit at my humble table with me while Rayna gets the ruby for you to inspect."

"Thank you, Mr. Riggs. You've met Sir Gavin, of course. This man, Sir Wade, will be inspecting the ruby. He can spot a fake a mile away, but from what I've heard around town, you trade in quality products," Prince Theiandar said with only a twinge of unease present in his tone.

Roache jumped on the pronouncement. "Oh, yes, most assuredly, Sire! *All* my wares are top quality and worth the price."

Rayna returned carrying a locked wooden box which she gingerly placed on the table between the men. The prince removed the ruby and held it up to the light before handing it to Sir Wade. The soldier took out a special magnifying glass and peered through it at the gemstone. He turned the ruby this way and that, while the others waited in silence for his inspection to be complete.

With a nod to Prince Theiandar, Sir Wade returned the gemstone to the box.

"All right, Riggs, what is your price for this ruby?" Theiandar said.

"Oh Sire, the gem you see before you did cost me a great deal, and I couldn't part with it for any less than ninety-five gold pieces."

"That is far too much, even for a ruby of this size and clarity. I will offer you forty-five gold pieces."

"Dear Prince, *that* is robbery!" Roache feigned insult, as he'd gotten it for free when he stole it from a merchant ship.

"But because you are our high prince, most respected and beloved ruler, I will offer it to you at eighty-two gold pieces."

"I will give you fifty-five gold pieces for this ruby," Theiandar said, countering again. When Roache hesitated, Theiandar added, "There's a merchant who may have what I am looking for. If we cannot come to an agreement . . ." He let the threat hang heavy in the air between them.

Roache raised his eyebrow. "Well, Sire, I value your business as much as your throne. I will sell it to you for sixty-two gold pieces, but I can do no less!"

"We have a deal," Prince Theiandar said.

Sir Gavin produced a leather pouch full of gold coins and counted out the agreed-upon amount. With the ruby tucked safely away in his coat, they exited.

Roache walked them out and closed the door behind them. He put his ear to the wood and listened, doing his best to make out their hushed conversation. Again, he was in luck.

"Raz, we need to gather the other men and leave as soon as possible. If we're going to make it to the Wyeth trail in time to meet the others, we don't have a minute to waste."

"True, Gavin. Silas and Daray are down the street at another merchant's establishment. Rance and Lieve are at the grocer's getting supplies for our journey back. Wade, you and I will get Silas and Daray while Gavin gets the others. We'll meet you at the livery."

The men separated and all was quiet.

Roache grinned and ran for the back of his store. "Rayna!" he bellowed. "I need you to tend the shop for a week or two. We will be out on a job." Full of malicious intent, he darted out the back door. As he exited, Zaide jogged around to the back of the building. "I heard everything, Zaide. We must go now if we are to beat the prince to the prize!" A crooked smirk etched its way across Roache's face. Luck was on his side!

* * *

King Trygg was truly one of the jolliest, most hospitable people Caityn had ever met. She thought back to earlier in the day when he'd come out to greet them. His middle section was round. His beard was gray, but his smile encompassed everyone with whom he came in contact.

"Welcome," he'd called from the far end of the room. His arms were spread wide, as if hugging them all at once. "I have read the letter from our very own High King Dante, and I must say I am happy, splendidly happy indeed, to be of service to our great realms.

"Now, I must make sure you are well accommodated. Your father, King Othniel, is one of my oldest friends, you know." He patted her hand as he laid it on his forearm. "Your lady will have a room adjoining your own. I shall have the pleasure of escorting you to your chamber.

Idra followed close behind the king and Caityn. The king left them to rest and prepare to have dinner with him that night.

When it was almost time for the evening meal, Idra stepped across the threshold into Caityn's room. "Oh, I was coming to offer to fix your hair before dinner, but I see you've already finished it."

Caityn frowned. "Yes, I find it relaxing, doing my own hair. I think about things while I do it. Sometimes I don't even realize what I've done with it until I've finished."

Idra smiled. "I remember the time you braided one side of it and put the other in a bun below your ear. At the time, I couldn't believe you'd come to the dinner table looking like that!"

Caityn almost smiled at the memory. "Yes, I remember wondering why everyone avoided looking at me throughout supper before I finally leaned over to you and asked for an explanation."

The princess closed her eyes to picture it again. "I was horrified until Adair said he'd never seen a more eye-catching hairdo in all the world. He always knows the right thing to say to lighten the mood." Caityn frowned. "I have been an awful sister to him, haven't I, Idra?"

Idra rested her hands on Caityn's shoulders as they made eye contact in the mirror reflection. "Don't worry, Caity. He knows this is not the real you. He forgives you. Don't be discouraged. There is still hope."

"You keep saying there's hope, Idra, but I don't feel it!" Exasperation pulled the tension in her shoulders tighter. "I may have my looks back, but I'm not stupid. I know, in the end, looking attractive will not make people accept or like me better. I'm struggling with the thought of ending it all and saving myself any more trouble, but there is something in me or around me or . . . or . . .something. I don't know. Something is holding me back. I'm confused."

Idra leaned over encircling Caityn with her arms. "I don't know anything, Caity, but I still have hope. I know we have time. I'm not giving up on you, no matter what you say or do."

It was time to go have dinner with King Trygg. As she opened the door, Ahmad was standing there, hand raised, ready to knock on the door.

Startled, Caityn gasped. Ahmad said, "Ah, you're ready. I was invited to dine with the king. Mistress Sarah has authorized me to escort you to the dining room." He bowed.

They walked in relative silence, and Caityn's eyes were drawn to the candlelit portraits lining the hall. One in particular caught her eye as they walked by.

It was a painting of an old woman with laughing eyes. She was ugly and bent, but the artist had captured something in her . . . whatever it was radiated out from the depths of her haunting eyes—eyes calling out to Caityn, begging her to step into the woman's soul.

Caityn stopped and stared. She tipped her head from one side to the other and longed to see or feel what this old woman held in her bosom. Ahmad and Idra, both concerned and curious, came to stand beside her as she gazed up at the painting.

"Who is she?" she finally asked, her voice breathy.

"Ah . . . I think this is Queen Isabella. She was the oldest monarch of the realm of Nevin, living to be one-hundred-three. By all accounts, she was a lovely woman and beloved by all our people. If memory serves, this particular portrait was painted for her one-hundredth birthday," Ahmad replied.

"She's beautiful," Caityn murmured.

Another minute passed. Caityn was lost within herself. Alone in the dark depths, she didn't take heed of the lone tear slipping down her cheek. She breathed deep and shook the tension from her shoulders. Without acknowledging her companions, Caityn headed toward the dining room once again, Ahmad and Idra in tow. The image of the old queen with laughing eyes never left Caityn's mind for the rest of the evening and into the night.

"We will be spoiled, sleeping in real beds tonight, Caity," Idra remarked as they returned to their rooms. "Do you want me to stay in your room tonight?"

"Of course not, Idra. You should sleep in a real bed, too. There is only a door between us."

"Do you promise not to do anything foolish?"

"Foolish? It all depends on your definition of the word, but I promise to go right to bed. Does that help?"

"I suppose. Good night, Caity. I'll be in to wake you in the morning."

The princess dismissed Idra with a wave and crawled into the sprawling four-poster bed.

CHAPTER TWENTY-THREE
Weathering the Storm

Theiandar and the others with him stopped late that night, ready to drop from pure exhaustion. They didn't bother building a fire but ate what food they'd gotten from the grocer in Larue City.

The prince was too anxious for sleep, so he took the first watch. All was quiet. He sat with his back against a sturdy, old oak. It stood alone beside the road, as if overseeing the people as they traveled to and fro, keeping track of the commerce of the realms . . . always a vigilant sentinel.

Theiandar found it comforting, the thought that something this ancient could be so sturdy. This oak had weathered every storm and drought. He hoped his love could do the same. All his dreams would be crushed if they could not save Caityn.

Before this whole ordeal, Theiandar hadn't realized how essential love was to the human existence, how a heart left void of it could wither a person's soul. Now he was painfully aware of the need to protect love, cultivate it, shower it on others, freely give it in the face of rejection, and speak it—not only with words, but through actions. How could it be only now was he beginning to truly appreciate that love, though multifaceted and complicated, was the most precious language in the world?

His tormented mind had lost track of time. It was time for Daray to spell him on watch. He woke his friend and then lay down in an attempt to rest. Theiandar's exhausted mind drifted off while contemplating the shadow of the mighty oak against the moonlit night sky. He prayed his love, like the tree, would stand strong in this storm.

* * *

Roache and his men had only a narrow lead on Prince Theiandar's troupe. He assumed the prince would travel toward High Castle on the main road and then turn northwest on the more traveled path to Nevin. Roache, though, was familiar with a little-known, more-direct route through Nevin. He was confident they would be well ahead of the other group and anticipated no problem in making it to the head of the trail leading out of Nevin's north country. Roache only needed to work out the best way to capture the old woman and maiden before Prince Theiandar arrived.

Another disturbing speculation about the trajectory of the prince's path had also crossed Roache's mind. What if the prince and his group were already heading in the exact direction Roache needed to go? All Roache knew was the prince was meeting the other half of his group at the trail. Roache had to get to the trailhead first.

There's nothing like an easy job. Roache grinned. He extended his arms over his head in satisfaction, like a cat stretching after a nap in the late-afternoon sun. He leaned back to rest on his makeshift bed and fell asleep with no qualms about their mission. He dreamed of Nox handing over the payment and stacks of gold littering a ship's hull.

The band of mercenaries didn't worry about being followed or tracked. Everyone slept without concern in the abandoned wasteland between Larue and Nevin.

* * *

The next morning, Ahmad entered the castle's great hall and found Caityn reclining in a plush tapestry chair, blankly staring into the behemoth fireplace sporting a roaring fire.

"My lady, I hope you slept well."

"As well as can be expected, I suppose."

"Zaccur, Florian, and I are on our way to the monasey. Tis only two hours south of here. We will be back with the needed items before dark. The king's son, Prince Melvyn, has offered to show you and Lady Idra around the castle grounds today. If you need anything, Hanif, Jarl, and Parker will be here. I would assume they'll be at the training arena or barracks. Mistress Sarah can send for them if you need. And my father is at the gate," he said.

Ahmad was hesitant to leave her here in an unfamiliar place. It was a place he loved and knew well, having grown up here, but Caityn seemed vulnerable and alone even when surrounded by kind and loving people.

She obviously didn't notice his sensitivity to her needs. As for needs, she didn't know her own. She looked back at the fire and said, "Good-bye. We'll see you this evening, then."

He stood there another moment before bowing again and leaving through the front entrance. Ahmad waved to his father on the way out. He sent up a prayer for their journey's success, Caityn's protection, and the final victory of their quest to restore her beauty. He could not see how life without hope or love could be worth living. The thought made him fearful, especially for the poor princess who suffered under the weight of it.

* * *

Caityn continued to stare into the fire after Ahmad's departure. Idra rested her hand on Caityn's shoulder. She jumped, not having heard Idra's approach.

"Don't scare me like that! What do you want?"

"Sorry, Caity, I didn't intend to frighten you. Do you still have the necklace with Kendra's ring on it?"

Caityn reached up and touched the chain around her neck. "Yes, I do. I suppose I should return it while we're here."

"Yes. I'll get Hanif or one of the others to accompany us. Do you remember where Bimala said she lives?"

"I do. It should be easy enough to find. She's the daughter of the local clothier and is a seamstress. She's likely at her parents' shop. Bimala says they live behind their store," Caityn explained.

"All right. I'll—"

Caityn watched a blush creep over Idra's cheeks. Curiosity got the better of Caityn, and she looked to see what had distracted her cousin.

Prince Melvyn stood behind Caityn. He didn't fit his name or look anything like his jolly father. He was tall, slim, and dark. There was no denying he was attractive. His chocolate-brown eyes were brooding and trained on Idra. The heat in her cheeks spoke volumes before she pursed her lips and curtsied low. It was not so much a show respect as to hide her blush.

"You must be Prince Melvyn," Caityn said.

He reached for her hand and kissed it before meeting her eyes. "And you must be the beautiful Princess Caityn. Word is spreading of your plight, but the story must be wrong. You look neither old nor ugly to me. Maybe it was all a ruse to stop the wedding." Before she could reply, he angled himself toward Idra. "And who are you, my lady?"

Idra's blush deepened. "I'm Idra, cousin to the princess and lady-in-waiting." She curtsied and then dared to look at him again. "And it isn't a ruse of any sort, Your Highness."

"I see," Melvyn said, a smile on his face and a twinkle in his eyes.

Caityn noticed the look of infatuation on Idra's face and rolled her eyes. Idra must have been quick to realize her own reaction to the handsome man, because she wiped the besotted look off her face and her posture became regal and distant. Caityn was caught off guard by the laughter she had to struggle to contain.

"Idra, go get Hanif. We should be on our way to the clothier's shop. I want to get this over with as soon as possible."

"What takes you to the clothier's shop?" Prince Melvyn said. "Are you in need of a new dress on your journey?" His teasing tone was lost on her.

"Nonsense. We have a commission to fulfill."

"Then please allow me to escort you today. I am happy to take you anywhere your heart desires. It will be my pleasure and an honor to spend the day looking upon your loveliness."

Caityn rolled her eyes yet again. "That's fine, but only because you know the way there better than either of us."

She waited for him to move, but he stood there. Caityn finally had to shoo him away. "Now would be appropriate. We don't have all day."

Melvyn laughed. "Of course, let's be off." He looked at Idra and winked.

She frowned at him. He offered his arm to Caityn, and they headed from the great hall into the gray, overcast, late-morning light. They walked for several minutes before Caityn interrupted the silence. "Well, you seem much more like your father than I thought at first, but you don't talk as much."

He laughed. "Well, to be honest I wasn't looking forward to spending time with an old hag and her maid, but neither of you are what I expected. That must sound vain of me, and it wouldn't be the first time I've been accused of it.

"I just spent the last week doing nothing except helping old women and children prepare the vineyards for the summer season. It was tedious work, with the elderly ladies complaining of creaking, achy bones. I was afraid I would encounter the same with you.

"I only arrived home last night and was too tired to come to dinner. I promise that is the only reason I was absent last night. I hope you can forgive my rudeness and any vanity which may have spoiled our first meeting."

"You'll have to ask Idra about forgiveness. I can't even fathom it," Caityn said.

The prince chanced another look over his shoulder at Idra who was window-shopping and pretending not to listen to their conversation. Caityn was sure she'd heard every word.

"We are almost to our destination, my lady. Can I ask what business you have with our clothier?"

Caityn fingered the chain at her throat. "Before I was cursed, I made a promise to return something. Since we're here, and I still have the item, it seemed natural to do so."

She released his arm as he reached to open the shop's door. The opening of the door had caused a bell to jingle, announcing their arrival. An older woman entered the room.

"Welcome to Tanner's Clothier. How can I help you, Your Highness?" she said to the prince.

"Thank you, Mistress Tanner. I'd like to introduce to you the Princess of Taisce. She says she has some business to conduct here at your shop."

"Actually, I have something to return to your daughter, Kendra. Is she here?"

"Your Highness," Mistress Tanner said, curtsying to Caityn. "She is here. She's back in the house, having some tea. Please, come join us."

"Thank you, Mistress Tanner. Tea would be lovely," Idra replied before Caityn could refuse.

Caityn didn't argue. They followed the clothier through the shop and into the storage room, exiting through another door leading to the living quarters. At a table on the far side sat a young woman about Idra's age.

The young woman clattered her teacup on to its petite plate and hastily stood, curtsying low.

"Princess Caityn! Lady Idra!" After her obvious shock at their presence wore off, Kendra said, "What brings you to our humble home, Your Highness?"

"It has been a long time, Kendra. I was asked by Bimala to deliver something to you. I thought it best to complete the task while I'm here in Nevin." As she removed the chain from around her slender neck, the ring caught the light streaming through the one window.

Kendra recognized it immediately. Her breath lodged in her throat as tears slipped down her cheeks. Caityn held it dangling from the chain. The ring danced back and forth in a gentle rocking motion until Kendra reached out for it.

The widow lovingly examined the plain gold band and the awkward silence dragged on. Just as Caityn was ready to bolt from the room, Kendra whispered her thanks to the princess. In an unexpected gesture, she took Caityn's hand, kissed it, and kissed it again.

"Thank you, Your Highness. Please forgive my outburst. Braden was my only love. He . . . I miss him terribly." Kendra's tears began anew.

Caityn fidgeted. She didn't understand Kendra's feelings about this dead man at all. Awkward could not even begin to describe how Caityn felt right then.

Idra spoke for Caityn. "Thank you for the offer to stay for tea, Mistress Tanner, but we cannot impose on your hospitality any further. We must go. There are preparations to make before we leave Nevin."

"Yes, thank you for your hospitality," Melvyn added. "Please excuse us, dear ladies."

The clothier did her best to hold her emotions in check. "Thank you for giving my sweet daughter this gift. She longs for her husband still, and this gives her one physical thing, a part of their life together. She will cherish it, I'm sure, and we are deeply grateful to you, Princess. Thank you."

Caityn's expression was unreadable. She scurried from the room, retracing her steps through the shop and out the front door. She didn't wait for the others to follow.

Safely outside, Caityn pressed her hands to her belly and took a deep breath. She sought an answer in her mind as to why watching Kendra had made her uncomfortable. What did it matter that she cried over a dead husband? Caityn's agitation only grew as the struggle of confused emotion weighed on her.

* * *

Idra and Melvyn were quick to follow her from the shop. Idra tucked Caityn's arm in hers as they headed down the street. Melvyn studied the princess.

"Come, Caity. Let's go back to the castle and get some rest before tonight. I thought we'd be leaving in the morning, but Sir Ahmad told me earlier, when they get back from the monasey, he wants to go northwest and camp at the trailhead. He doesn't want to lose any time."

"Hmm?" Caityn muttered. "Leaving when?"

"Tonight, Caity. Tonight," Idra replied.

* * *

It was well into the afternoon when Ahmad and his retinue rode through the castle gates. He was exhausted, but he knew each passing day brought them closer to the lunar eclipse. The monks explained the eclipse was expected in nine days. Who knew how long it would take to find the Beauty Thief's hideout on Ophira's Peak? Too many variables, with no sure answers, made one feel weak.

Mistress Sarah greeted him in the great hall. "I will retrieve the princess myself, Sir Ahmad. Please wait here until I return."

Exhausted, he flopped into a chair by the fire.

"Ahmad, my friend, how are you?" Melvyn asked as he approached the fire.

Ahmad's smile was genuine upon seeing the prince. He bowed before taking Melvyn's arm. "Well, if it isn't the handsome Prince of Nevin! I thought you were overseeing the vineyards, Sire. What brings you home?"

"My aunt. She is causing my father all kinds of trouble. You know how kindhearted he is with everyone. She's up to her usual shenanigans and taking advantage of him. I came home to talk some sense into my father. If he isn't stern with her, I'm afraid he will bankrupt the kingdom! I have to head back to the vineyards in a few days."

"I'm sorry to hear it, Sire, but you're a wise adviser to your father. He may be generous, but he's no fool. I'm sure he'll listen to your counsel."

"You're a great encourager, Ahmad. I'm certainly glad I ran into you right now. May I ask you a question? I spent the morning with the lovely princess and her lady. How can you stand to be traveling with her? She's prickly and . . . odd. How can Theiandar be marrying that girl? She's not only abrupt, she's rude. She's a beauty, but she's got no heart!"

"But she does have a heart, Highness, only the essence of it has been stolen. This is exactly the reason why we're here. We're trying to get it back," Ahmad said.

"Well, Godspeed, my friend. I've heard it said that the princess refused to marry the prince and caused the wedding postponement. There was talk of it being canceled altogether. All manner of nonsense is spreading. Be aware, it has caused tensions to mount, even this far from Taisce. I wish you luck."

He patted Ahmad's shoulder in consolation and strode across the massive room. Ahmad watched him go, unable to ignore the new concerns brought on by Prince Melvyn's words of caution.

CHAPTER TWENTY-FOUR
Ambush

Theiandar and the guards were making good time, but the horses were showing signs of exhaustion. There was a chance that pushing them harder would only bring added delays.

"The horses have been ridden hard. We'll detour to Castle Nevin and borrow some fresh mounts," Theiandar said.

"Raz, doing so will surely delay our arrival at the head of the north trail."

"I realize that, Gavin, but it cannot be helped. We'll get less sleep, but this way we can travel from the castle with the rest of the unit. We should arrive at Nevin just after midnight."

Theiandar was missing Caityn—or at least the Caityn he'd come to love. *Perhaps my eagerness to see her is clouding my judgment*, he thought. But he made no effort to contemplate his motives beyond. The anticipation of seeing her was sure to lead him in to some disappointment, though. His subconscious had to work overtime to deny the fact that he hoped this had all been a bad dream.

His love for Caityn as she used to be was the lens through which he continued to perceive her. In his haste, he forgot she could not feel anything for anyone but let his own emotions guide him.

* * *

Caityn and her entourage left Nevin Castle after dinner. Ahmad pushed them to ride at a steady pace, hoping to reach the head of the path to Wyeth before midnight.

The wagon trail was well-trodden but not quite a road. The path was one leading to the vineyards. Instead of continuing in that direction, they stopped at the place where the trail forked, providing a more direct route to the northern realms.

Ahmad's concern over the size of their company was notable. He stood with his back to the camp as he stared out into the darkness. His unease wouldn't be shaken.

"Is something bothering you, Ahmad?" Jarl asked.

"Yes and no. Something doesn't feel right. I can't place what it is. I feel it in my bones."

"There's nothing out there, Ahmad. It'll be fine."

"You're probably right, Jarl."

Ahmad didn't take his eyes off the dark forest. It was midnight, and it had taken five hours of hard riding to get here. There was no turning back. The camp was in an alcove made by a rocky hill and dense forest. It was protected on two sides, but it still left them vulnerable.

"I'll be placing two men at watch tonight. Hanif and I will take first. Zaccur, you and Florian will take second. Hopefully Raz and the others will be here by morning," Ahmad said.

"Well, if Gavin timed it right, they could sleep for most of the night and still get here by early morning," Jarl said.

* * *

Zaide crept back out of the bushes. With impressive stealth, he slunk to where he'd tied his horse. The distance between kept all sounds of the horse clopping through the forest from attracting any unwanted attention, but it was three-quarters of an hour before he arrived back at the camp where Roache was waiting for his report.

"Well, what did you find?" Roache asked as soon as Zaide trotted into their midst.

Zaide hopped down from his horse, his swagger exuding confidence.

"More good news, sir. Not only have we arrived ahead of Prince Theiandar, but there are only six men and the two women. They brought no extra guards."

"What a stroke of luck! We have a few hours before the others arrive. Let's get our plan set. It will be a simple thing to take our prize." Under the cover of darkness, Roache's impudence took on a life of its own, radiating like waves of desert heat off sun-scorched rocks.

"There are two points of entry, Roache—one from near the path and the other from a spot with less dense forest or ground cover," Zaide said.

Within half an hour of Zaide's return, the mercenaries had a plan in place and were on their horses, prepared to ambush High Castle's special guard and steal away the women.

Of course, none of Roache's men would be upset if forced to kill the High Castle soldiers in the process. Doing so would save them trouble in the years ahead. Half the future king's personal guard was out there in the forest tonight. They were Prince Theiandar's most trusted men. Roache contemplated the pleasure of extinguishing them from existence.

They stopped in the same spot where Zaide had left his horse on his previous scouting mission. "Fink, you stay with the horses," Roache said. "The rest of you follow me. Tis time to make some money, my friends."

They crept through the forest, surrounding their target. "There are two guards over there, both awake," Zaide whispered.

As they inched closer, it appeared their approach had gone undetected.

This time of anticipation was one of Roache's favorites. He allowed himself a moment to enjoy the mounting exhilaration before making the call to strike.

He waited a second too long. One of his men stepped on a twig, its crackling like an explosion in the nighttime silence.

"Ambush!" Roache heard a High Castle guard yell.

Zaide didn't waste another second. He jumped out from behind a tree and swung his eight inch long knife at the man, hoping to silence him with a slit to the throat.

The guard, prepared for attack, dodged the worst of it as the blade grazed his shoulder. Voss had been quicker with his strike. He jabbed his sword through the gut of the other lookout before the guard had a chance to dart away from where he stood against the tree trunk.

"Move!" Roache yelled, his anger boiling. The raiders obeyed without hesitation. Pure chaos ensued as the two factions met in fierce battle.

Roache heard a woman scream from somewhere in the camp. His part in the melee was about to begin. He leaped out of the shadows, and with impressive agility, hustled to where he'd heard the woman's cry.

* * *

Caityn sat up when she heard Ahmad yell, and it took her eyes a moment to adjust to the dark. She heard men's harsh voices calling out from the blackness of the woods surrounding them. In the confusion of events, Caityn stared at their guards who drew swords and stood in a half circle around her and Idra.

"Help over here!" Ahmad cried out.

Zaccur, hearing the call, broke away from the circle. Florian ran the opposite direction, to where Hanif had stood guard, having heard his loud cry of pain in the same instant. Caityn's eyes tracked his movement to where she saw Hanif slumped against a tree.

Idra's scream pierced the air next to Caityn's ear, causing her to cringe at the horrified sound.

Before Caityn could process what was happening, Jarl ran forward, a fierce yell escaping his lips as he charged, sword raised high over his head.

The women were left with one guard: Parker.

Caityn noticed a host of shadowy figures moving toward them from the woods. Parker spread his legs in a wide stance and held his sword with both hands, ready to engage.

Idra scrambled to her feet. With great urgency, she pulled on Caityn's arm, but the princess was too stunned to move.

"Caityn, come! Please, we have to move. Please, Caity! Get up!"

Caityn yanked her arm from Idra's tight grasp. "I'm getting up," she hissed, pulling a dagger from her boot. It was the one Adair had given her a few days before. She took Idra's hand as they backed away from the camp.

The princess stumbled on tree roots in her hasty retreat, but her eyes never strayed from Parker as he brandished his sword in their defense.

Before Caityn knew what was happening, a man came up from the side. He jerked her against his chest, grabbing her around the waist and clapping a hand across her mouth to silence her. Idra screamed once before the same fate befell her.

Ahmad's voice could be heard in the distance, but his words were drowned out by the clashing of battle. The metallic *ting* of swords rang hollow in the chill night air. The only sounds more horrifying were the anguished cries of men in rage and pain.

The whispers of her captor, his breath hot as his mustache scratched against her neck, blocked every other sound from Caityn's mind. "Well, neither of you look old to me, precious. Maybe our friend, Nox, was telling lies. We'll find out soon enough, but I certainly hope you're my prize. Maybe I'll just keep you for myself, hmm?"

She screamed into his hand and then bit it as she stabbed with the knife. He released her mouth to block the blow and wrenched her arm behind her back.

The man swore at her and ripped the knife from her grasp. He grabbed her hair, giving it a ruthless yank. The motion forced her head back and exposed her throat. Her captor leaned his head into the crook of her neck. "Don't you *ever* think of doing that again. I'll make you suffer; you can be sure of it."

His lips were but a hair's breadth away from her neck. Caityn wasn't sure why she shivered. "Let us go, you fool, before you regret it."

The man laughed. He released her hair but kept an ironclad grip on her wrist. He and his cohort dragged the women into the dark woods. None of the castle guard came to their rescue. Caityn struggled the entire way, even when he threatened to hurt her again.

It seemed like forever as Caityn pulled and clawed against the beast-of-a-man's hold. Soon, she was too tired to do more than drag her feet in protest. It was obvious Idra's fear was greater, as her sobs punctuated her unwilling participation.

When they'd moved far enough away to where the sounds of battle became non-existent, they arrived at a cluster of horses. The man holding Caityn, the obvious leader, spoke to the horse wrangler. "Stay here with the rest of the horses. When the others return, head toward the river's mouth."

"Yes, sir," the squat man replied.

Roache pulled a rope off his saddle and, with quick motions, bound Caityn's hands together. He lifted her onto the saddle. The other man did the same with Idra. In no time they were headed north toward Wyeth.

* * *

Ahmad didn't miss the sight of Caityn and Idra being dragged off, but he was engaged in combat and couldn't help them. It would seem his company was outnumbered.

He was infuriated, not only because of the fight and the danger the women were in, but for not heeding his own instincts. If only they'd stayed at the castle until early morning! They still could have made it here in time and not risked an ambush in the dark. They wouldn't have been outnumbered. No one would have gotten hurt. The princess and Idra would still be safe.

A strange signal reverberated around them, carried through the woods on the crisp air. His opponent used the distraction to give Ahmad a hard shove, knocking him to the ground. Instead of taking the opportunity to run Ahmad through, the ambushers retreated.

Ahmad scrambled to his feet, chasing after the attackers. He was within arm's reach of one of them when someone shot an arrow at him. He couldn't identify the place from where the deadly shaft flew, but he had to avoid it—and others—as more arrows whizzed past him.

He ducked behind a tree. It was all the attackers needed in order to escape. When he heard no more arrows whizzing by, Ahmad tried to follow in the opponents' footsteps, but he soon lost the trail.

He stopped and rested his head against a tree trunk and worked to catch his breath. He knew he'd have to satisfy himself, at least for now, with knowing they'd headed in a westerly direction.

There was no way he could go after them by himself, and as Raz's second, he needed to check on the others. It looked as though the women were what the ambushers had been after. He would need all the help he could get to save them.

Ahmad jogged back to camp. He didn't bother with stealth; he was certain the abductors were not coming back. Upon reentering the camp, he found a fire had been made in the midst of the battle-torn space. The horses were nowhere to be seen. The injured attackers were apprehended and one tied up, the other dead.

Jarl and Zaccur were with Hanif, by the tree near which he'd fallen. Jarl was putting pressure on the wound to Hanif's belly. Ahmad spent close to a minute scrutinizing Hanif's face and chest, looking for signs of life.

"He's gone," Ahmad said, resting his hand on Jarl's shoulder.

Jarl sat back on his haunches, his jaw clenched tight enough to see the tendons along his cheek move.

Ahmad stared at Hanif's body and was caught by the sight of his young friend's lifeless eyes staring out through the underbrush.

Jarl startled Ahmad when he stood and punched the tree trunk with all the force he could muster. It was impossible to miss the cracking sound made by the impact.

He cried out with a gut-wrenching agony. No one was sure if it was from the pain of his bleeding, damaged knuckles or the crushing sorrow of losing his friend. Ahmad suspected it was both.

Ahmad had experienced skirmishes and battles, but he'd never lost a man before. He stared at Hanif, one of the youngest at eighteen years old. How could he have never noticed how blue Hanif's eyes were?

Ahmad's nostrils flared. He fought back the tears threatening to escape and took several short, deep breaths. He held the last one until he thought he might pass out, until he hoped his emotions were under control.

He couldn't tear his eyes from Hanif, but he couldn't look in to the emptiness anymore. It made him think of Caityn. There were others who still lived and breathed. Ahmad could see Parker in the distance, propped against a tree. Florian pressed an impromptu bandage against a wound on Parker's side.

Ahmad crouched down next to the injured man. It was taking a great deal of fortitude to contain his tumult of emotions. "How are you, my friend?"

Parker groaned and tried to laugh as he attempted to readjust his position against the tree. Ahmad watched him struggle to work past the pain. The wounded soldier gritted his teeth. "Oh, you know me, just enjoying the evening."

"Hang in there, Parker. Raz and the others will be here soon. We'll get you back to Nevin and get you the best care."

Parker made one brief nod and whispered, "Hanif?"

Although Ahmad knew the emotional pain he was about to inflict would only add to his friend's torment, he couldn't deny him.

"He's gone."

Parker's cry filled the woods, echoing off the rocky hills. He clutched his aching side. "Who attacked? And for what?"

"I don't know, Park, but I'm going to find out. All I know is they took the princess and Lady Idra. We'll go after those blackguards as soon as we have backup." Resolve etched his words as though written in stone.

"Ahmad, you're bleeding," Florian said. "Here, put this on it for now." He wrapped an extra piece of cloth around Ahmad's arm.

He barely registered the pain of his injuries. Once the temporary bandage was in place, Ahmad walked over to the prisoner who lay subdued near the low fire. All he could think about was revenge.

"You and your men killed a dear friend of mine and took some important people. Tell me why."

The man laughed, his refusal to answer evident in the malevolent smile he wore. He coughed, spattering blood on the ground. The rest he spit on Ahmad's shoes.

That was the final straw.

He squatted down in front of the man, grabbed his shirt, and yanked it over to wipe the bloody spittle from his shoe. With his grip tight on the man's shirtfront, Ahmad punched him in the jaw. There was enough force in the blow to rip the man's shirt from Ahmad's white knuckles. The reprobate went flying backward, sprawled across the ground, and bleeding afresh from his mouth. He spit again and laughed. It was obvious he enjoyed the look of hatred he'd brought to Ahmad's face.

Ahmad was seeing red, his anger masking his vision. He growled low, beast-like. "I'm in no mood. You'd better answer my questions before this gets out of hand."

"I can tell you, Nox is a greedy man. He wanted himself a little old lady." His laughter grated on Ahmad's already frayed nerves.

"Nox? Who's Nox?" He tried to ignore the satisfied look in the man's eyes.

"He's the scariest miniature man you'll ever meet! You don't want to mess with him, let alone Roache. You can be sure he'll take his revenge on you for killing Voss there," he said with a nod in the dead mercenary's direction, "seeing as how that's his nephew."

"What does this Nox want with the princess and her maid?"

"Who knows? He's crazy. Roache deals with him because he's got tons of money and pays well. Otherwise, we stay away from him. Rumor has it he can tear a man's heart right out of his chest." Ahmad could tell the man believed it to be true.

Ahmad ignored the man's demented grin as he rifled through the captive's pockets. Empty-handed, Ahmad moved to the dead man, Voss, and rummaged through his pockets as well. There were several coins and a folded piece of paper. Ahmad smoothed it out and was surprised to see a map with the Saddle Ridge Mountains as the focal point.

He held the map out to the captive. "What's this map for?"

The man ignored Ahmad's question, which only served to incite him all the more. Ahmad grabbed the front of the man's shirt again, hauling him to his knees. He posed the question again, mere inches from the scoundrel's face. "What is the map for? And where are they taking the princess?"

He spit in Ahmad's face. "I'm not saying anything else."

Ahmad didn't contemplate his next move. His hand was lightning-quick, so quick the lowlife never saw it coming. Ahmad's knuckles made impact like a battering ram straight to the face. The man's head snapped back and then lolled to the side; he was knocked out cold.

Zaccur must have seen the look on Ahmad's face, but hadn't moved fast enough to stop him from completing the act. When he reached Ahmad, Zaccur laid his hand on Ahmad's chest to prevent him from doing anything else he might regret.

Ahmad looked at his friend through rage-filled eyes. Still, it was the look on Zaccur's face that stopped him, more than the hand resting on his chest. The brigand dropped to the ground with a loud thump when Ahmad released his cramped hold on the man's shirt.

Ahmad wiped the bloody spittle from his cheek and stared at its ruby stain on the heel of his hand. His shoulders drooped as his vision cleared. He was defeated in more ways than one.

CHAPTER TWENTY-FIVE
Tracking Thieves

An hour had passed since the women were abducted. Hanif's body had been wrapped in blankets to make it easier to take him home for a proper burial. As they were securing the captive to a tree, Ahmad and the others heard the rumble of horses approaching from the south.

Theiandar's partial unit pounded into the camp. Their horses' breaths came in heavy snorts as they stamped around on the forest floor. Ahmad cringed at the look of confusion on Theiandar's face while he surveyed the campsite, his eyes in continuous motion as he scanned the area for what Ahmad assumed was a sign of Caityn.

"What's happened, Ahmad? Where's Caityn?" the prince asked as he dismounted and marched over to Ahmad.

Wallowing in his shame, Ahmad struggled to speak. "I'm sorry, Raz . . . sir. I lost Caityn and Idra. The attackers . . . they took them. And they killed Hanif. Parker's wound could be life threatening. He needs a doctor."

Ahmad bowed his head, unable to look Theiandar in the eye. "I'm sorry. I failed you. I failed Princess Caityn and Lady Idra, and I failed the men."

Theiandar's expression was grave but not unkind. He rested his hand on Ahmad's shoulder and stood silent for what seemed an eternity before he spoke. "We're all sorry for the loss of our friend, but you cannot take the blame for his death. Each of you was handpicked for this unit, brave men who I am proud to battle alongside. No one here blames you for this."

Ahmad shook his head, still refusing to make eye contact. Theiandar repeated his heartfelt absolution but in a tone of finality.

"Now, I cannot waste another second. We must find the man who took Caityn and Lady Idra. Tell me all you know. Did you get a good look at him?"

Ahmad took a deep breath. He worked to steady his voice and looked up. "I questioned that man." He pointed to the thief in custody. The man's nose was broken; there was no doubt. His eye was swollen shut. "I'm afraid I lost my temper and was overly rough, unfortunately, Raz. But he did end up providing some information.

"The man who took them is called Roache. The name is familiar, but I can't think why. They're taking the girls to a man by the name of Nox, who I think must be the Beauty Thief, Sire. Our prisoner described him as a small man and alluded to him doing things beyond the realm of human capability. Oh, and I also found this on the dead man."

Theiandar took the map Ahmad held out to him and unfolded it. "Roache? Isn't he the trafficker—the one who pirates merchant ships and sells people into slavery? What would he have to do with the Beauty Thief?"

"I don't know, Raz, but it sounded like it was a business dealing of some sort. The prisoner refused to say more, and Zaccur stepped in to keep me from doing anything else I might regret. Sire, we need to get Parker to a doctor as soon as possible."

"Agreed. Listen, Ahmad, I know you feel responsible for Parker, but I need you with me. You're the best tracker we have. Silas, Rance, and Jarl can take Parker to Nevin for help. King Trygg will see to the prisoner. After they make sure Parker is in good hands, the others can take Hanif home to his family.

Ahmad wanted to protest. He was responsible for Hanif's death. He was responsible for the princess being kidnapped. He was unworthy. He did not feel equal to the task, but he also knew better than to argue with the prince once his mind was made up.

Theiandar called all the men over and issued their orders. He also asked them to bury the dead assailant. It would free up the rest of them to follow the trail while it was still fresh.

When Theiandar saw Zaccur, he stopped him. "Maybe you should head back with the others and have a doctor look at that, Zac."

"No sir, I'm coming with you. I'll be fine." He sported a cocky grin as he touched the gash that trailed diagonally across his chest. "Besides, 'tis only a scratch."

A hint of a smile crossed Theiandar's lips. "Fair enough, but only if you're sure."

"As sure as I am a tiger's got claws."

Theiandar clapped him on the back. "Well then, let's move."

The men going with Theiandar retrieved their horses and mounted up for the journey.

* * *

While Ahmad led the way, his eyes peeled for signs of those who'd gone before them, Theiandar studied the map. Though the handwriting looked hasty, he could make out the mention of Ophira's Peak at a point across the river west of Wyeth. If that was the case, it would take two days to get there once they had the arrowhead, perhaps a bit less. This was where they hoped to find the ladies and the little thief Ahmad had said was named Nox.

A fitting name, Theiandar supposed. He stole beauty in the night, and his heart was dark. He'd already stolen Caityn's heart. What more could he want with her? It didn't make any sense.

While Theiandar was mulling over this question, Ahmad reined in. He jumped down from the saddle and walked over to a bush to pluck a soiled piece of cloth from its branches. He studied the tiny, embroidered initials it bore.

"Lady Idra's handkerchief, Raz! We're on the right trail." Ahmad held it aloft for Theiandar to see then pocketed the soft square of material before remounting.

They continued in relative silence, though the spark of renewed hope lifted the pall about them a bit. All eyes searched for more signs to follow.

It was easy to find where the attackers had stashed their horses, but tracking them from that point became complicated. The abductors had split up. The tracks went in several different directions in an attempt to throw Theiandar and his men off the trail.

"They're likely headed north, Ahmad."

"Agreed, Raz. That's the easiest route to Ophira's Peak. We must assume that's where Roache is taking them."

They followed the trail with the deepest hoof prints. It seemed to be headed toward Glass Lake. "I'm not aware of any good places to cross the river near the lake," Theiandar said. "Are you sure we're on the right trail? We could be adding time and distance."

"Anything is possible, Raz, but we followed the most deeply carved tracks. Either there are some hefty men on those horses, or they're carrying more than one rider at a time. I'm as certain as anyone could be. This is the best one to follow," Ahmad said.

Theiandar agreed. There was nothing else he could do. Besides, Ahmad had proved himself trustworthy over and over in the years they'd known each other. Now was not the time to let doubt cloud his judgment.

His trust in Ahmad's tracking capabilities was confirmed a mere fifteen minutes later as more horse tracks converged on the trail. Theiandar knew they were at least two hours behind. It was too much.

* * *

She watched Idra. Caityn saw the tears slip silently down Idra's cheeks. *I should feel . . . something*, she thought.

There were some emotions threatening to surface, though she couldn't quite pinpoint what they were. Anger and annoyance, perhaps, and a touch of fear, but otherwise she felt nothing.

Idra sat facing backward, chest-to-chest with the man who held her captive. Caityn faced forward, the strange man's arms encircling her, holding the reins. He smelled of sweat—repulsive, fetid sweat; it was as though he never bathed. Its sticky wetness seeped into the clothes on her back.

Her captor had become irate when the rest of the party caught up to them. One of the late comers informed him of his nephew's demise and the other man's capture. Apparently, the rest had managed to escape. This man, their leader, made his displeasure clear, ranting and raving for what seemed like forever. He finally calmed down and ordered the group to start moving again.

Every once in a while he would nuzzle her ear. He seemed to take pleasure in making her cringe. She was persistent in ignoring his questions. He kept asking her which "pretty" she was, but Caityn refused to answer. It seemed to matter to him, and she wasn't about to aid him in his twisted cause.

He must have grown tired of playing nice. Without warning, he squeezed her body against his. "Maybe she's the one old Noxy wants. For what, I don't know, but I think she's older than you. Nox wants the older one, and he wants her unharmed. Since I think you're the younger, I get to keep you for myself. How does that sound?"

She did her best to ignore the unfamiliar tickle of fear raising the hair on the back of her neck. He removed his arm from her waist and yanked her hair back again. "Answer me when I talk to you, she-devil."

Something resembling protectiveness caused her to speak up. "I'm the younger," she said.

He shoved her forward onto the horse's neck as he released her hair.

"See now, my pretty pet? That wasn't so hard, now was it?"

Caityn tried her best to piece it all together. Apparently she was the one this Nox person was after, but if it would keep Idra unharmed, she would pretend otherwise. She would trade places with Idra and protect her from these foul men. Caityn didn't know why this was important, but it felt right.

Roache prodded his horse to move forward a bit, coming abreast of the one in front of him. He spoke to the man holding Idra. "It looks as though you've got the one Nox wants. Be careful with our lovely plaything."

The other rider replied with the same malicious evil seeping from his heart. It was evident in his eyes and every word that slithered past his tongue. "Oh, I can be careful, very careful." He reached up to caress Idra's cheek. "Can't I, pretty thing?" Idra, still perched facing her captor, drew her cheek away from his touch. He slapped her.

"I mean it, Lon," Roache said. "Keep your hands to yourself. Nox wants the old one unmolested, and he'll be able to tell if she's been mistreated."

Zaide was leading the way to the rocky terrain around the south side of the lake. Once on the dried up, rock strewn lake bed on the eastern shore, the horses would have to go slow, but the way would make it simple to mask their trail. It was helpful few men knew this pathway was passable, instead choosing to cross miles up the river.

"Zaide, how much farther to the river crossing?"

"We're two hours from it, but we'll have to get off and walk up ahead. With the ground as rocky and uneven as it is, there's too great a danger of a horse turning an ankle. We'll have to take it slow, but I'm sure we have a good head start."

"Excellent. Let's pick up the pace." Roache drove his heels into his horse's flanks and cantered past the other riders to take the lead.

* * *

Their forward momentum was brought to a standstill. The trail disappeared. Standing in the midst of endless river-smoothed rocks, Theiandar picked one up and hurled it. He watched its graceful arc through the air until it disappeared, listening for the dull smack it made upon impact somewhere beyond. His frustration was doing almost as much to blind him as the descending darkness.

Ahmad had tracked the other group all day, but when they arrived at the dry portion of riverbed, the tracks disappeared. They'd gone back and forth across the terrain, looking for any sign of Caityn or Idra, but their search came up empty. None of Theiandar's men knew of the shallow pass in the river.

"I think we've wasted enough time here, men. The crossing is to the east. Let's head there now. My hope is that we'll be able to pick up the trail again in the morning," Theiandar said.

They headed out again, the additional two hours on horseback giving Theiandar more time to think. His heart was breaking. The only thing to keep him from suffering a complete breakdown was hoping and praying nothing would happen to Caityn and Idra. *There must be some reason Nox wants them. Maybe they'll be left unharmed . . . at least for now.* It was all he had to resist the fear that threatened to cripple him.

The growing brilliance of the moon served to remind them time was running out. The path at the common river crossing was wide and easily seen, even in the dark.

"We'll cross in the morning," Theiandar said as they dismounted. In order to cross safely, they would need to wait for daylight. The melting snow and previous month's spring rains had raised the water levels, and they were still above normal.

The soldiers were tired and disappointed. They ate what was available and then lay down to sleep for a few hours. Theiandar took first watch. He used the quiet time to pray.

"Great One," he spoke into the darkness, "I don't know what you have in mind with all this. I don't think I'm strong enough."

He stopped as tears welled in his eyes. He hadn't cried since he was eight, when he'd broken his arm falling out of a tree.

"I need you, Great One. All I want to do is save Caityn and hurt the ones who've abused her. . . . Somehow I have to be a leader, but I don't know what to do next or where to go."

He buried his head in his hands and begged. "Please, Most High One, help me! I'm lost. I need you and Caity does, too. Please, protect her because . . . I cannot.

"Help me find her." He raised his head and took a deep breath. *I will not cry* was the only thought he could muster and control. He was a soldier, a strong man. Could he not escape this weakness?

Ahmad chose that moment to sit down next to Theiandar. There was no need to say anything, really, as the unique night sounds of the forest closed in around them. The two were as close as brothers. Ahmad had always been courageous, but his gift for encouragement was what stood out to Theiandar the most. He wished his friend had some uplifting words to share, but the silence continued.

* * *

"'O Mighty One, there is nothing in me you do not know! No matter where I run, no matter the shadow under which I hide, you are there. Great One, you know all my thoughts, and you comprehend the depths of my life.'"

Ahmad stopped reciting from the Great Book, but Theiandar knew his friend wasn't finished.

"He knows exactly where she is and what she's going through. His thoughts are bigger than yours or mine, and his plan is beyond anything our minds could fathom."

Theiandar listened, but his heart wasn't in it.

Ahmad must have recognized Theiandar's reticence. "Don't despair, my friend. Our Most High knows the pain of your heart."

Theiandar worked to refocus his mind. Eventually, he let the words from the Great Book speak for him.

In a hushed voice, Theiandar recited assurances he had memorized as a boy. "'If Most High is on our side, what matter is it what forces come against us? We have been given ultimate love in ultimate sacrifice through the Son. He cries out on our behalf and his love is forever upon us. What adversity, or anguish, or oppression, or misery, or peril, or weapon can take us out of his love? Nothing, not one circumstance can do it!'

"I'm glad you're here, Ahmad. I've been wrapped up in saving Caityn and forgot to lean on the one thing that always keeps me upright. I love her so much, and I'm afraid of losing her. I can't think straight. We've lost Hanif. I feel like I'm making all the wrong choices."

Ahmad was quiet. Theiandar was sorry for mentioning Hanif, but it was too late. He had to move past his regret. He said, "What do we do tomorrow, my friend? We're running out of time. Do we try to find their trail on the other side of the river, or do we go to Wyeth and have the arrow crafted? We've got to have it before we make our way to Ophira's Peak."

The question hung in the air like a ghost.

When Ahmad didn't speak up, Theiandar filled the silence. "I'm aware the Great One knows his plans and why we're going through all this, but I wish it was clear to me, too."

Ahmad's voice, though quiet, was heavy with conviction. "That is where faith comes into play. You know what the Great Book says: 'Faith is the credence of things yearned for, the full reliance on things unseen. Leave Princess Caityn in the Mighty One's hands, because when all is said and done, she belongs to him first."

"You're right. I know you're right. Tis just hard to let go and trust in the unseen when I've experienced the evil in this world. I still have an inkling of hope, so don't be troubled. I'll have a decision about our course of action come morning."

"You need to get some rest, too, Raz. You're not invincible, and you'll be no good to anyone if you don't rest."

"Again, you're right. Go wake Gavin. I won't stay up much longer."

Ahmad patted Theiandar's shoulder as he left his side.

Gavin was groggy but made his way over to sit next to Theiandar.

"Raz, I'm here to take over. You can get some shut-eye."

"Thanks Gavin, but I've got some things to work out before the morning."

"If you're trying to decide between tracking the kidnappers or going to Wyeth . . . well, I've been thinking on that myself. It seems to me Caityn's life is important to this Nox fellow. I don't think she'll be in any immediate danger from anyone until after the eclipse. I think we should head to Wyeth to get the arrow made and then follow where the map leads."

"I think you helped make up my mind, Gavin. My hope is Saar and his men will return quicker than expected, and we'll have backup. Make sure to wake us no later than first light."

"Yes, sir. G' night."

Theiandar trudged to his bedroll, weighted down by his heavy spirit. Squeezing his eyes closed, he endured another night of fitful sleep.

CHAPTER TWENTY-SIX
The Mighty One is Over All

The kidnappers were confident when they stopped to rest, so much so that they freed the young women's hands and removed the gag they'd had to resort to in order to silence Idra. She and Caityn were kept on opposite sides of the fire to discourage their conversing. Drinking water was provided them, but no food was offered.

Caityn glared at the man sitting at the fire with them. He was poking at it with a stick, sending embers floating into the air. She was angry and felt strangely inconvenienced. She saw fear in Idra's eyes and didn't like it. These men were horrible; it was obvious by the way they spoke to each other, especially in reference to Idra and her. They had some sinister plans in the works. There had to be a way of escape.

She'd already tried to break free when they finally stopped for the night, but their skill as kidnappers was apparent in every move they made. Besides, she had no idea where they were or how close civilization might be. It would be hopeless to try to escape on foot. She couldn't leave Idra alone with them anyway.

A hand on the back of her neck stopped Caityn's contemplations. Its vice-like grip tightened until she cried out in pain. Roache laughed as he slid onto the log next to her and put his arm around her shoulder. She shrugged him off, which served to increase his amusement.

"Now, now, vixen, you are part of the payment for delivering the other one to Nox," he said with a dip of his head in Idra's direction. "I haven't decided whether I'll keep you or sell you, so you better be on your best behavior."

Idra had her eyes trained on the fire. "How can you be sure you have the right girl?" she said, surprising Roache and Caityn.

Roache's eyes narrowed. "What do you mean?"

Idra shrugged, her fear having been replaced by something steel-like. "I heard you talking about an 'old one' earlier. Certainly I'm older, but are you sure that's what he meant? What if you're wrong and you hurt the one he wants, the one you're to take care with?"

His expression flitted from curiosity to anger in a matter of seconds. He jumped up, tromped around the fire, and grabbed Idra's jaw, jerking her face close to his.

"I suppose you could be right, shrew, which would mean you are the one I get to keep. Sound good?"

He saw the flicker of fear return to her eyes and released her, his evil laughter echoing across the campsite. "Tie them both up," he ordered a man hidden in the shadows. "Nox has some explaining to do when we meet."

The man, the one with the intelligent eyes who'd led the group of kidnappers all day, tied them both to the same tree trunk. Their hands were bound in front, separately, but Caityn and Idra's bodies were wrapped snuggly against the rough bark with one long rope.

He squatted down in front of them. His methodical assessment of the knots securing their hands was slow, but when he was done, he held up Caityn's dagger before their eyes. "Roache gave me a little gift. This isn't a ladies' dagger. I wonder who it belongs to. And don't even think about trying to get free from these ropes. Knotting is a specialty of mine."

Without another word, he backed into the darkness, his eyes trained on Caityn's until she couldn't see him anymore. A moment later, they heard the whiz and smack of the dagger blade as it hit the tree between their heads.

He emerged from the darkness, unable to hide his smirk. He yanked the well-buried dagger from the tree. "But my first love is knife throwing."

The man at the fire laughed and took a swig from the bottle he held. The blade thrower towered over the women before he melted back into the blackness.

Idra tried not to cry, but her efforts were useless.

"I'm fed up with people ordering me about," Caityn said. "I knew this whole journey would turn out to be an idiotic venture. Now your life is in danger, too. I wish I'd died in the river and saved everyone the trouble."

Idra used her bound hands to wipe the tears from her eyes. "Shhh!" She sniffled. "They don't have to know you're the one Nox wants. Right now they're confused and unsure. We need to keep it that way—for both our sakes."

"I don't know what to say, Idra. This is my fault. Men have died because of me! I don't think I can live like this, not knowing myself, not understanding what my feelings are. Tis like the mirror I see myself and my surroundings in is cracked and distorted. What's worse, when I step away from this broken mirror, I can't see—I can't feel—anything at all."

"Just don't give up. From everything they've said, I think this Nox fellow is the Beauty Thief. Maybe we can steal the necklace from him and find a way to get back to Prince Theiandar and his arrow."

"I thought so, too, but who's to say Theian will even have the arrow in time?"

"Let's not think that way, Caityn. Remember, our help comes from the Most High, maker of all there ever was or will be. Everything—"

"Be silent! No more talking or I'll gag you both!" Roache bellowed from the fire, barely five feet away.

We must be truly alone if he can yell without fear of being heard, Caityn thought. She rested her head on Idra's shoulder and was silent. It was their only comfort, being close together like this. The night air chilled them, but no blanket was offered. After a time, shivering and exhausted, they both fell asleep.

* * *

The sun made its appearance the next day to the sound of birds chirping and blue skies. Gavin roused the others, and after changing the bandages of the injured ones, they mounted their horses without their boots on and rolled up their pant legs as far as they would go.

The horses had to be urged into the deep, cold, fast-flowing water. Inching forward, they were able to cross the river with little difficulty.

The plan was to ride as hard and fast as they could to Wyeth. Florian was from there and was familiar with the most renowned fletcher. He took the lead.

While the fertile soils of the area were perfect for the many willow trees growing there, it was the forests of birch and cedar in the south and east of Wyeth which made the area famous. This was the land where the master bow and arrow crafters settled, and if you needed the perfect arrow, there was only one man to see.

"Raz, we'll be able to reach Rusty's place within a day. He's actually south of the castle of Wyeth by at least half a day. There is a village not far from his home. We'll be able to get supplies there," Florian explained.

"Let's just hope he can make an arrowhead out of a ruby. I've never heard of such a thing," Theiandar said.

"I believe 'tis uncommon, but Rusty is a master fletcher. If anyone can do it, he can."

The forest thinned out the longer they traveled. When they stopped to camp for the night they were near a creek and open meadows. Scattered about were the willow trees giving the realm its name.

That night, the men rested their weary bodies on the mossy shore of the creek. The soft gurgle of water over rock should have been comforting, but nothing could distract Theiandar from his thoughts of Caityn and Idra. Exhaustion had a way of either keeping him awake or drowning out all other thoughts. The latter was slow to come, but when it did, his sleep was fraught with nightmares. He woke with a start, pulse racing, sweating despite the coolness of the night. It took a minute to calm down, but he couldn't go back to sleep.

* * *

The birch forest they rode through the next day was ethereal. The tree trunks—deathly white, save for the countless dark spots that freckled them—stood in stark contrast to the delicate green leaves sprouting above. The breeze rattling through them produced a near-constant hum, as if a thousand rattlesnakes lurked, waiting to pounce.

Theiandar was resolved to stay focused on the plan, but as the day dragged by, he was tormented by thoughts of Caityn and what might be happening to her and Idra. When Florian interrupted his musings, he lashed out at him.

Florian seemed to ignore Theiandar's harsh tone, not taking offense. "We're almost to the village I told you about yesterday, Sire. I can see smoke beyond the hill. If we turn here, Rusty's place is another hour east."

His frown remained in place, but Theiandar nodded in reply. He pulled ahead of Florian, steering his mount in the direction the knight had indicated.

Ten minutes later, they rode into the quaint village. You could see all the way from one end to the other. At first the people seemed apprehensive. Some children hid behind the skirts of their mothers. It didn't take someone long to recognize the seal of the High King's Guard and pass the word. It was amazing to watch the change in the villagers. Theiandar wondered at it.

One little girl in particular, with no fear of being trampled, ran up to Theiandar's horse. She held out her arms, begging to be picked up. "Please, ride, please!" she asked in her sweet, toddler voice.

Theiandar's heart melted at the sight. He was reminded of the day he'd first met Caityn. She'd been a brave girl, too, with no fear of horses. He smiled down at this tiny one. Her mother rushed over to shoo her daughter away.

He said, "No, please, if you find it acceptable, I'll give her a short ride on my horse. I'll keep her safe."

His promise, though, caused his smile to falter. He realized he'd pledged the same to Caityn, and yet he hadn't been able to keep his word.

"If you're sure, milord, but dunna' let her be a bother to ye." Then to her daughter, "Now mind the man."

"Yes, Momma," she replied. They rode to the other end of the village and dismounted. Theiandar handed the girl back to her mother before he got down.

The girl, barely more than a toddler, engulfed him in her innocent joy. The girl's mother said, "We thank ye, Sire, for my sweet girl here has wanted to ride a horse since before she could say a word. Ye've given her a great gift today."

"No, 'tis I who received a gift, madam. If not for this precious child here," he said while tapping her button nose, "I might have spent the rest of the day wearing a frown." Theiandar turned his attention to Florian. "Gather what we need, and then we'll head to Rusty's."

In no time they had everything they needed. Theiandar was anxious to arrive at the master fletcher's home.

It took an hour to arrive at Rusty's. His home was a single room cabin in the middle of a perfect circle of willow trees. Behind the cabin was a large covered building with open sides and a barn not far from it.

They had to bend forward on their horses to move through the covering of willow branches at the entrance to the property. There was something majestic about entering through the hanging limbs of the willows. It was as if they'd moved into a completely different world.

Florian called out to Rusty to announce their arrival. Theiandar was so busy taking in their surroundings that he failed to notice the sturdy, red-headed man standing on the front porch, his loaded bow pointed in their direction. Theiandar's first instinct upon seeing it was to reach for his sword, but Florian anticipated the move and caught his hand on the hilt.

"Don't draw it, Raz. He doesn't recognize us, and he doesn't like strangers. Just take it easy, and he'll put the bow down as soon as we introduce ourselves."

"I hope you're right, Florian." Theiandar smiled as he removed his hand from his weapon. "Besides, I think bow beats sword, at least from this distance."

Florian smiled as he addressed the man on the porch. "Rusty, 'tis me . . . Fidget. We've great need of your arrow-crafting skills."

Theiandar heard snickers behind them. He had to admit, he found it to be a silly nickname, too, but he was more interested in the reaction of the man on the porch. Rusty lowered the bow.

"Fidget? Is it really you?" He held his hand over his eyes as if to shield them from the sun. "Well, if it isn't! You rascal, all growed up and fancy! I can't believe my eyes, boy! Get over here and hug this old man!" Rusty hopped down the stairs on his thick legs.

Florian jogged across the yard, wrapped the old man in a bear hug, and lifted him off his feet.

"You old coot! How've you been?"

Rusty laughed. "There was a time when you couldn't have hefted me, youngster, but I see you took after that behemoth of a father of yours. Ha! I'm as right as rain on drought-dry land. Now, who have you brought with you?"

"This is Prince Theiandar and most of his guard unit."

"Well, I'll be! I think I should be bowing or curtsying, or some such, but I don't have a clue which. I hope you'll take my hand, Sire."

Theiandar smiled at Rusty and shook his hand. "Thank you for the kind welcome. I hate to rush past the pleasantries, but we are in desperate need of your help."

Rusty's red, bushy eyebrows shot up. "What help can I be to you, Sire? I'm happy to do whatever I'm able."

Theiandar reached into his inner pocket and pulled out the leather pouch. He shook the ruby into his palm, holding it up for Rusty to see. "I need you to make this into an arrowhead. And you must make me the best arrow you've ever made. It has to shoot straight and true. This is one arrow which must save a life."

Rusty took the gemstone from Theiandar's outstretched hand and held it up to the light. He turned it over, examining the ruby. "Tis been ages since I've made one out of anything but flint or obsidian, but I think I can work my magic on it."

He flipped the ruby high into the air and caught it in his weathered hand. "Come on in, my fellows, and rest your weary selves by my fire. I'll get to work on the arrow at first light. The hour draws on far too late to start it now. I'll add some extra venison to my hearty stew, and we'll have a feast tonight."

The sun had started its downward slant in the sky. Theiandar felt he had no choice but to comply, though it took great restraint not to insist Rusty start on it right away. Leaving it all in the Mighty One's hands was what he'd resolved to do. It was what he would do, even if it meant literally biting his own tongue.

CHAPTER TWENTY-SEVEN
Forming Plans

The kidnappers were close to the base of the Saddle Ridge Mountains. They followed the expanse of Glass Lake's shore for miles before leaving the trail-masking safety of the rocky terrain. As evening approached, they stopped at the edge of the fast-flowing Bear River where they planned to cross to the west.

There was a better crossing to the north, but a village was too close for comfort. This far north in the Twelve Realms, people were less familiar with Roache and his group. The locals were far more likely to be curious about the strangers' presence.

Caityn and Idra had finally been given blankets on the morning of their second day in captivity. Roache must have rethought the wisdom of their treatment the night before. Since then, he'd changed his tune to one of relative protectiveness.

Caityn knew he was protecting an investment. He didn't care one iota about her or Idra, but at the moment, being treated as a valuable commodity was better than freezing to death. She couldn't leave Idra alone with these people. *I cannot die. Who knows what would happen to Idra?* she thought.

She and Idra were tied up, sitting back to back on the shore while the men searched for the best place to cross the river in the waning light. The princess couldn't ignore the rumble in her stomach. She muttered something about longing for a pastry slathered in sugary cream.

Idra, having gained a dab of courage over the last day, spoke up on their behalf. "Sir, we're starving. We've barely eaten anything in the last two days."

"Well, we can't have you wasting away, now can we, my pretty, pretty princesses." Roache took great pleasure in mocking them. "You can be sure, when I find out who's who here and get what's my due, whichever of you belongs to me will be paying for your deceit. Devin! Feed these wenches."

Caityn glared at him but said nothing.

"Thank you . . . for the food," Idra said. "We're grateful."

He spit at the ground near their feet and walked away without a second glance. Caityn took the stale bread the man offered and attempted to see Idra out of the corner of her eye. "Why thank him? He deserves no thanks for anything at all. He's an awful beast!"

"Nevertheless, Caity, he didn't have to feed us. He could have refused. That's something to be thankful for, I think."

"I don't understand you, Idra."

"There was a time when you would have." Idra chewed her bread methodically, savoring every precious bite. "I pray desperately for that time to be restored. I'm so scared. What if Sir Ahmad and the other men can't get to us?"

"Well, once we get to Nox, I'm going to take the amulet from him, maybe choke him with it in the process, and then, hopefully, this whole nightmare will be over," Caityn said.

"There is no way Roache would let either of us get that close. And remember, he's likely a persuasive man, seeing as how he was able to convince Eliya to administer the sleeping draught. He'll be able to convince Roache of just about anything, and that gives me chills."

"Idra, you've got to escape and get help. I think I'd be in less danger than you if they find out who we are. We've got to find a way to get you out of this camp and to safety."

"That is not happening. Besides, how could I leave you alone with these creatures? I wouldn't be able to stop worrying about the horrible things they could—"

"Don't be silly. You heard what they said. Nox wants his girl protected. If you get away, and they find out I'm her, then I'll be fine. You can lead help back to rescue me. Understood?"

"It sounds simple enough, Caity, but I can't see myself doing it. I don't even know where we are! What if I get lost in the woods and never reach help? Tis almost as frightening as staying with these . . . I don't even know what to call them."

"I know 'tis frightful, but is there a better choice? If you stay here and they find out I'm the old one, I'm sure your fate will be unpleasant. You're not safe. The longer this goes on, the more likely it is they'll discover the truth." She paused but Idra made no comment. "I've been thinking . . . can you swim?"

"Yes."

"Do you think you could do it with your hands tied?"

"I don't know, but I do have these ropes loosened. Maybe I can get my hands free," Idra replied.

"Don't do it now. Listen, I heard them say there is a village to the north. I think I have a plan." Caityn whispered it to Idra, her eyes scanning about to be certain no one was listening.

Idra took a deep breath after hearing it all explained. "Oh, I don't know if I can do it! But you make a good point. I'll do the best I can," she said, resolve steeling her voice.

"Tis the best chance we have, Idra."

They both knew the plan was incredibly risky, but their situation left little room for safety concerns. It was decided. Idra was to escape during the river crossing.

The chance to implement the plan came sooner than either of them expected. Less than fifteen minutes later, Roache ordered the men to mount their horses.

A man by the name of Lon loosened the rope which bound the women together. He grasped the tie still binding Idra's hands and jerked her to her feet. The forward motion propelled her body into his. Lon wrapped his other hand behind her back and pressed her to him. She struggled to push away.

Lon laughed as he leaned in to kiss her neck. Hearing her cries, Caityn got to her feet with one thought in mind. She ran at him with all the force she could muster, hitting him with her bound hands. "Let her go, you ugly brute!" she yelled, her emphatic cries as useless as the blows she struck.

He stopped laughing. Incensed, he backhanded Caityn across the face. She cried out as she crumbled to the ground. Idra dropped to her knees beside the princess in a feeble attempt to protect her from further injury.

"Don't you ever touch me again, you little hussy!" Lon roared down at her.

The next thing they knew, he was toppling to the side, a look of shock and pain forever etched on his ghastly face. Roach stood behind him, expressionless. "When I say keep your hands to yourself, I mean it," he said, no trace of anger in his voice. It was more than a little disconcerting when he gently lifted Caityn from the ground. He motioned for the one called Zaide to take hold of Idra.

For the first time in a long while, Caityn was afraid. This man had killed his own henchman without batting an eye! It made her blood run cold. Over his shoulder she tried to make eye contact with Idra, to stop her. There was no telling what he would do to them if the plan didn't work.

Preoccupied with the struggle to free herself from Zaide, Idra never even looked in Caityn's direction. The urgent plea in the princess's eyes went unnoticed as they were tossed onto the horses. Their captors mounted behind them.

"We found what looks to be the best place to cross, upriver about half a mile. We'll still be well away from any villages," Zaide said.

"Well done, Zaide. We'll make camp on the other side. Getting over will be more difficult than I'd like, but it'll be dark soon, and it will put a nice barrier between us and anyone who might have followed us."

"I doubt that happened, sir. We had a good lead, and I believe our trail was untraceable."

"Let's hope you're right."

They rode a short distance to the crossing spot Zaide had scouted out. Roache took the lead, urging his mount into the dangerous waters. His horse hesitated, but with plenty of prodding and swearing from his rider, the steed plunged its hooves into the icy-cold depths. Caityn's heart beat faster from cold and fear.

With slow, deliberate steps, they made their way to the middle of the river. The horse struggled to stay upright as the swirling water rose past its chest. Before long, though, they'd passed the deepest point and made it safely to the far shore.

Zaide was the last to enter the water. He sat relaxed in the saddle with Idra seated in front of him, his arms on either side, holding her in place.

Wet all the way to her waist, Caityn shivered as she watched from the other shore. She wasn't sure if she was more worried Idra wouldn't follow through with the plan or that she would. Either way, the unknowns made her anxious.

Before anyone knew what was happening, both Idra and Zaide were in the water. Fearful neighing mingled with the sounds of rushing water as the frenzied horse worked to right itself.

Zaide surfaced next to the horse, his hand holding tight to the saddle horn.

In desperation, Caityn scanned the water's surface for any sign of Idra. She was nowhere to be seen.

Roache barked obscenity-laced orders at his men, demanding they search for the missing girl. His anger was directed at Zaide, who had regained his seat on his mount.

In the moment, Caityn was shocked to find she was praying: praying Idra would be safe, their captors wouldn't find her, and she would return with someone who could help them.

Then it dawned on Caityn. She might be able to halt the search for Idra. She twisted in the saddle to look at her captor. "Roache, I'm the one you really want. I'm the old one, not her."

His wary eyes narrowed as he studied her. "I don't believe you. She was obviously older than you."

"That's only because of Nox. He has some kind of . . . of power. His evil curse has worn off—the part affecting how I look on the outside. He really does have some sort of magic, like we heard your men talking about the other night. Besides, there's no way Idra could survive in that river. Just take me to him and . . ." She struggled to find the right words to convince him. "I'm sure this Nox will pay you double what he offered you before. The money would be more worthwhile." She infused her voice with as much false confidence as possible. *Please let him believe me!* She waited with bated breath.

Roache stared at her. "You better not be lying to me, witch, because if you are, you can be sure there will be hell to pay." His threat hung in the air as he called off the search for Idra. Caityn was relieved, but she couldn't shake the image of the dead man on the other side of the river. She knew exactly what Roache was capable of. They cantered off into the cover of the forest.

* * *

Idra held her breath as long as she could. She was still amazed it had been such a simple thing to get her hands out of the restraints. Once she had, she'd made quick work of knocking her captor off balance and scurrying into the water. It was deep and she tried to stay under as long as possible before resurfacing, hoping distance and fading light would mask her appearance when she surfaced for air.

Though she was a strong swimmer, her skirt was heavy and threatened to drag her down. She worked at undoing the ties and wriggled out of it. Once freed from the excess weight, she struggled to the surface and made her way to the east bank of the river.

She tried not to gasp for air as she swam to shore. All the while, she strained to detect sounds of her captors. Soon it would be completely dark. Idra tried to ignore the fear growing inside her chest, already trembling with cold. She scurried up the bank and into the underbrush next to the river's rocky shore. After waiting several minutes, she crept farther into the woods but stayed within earshot of the river's rushing waters.

It was hard to pick her way through the bushes, but she dared not go close to the river. Her teeth were chattering, and she couldn't stop it. She was deathly cold.

The light continued to fade, but Idra forced her feet to keep moving forward. She focused on the sounds of the river, always to her left. Throughout the midnight hours, the crackling of branches or the unfamiliar cry of some forest creature would frighten her. Her muscles continued to become stiff and uncooperative.

Idra promised herself she'd only stop for a few minutes. The numbness of cold addled her brain, disrupting her ability to reason, but she started moving again. She simply wanted to stop and sleep, but she pushed her aching, bruised muscles to keep moving.

Finally, well past midnight and with the sky starting to lighten, she could take no more. Idra collapsed at the base of a tree. Adrenaline long gone, a weariness beyond the physical took its toll on her and she slept—a deep, death-like slumber neither fear nor fortitude could prevent.

* * *

Late into the night, Zaide approached Roache as they dried by the campfire. "Sir, I'm sorry I lost the other woman. If you agree, I will set out to track her down. If she's still alive, I will bring her back."

Roache regarded Zaide with a severe look. "You're lucky I haven't killed you for your incompetence. But she is not the one we need to finish the job. While I know she'd be valuable at market, more gold from Nox would be less trouble." He stopped to consider it. "But if you find the girl, and I get the extra bag of gold from Nox . . . we'd be even better off." He nodded, deep in his plotting thoughts. "Yes, go find her. If she hasn't drowned, bring her back. We'll have to teach her a lesson about running away."

Zaide smiled at his commander, more than a little relieved. He'd been given a second chance to make things right, and he had no intention of blowing it. Zaide mounted his horse, and the two of them melted into the darkness of the forest as if they were a part of it.

CHAPTER TWENTY-EIGHT
Piercing Perfection

Theiandar woke to the *tink-tink-tink* of chisel on rock. He and the remaining men from his guard had bunked under the cover of Rusty's open workshop. The night before, he'd sat listening to their host tell stories of when Florian was a young boy—the runt of the bunch who couldn't stand still.

He revealed how the young man had gone to live with his uncle near the castle of Wyeth after his parents were killed by a group of raiding marauders from the Crescent Cave Nation. It explained a great deal about Florian—his drive and determination to protect widows, orphans, the elderly . . . anyone who could not fend for themselves.

Theiandar tried to gather his groggy, morning thoughts. The tapping sound continued with melodic precision. He sat up to look in the direction from which it came.

On a bench near the edge of the open room, Rusty sat hunched over a table. He tapped on the end of a chisel, deep in concentration. His body was angled in such a way that the radiant rising sun shone directly on the object in his hands. The fiery fletcher looked up from his work and removed the strange, thick spectacles from the end of his nose.

"Ah, you've decided to wake, have you? Well, good. Breakfast is waiting for you over yonder in the cabin. Tis a hearty oatmeal, and there's some goat's milk in the pitcher on the table, too," Rusty explained. He returned the magnifying glasses to his nose and went back to his work.

Theiandar wanted to ask Rusty how long it would take to make the arrow, but didn't want to be rude. Instead, he thanked him and led the way back to the cabin.

During breakfast they planned. "Here's what we'll do. Gavin, Ahmad, and Lieve—you will go ahead to the castle of Wyeth to meet with Saar's unit. When the arrow is complete, the rest of us will meet you there. Florian, you're sure it will take two days, at the most, to finish the arrow?"

"That's right, Raz," Florian said.

"Two days? We have less than a week left until the total lunar eclipse. I certainly hope it takes less."

"I agree, Ahmad, but if Saar has found Ophira's Peak, we should still have enough time. This arrow has to be perfect; otherwise, we'll certainly risk Caityn's life." Theiandar hesitated over the thought. *Who knew if they'd even find Caityn before it was too late?*

Gavin sensed his leader's unease and rested a hand on Theiandar's shoulder. "Don't worry, Raz, we'll find her."

"I pray you're right, my friend. Let's get to it, then."

With breakfast finished and all necessary preparations complete, the three soldiers mounted their horses.

From his saddle, Ahmad said, "If the Mighty One wills, we'll see you on the eve of the morrow night."

"I hope it be so," Theiandar replied. "If we do not arrive by midday of the day after tomorrow, and Saar has, you'll have to go on ahead of us. If one of his men stays behind, he could guide us to you."

"Understood. And Raz? Caityn is *his* first, remember."

Theiandar waved farewell to his friends, men he trusted with his own life and the life of his beloved Caityn.

* * *

She stirred from her exhausted slumber. The *chirp-chirping* of birds in the distance was the first thing Idra heard. She was still cold and stiff but more aware now than she'd been earlier. As she lay there against the thick, knobby tree roots, she urged her body to respond, but it wasn't going well.

Idra froze in place like a frightened animal when she heard voices from the other side of the tree. Her instincts kicked in, and with a heady rush of adrenaline, she jumped to her feet and ran, dashing head-on into a young woman carrying a basket of wild flowers. The blossoms went flying through the air as both women crashed to the forest floor.

A young man sprinted over to the girl. "Solwyn!" He reached out to help her up. "Are you injured?"

Solwyn pushed his hand away. "Of course I'm well, Dirk." She got up on her own and hustled over to Idra, crumpled and crying nearby. As she reached out to Idra, Solwyn recoiled in surprise. To touch Idra was to touch ice.

"Oh my! You poor dear! You're frozen solid!" Solwyn said. She removed her shawl, and threw it around Idra's body before helping her to a sitting position. "Come now, we need to get you to a fire to warm you up."

Dirk watched in wary silence.

"Don't stand there; help me get her up! We have to get her home. My mother will know what to do for her."

Dirk hesitated, but upon seeing the stubborn look on Solwyn's face, he quickly complied. Idra was too tired and too cold to argue. Between the two of them, they half dragged, half carried her the short distance back to the village where they lived. On the way, in a bit of delirium, Idra attempted to tell them about Caityn and getting help.

Solwyn shook her head. "No, no, young miss. You need to calm down. Everything will be fine. Mother will take good care of you. Just take it easy, and all will be well."

* * *

Zaide pounded his fist into the tree trunk. He knew he had scarcely missed finding Idra here. By the looks of the mess of flowers and extra footprints, he was sure she'd already made contact with the villagers who lived over the rise.

Seething, he jumped back on his horse and galloped south, away from the village. *We'll have to live without her,* he thought. His pride stung. It rubbed him the wrong way to know this woman had outsmarted him.

He knew Roache would be livid, but there was nothing he could do about it now. It was doubtful Roache would do the same to Zaide as he'd done to Lon. The man had been an idiot and bungler from the beginning. It was frustrating to have tracked the girl all morning only to lose her. He'd picked up her trail on the west side of the river, a mile south of where they'd crossed. She had made surprisingly good time. It looked as though she walked all night long.

This actually impressed him about her. It wasn't just anyone who could take a dangerous dive in a freezing river, swim to shore, and then walk all night in the cold. He loved women with fight in them. Zaide found it attractive. He had to admit to himself that someday he hoped to meet this one again.

* * *

When Gavin and the other men reached Wyeth Castle in the afternoon, the gate was wide open. Throngs of people hustled and bustled about. They dismounted and walked the horses to the stables at the back of the castle grounds and were recognized almost right away. Word of their arrival spread like wildfire.

On the way to the barracks, they were met by the steward who greeted them with a curt nod. "His Highness is quite put out by all this nonsense about finding a thief in our realm. You should know he is unhappy about being accused of harboring such a man."

Ahmad said, "I beg your pardon, Master Wayne. Please give our apologies to the king for any miscommunication. No one believes the important realm of Wyeth would ever harbor a man such as this Beauty Thief. We are merely here to capture him and rid the kingdom of this vermin."

Ahmad's diplomatic proclamation must have been exactly what the steward wished to hear. He replied, "Ah, well, in that case you must come in and tell the king yourself." He leaned in and lowered his voice. "And of course, I bear the brunt of his Majesty's peevishness! Do me the favor of explaining your presence in order that I might avoid the rantings of a grumpy monarch."

Ahmad smiled at the steward. "We would be honored to visit the king. Please, lead the way!"

Master Wayne led the men to the great hall of King Orn. They found the monarch seated on his throne, one leg thrown over the arm of the chair and a goblet of wine in his hand. He made no move to compose himself. Instead, he bellowed.

"Who are these fellows you've brought into my presence? I'm in no mood to offer assistance to intruders."

His steward bowed. "Your Highness, these are the High Prince's guardsmen. They are here on a mission to *serve* Your Grace."

"Oh? And how do they plan to serve me?"

Ahmad was well aware the king of Wyeth was a self-centered man who cared little for the needs of others. Keeping this in mind, Ahmad chose his words with careful deliberation.

"Your Highness, it is a great honor to be at Wyeth and in your presence. Please allow me to say that your home is as beautiful as it is welcoming."

King Orn set his goblet down on the arm of his throne. "Get on with it."

"Of course, Sire," Ahmad said, unruffled by the tone of dismissal in the king's voice. "We are here on behalf of Prince Theiandar, High Prince of all the realms, Your Majesty." Ahmad added a flourish to his bow. "It has been revealed that the graciousness of our realms has been taken advantage of by an evil man known to us as the Beauty Thief. Evidence points to his hideout being in Wyeth. By no fault of your own, Sire, he has sneaked into the Saddle Ridge Mountains and is wreaking havoc on our lands. We come to rid your beauteous homelands of his person and protect your honored people."

King Orn leaned forward in his seat, his eyes narrowed as he listened. Then, his laughter echoed across the great hall.

"Oh, now, *that is* fabulous! You don't think my men could find this buffoon? We don't need your help here or your swords. But, because I am a ruler under High King Dante and have agreed to our lands' covenants, I will acquiesce, and I suppose it doesn't hurt to have extra hands in battle." He made himself comfortable once again, held his goblet high, and swirled its contents around. "Well? You have my permission to stay. I care not what you do, but don't bother me again."

Ahmad, Gavin, and Lieve bowed and exited. Gavin shook his head as they crossed the open courtyard.

Ahmad smiled at him. "I can tell you've had scant time in the company of that particular monarch." He laughed at the sideways look Gavin gave him. "He's probably the only king in the Twelve Realms whose conceit rivals that of the ruler of the Crescents. I'm glad there are not more like him. I pray his son takes after his mother. Now, she's a saint!"

They entered the barracks to find no sign of Saar and his men. With only five days until the total eclipse, they were cutting it a bit too short for Ahmad's liking.

If they didn't find Caityn and the amulet, there would be no saving the princess at all. The thought was disturbing and daunting. Ahmad did what he did best: he stopped right there, amidst the hubbub of soldiers, and knelt in prayer.

Some of the men looked at him strangely, but a few, upon hearing his words, took the same posture and prayed with him on the hard dirt floor. Gavin and Lieve were the first to join him. When Ahmad ran out of words five minutes later, Gavin issued a reverent "Amen," and the soldiers returned to their tasks.

"Well, we should make sure our supplies are in order," Ahmad said once the three were alone again. "Then let's ride out on the trail leading to the river crossing. Maybe someone along the way will have news of Saar's unit."

"Fine by me, Ahmad," Lieve said. He elbowed Gavin to get his attention.

"Huh? Oh, right. Trail to the river. Got it. Let's do it."

Ahmad and Lieve exchanged a concerned glance over Gavin's distracted reply.

"Is everything well, Gavin?"

"I'm well. No, I'm not, but the gnawing of the thought is not worth mentioning." Sometimes trusting in the unseen, having faith, was harder than he'd like it to be.

After two hours of riding west with nothing to show for their venture, they turned back to the castle to get some rest and wait for Saar's return.

CHAPTER TWENTY-NINE
Send Help

Idra woke with a start. She was too quick to sit up, and it made her head spin. She fell back against the bed unable to keep a moan from escaping her lips. *Where in the world am I?*

"You're awake! I'm glad. Ma said you'd wake when you were ready, but I was beginning to get nervous. Oh, where are my manners? Let me get you some water."

Without sitting up, Idra cast a wary eye on the cheerful stranger as she crossed the room and returned with a glass of water. Parched beyond belief, Idra tried her best to sit up again and take the cup, but her incredible weakness prevented her from doing so.

"Here, let me help you," the girl said.

She sat on the bed and held the cup to Idra's dry, cracked lips. The trickle of water soothed the burning in Idra's throat. "Thank you," she whispered to the girl who appeared to be about the same age as Caityn. *Caityn!* "How long have I been asleep?"

"Only since yesterday morning. Barely more than a day, I would say. You were awfully cold when we found you! My name's Solwyn, by the way. What's yours?"

"Idra," she croaked, her voice rusty from lack of use. She shivered and Solwyn, quick to notice, reached for an extra blanket at the end of the bed and wrapped it around Idra's shoulders.

"Nic to meet you, Idra." As Solwyn refilled Idra's water glass, an older woman entered through the only door. She placed a basket of herbs on the table and approached the bed.

"How is our patient?" the woman asked while placing her soft, warm hand on Idra's forehead and then felt of her cheek and neck. "You are a little fevered, I think. Wynnie, soak this cloth with cool water and rest it on her head."

"Yes, Mother." Solwyn fetched the cloth. "Mama, this is Idra. Idra, my mother is a healing woman for the village, so you've come to the right place."

Before Solwyn could get the cloth in place, Idra remembered what she needed to do.

"Thank you for your hospitality, but I must go," she said as she struggled to her feet. "I must get help for Caityn! She's in terrible danger!" Hot tears streamed down Idra's face as her legs collapsed beneath her, the room spinning before her clouded vision.

The girl's mother gently moved Idra's hair back from her face, and took a dry cloth and wiped her tears away. She asked, "What is it, miss? What has happened to your friend?"

"Tis too much to explain, but I must get to the castle at Wyeth. I have to find Sir Ahmad or High Prince Theiandar. Terrible men have captured the princess, and I must get help!"

"You're too ill to go to the castle today," the woman said. "Tis a day's walk or a half-day's ride to get there from here. We have no horses in this village and no cart to take you. I can send Dirk to deliver your message, but you must rest."

"I promised Caity I would get help. I can't sit here while she's with them. Please, I must get help!"

"You lie back and rest, Miss Idra. Solwyn, go find Dirk and send him over. Tell his mother I need him to go to the castle to find the High Prince or one of his guards."

"Yes, Mama," she replied as she scurried out the door to find her beau.

While she was gone, Idra drifted in and out of sleep again. Before she knew it, Dirk was there. She woke when the door creaked open and listened as the older woman explained to him what he needed to do. She chanced a peek at him. He was listening intently to Solwyn's mother's instructions.

"I went back today," the young man whispered, "to where we came across her yesterday. I found another person's tracks near the tree. It looks like they were in a hurry to leave in the other direction. Are you sure 'tis safe to have her here? What if they bring others back to get her?"

"Well, Dirk, I think we'll leave it in the hands of the Great One. For some reason, she's here with us and needs our help. We will give her what we can and protect her in the meantime. Please hurry."

"Yes, ma'am," he said as he headed out to round up food and a bedroll for the road.

Once Idra relaxed and drifted nearer to sleep, Solwyn whispered, "I ran into Bodie on my way back and he says he saw the unit of High Castle guardsmen, the one that was here before. He says they're nearing the river crossing. Do you suppose they know this girl?"

"Anything is possible, dear." She paused. "Why don't you go down to the river and meet them as they cross? You can ask them then."

"Of course, Mama, I'll be back in a while. They're probably already across!" she exclaimed as she dashed out the door once again.

* * *

Rusty had worked from sunrise to sundown, meticulously forming the ruby into an arrowhead fit for a king. It was not perfectly smooth, but the shape and lines of it were aerodynamic enough that when attached to the solid, straight shaft, it flew with precision and ease. When Rusty had completed the arrow's construction the next day, Theiandar tested it multiple times, shooting it into a soft pile of mud to make sure it would fly straight and true.

After he was satisfied with the arrow's performance, he paid Rusty with a bag of gold coins.

"My gratitude is unfathomable, Rusty. Your service goes beyond what a bag of gold could ever suffice to pay. We must go now, but know I will never forget your service to me or to the kingdom."

Rusty dismissed him with a wave. "'Twas nothing, Your Majesty. It will always be my pleasure to serve. Safe journey to you. May you accomplish with success all you set out to do!"

Florian hugged the older man one more time, and they mounted up to leave. The shadows were lengthening as they rode through the gates of the castle.

Theiandar knew he should first go and announce his presence to the king, but his mind was focused on his task. He bypassed the keep and headed to the barracks instead, intent upon finding Ahmad and the others. He was hoping against hope that Saar and his men had returned.

At least they had the crude map in case they didn't encounter Saar. With it, they could find their way to Ophira's Peak, but finding the cave would be another matter altogether.

Upon reaching the barracks, Theiandar hopped down and handed the reins to Zaccur. "Men, take the horses to the stables. I'll meet you back here when you're done."

Theiandar marched into the simple barracks of Wyeth's castle guard. The room was dimly lit, and it took his eyes a moment to adjust to the dark.

Before he could make a full inspection of the room, Gavin clapped him on the shoulder. "You made it, Raz! Do you have the arrow with you?"

Theiandar smiled at the soldier's directness. "Yes!" He pulled an old brown sack from his shoulders. "Here it is. This valuable piece of work will be staying close to my person."

He placed the bag on the nearest table and unwrapped the bow and arrow with care. Ahmad and Lieve had joined the two as they gathered around the table to admire the Wyethian's handiwork.

Gavin reached out to grasp the arrow. He studied the shaft's smooth lines. He was impressed with its near perfection. Then he traded Lieve for the bow. Gavin admired the detail work upon seeing the upper and lower limbs.

Theiandar waited for them to complete their inspection and then wrapped both items.

"Nice," Gavin remarked.

"Rusty does impressive work." Theiandar replied. "Now, has Saar returned yet?"

Ahmad shook his head. "No, Raz, not yet, but we're hopeful he'll be here soon."

Before Theiandar could reply, a commotion ensued outside. He led the way out the door to find Saar and his unit cantering up to the barracks.

"Saar! Thank the Great One! The eclipse begins in four days. Did you find the peak?" Theiandar questioned Saar before he'd even dismounted.

"Sire, I'm sorry. We would have been here earlier, but there was an encounter at the village near the river crossing. It had to be attended to before we could make our way here. I left three of my men there as guards."

"What happened?"

"Highness . . . were the princess and her maid kidnapped?" Saar asked, a look of confusion on his face.

"Yes, but how did you know?"

"The maid, Idra, I believe. We rode here as fast as we could. She was at the village and in quite a state. She's taken ill, Sire. The locals who found her said she was rambling about the princess being in trouble and needing to find you."

"How did she escape? How ill is she?"

"They're not sure, but she's got a fever. She's sleeping more often than not and incoherent otherwise. A young man from the village was brought to my attention. He explained how he and a young woman had come across the lady in the forest. He returned to the spot later and found new tracks heading south along the river."

"Thank you, Saar. You've been most helpful. Listen, when we get back to the village, I want you to follow the kidnappers' trail. If they crossed the river south of the village then 'tis entirely possible we could box them in, if you track from behind and we come from above or the side."

"I believe we found the place you're looking for. Tis a two or three day ride, depending on what part of the mountain you want. The problem is we didn't locate a cave. We spent the better part of two days searching the mountainside for it, Sire," he said, his profound disappointment obvious.

"Don't give up hope, Saar. You've helped to restore mine with what you've told me tonight. Let's look at the map together. We were able to seize one from one of the kidnappers, too. Between your fresh knowledge of the terrain and this rudimentary map, we may be able to pinpoint the exact locale."

Before Theiandar could even unroll the map the steward rushed into the room. He was breathless from his mad dash. Before Wayne could utter a word, Theiandar said, "I'll be right there, Master Wayne. Don't trouble yourself." He thrust the map at Ahmad. "My friend, look over the map with Saar. I want a full report when I return."

"Yes, Sire."

The prince pressed the wrapped bow and arrow into Gavin's hands, giving him a look requiring no words to express his request. He followed Wayne to the castle.

Once Theiandar had taken all the pompous, self-inflated talk he could handle, he returned to the barracks to find most of the men were fast asleep. Ahmad sat next to the fire at the far end, staring into the flames.

"How did it go?" Theiandar said.

Ahmad looked over with a halfhearted smile. "Raz, the map is good. Tis a true representation of the area around Ophira's Peak. Our map still doesn't have the cave from the legends on it. The main feature is the gnarled-looking tree on the southwest side."

"Something else is bothering you, my friend. What is it?"

"Idra," Ahmad whispered after a moment's hesitation.

"She's only caught a cold. She'll be all right. I'm amazed she escaped at all."

Ahmad said nothing more.

"What is it? Are you worried for her health?"

Ahmad looked at the ceiling and sighed. "Sire, 'tis probably not my place, but . . ."

Theiandar waited in patient silence for his friend to find the words he needed. Finally, Ahmad plunged on. "I care for her, Raz. More than I should, I think. I didn't realize it until the kidnapping. I was worried for Princess Caityn, to be sure. But, Raz, when I thought of Lady Idra and how she's of no real use to these men . . . well, I was enraged. I know I'm nothing to her and could never confess my feelings to her, but I can't deny what I feel. And, yes, I'm worried for her health. At the same time, I feel profound relief that she is free from those men."

He stopped talking. Neither man spoke for a time. Theiandar rested his hand on Ahmad's shoulder. "Your feelings for Lady Idra only speak highly of your sensibilities, my friend. There's nothing in her station in life or yours to keep you apart, other than her returning those feelings.

"But, I caution you to consider this further. Be slow to act. You've been thrown together due to this ordeal. It could be harmful to both of you if your feelings were to change after our mission is complete."

"Of course, you're right. Thank you, Raz, for the advice. I'll consider it. Thank you for listening . . . and for not thinking me crazy."

Theiandar laughed. "I didn't say anything my father wouldn't have said to me. You're a good and honorable man, Ahmad. Any woman, Lady Idra included, would be blessed to have you as her husband and protector." Theiandar's mood sobered as the conversation died. He was relieved Idra was free, but what did it mean for Caityn?

CHAPTER THIRTY
A Princess for Gold

After Idra's escape three nights ago, it was decided Caityn would be placed on her own mount and tied securely to the saddle. She was resigned to the fact she would never escape, having tried unsuccessfully to loosen the ropes for hours and hours of the journey. She only stopped trying when she noticed blood staining her skirt and the ropes.

Other than ordering one of his henchmen to take care of her wounds, Roache ignored her for the remainder of the journey west. The other men knew to keep away from her unless they were following an order, so Caityn had been left to her own thoughts for much of the time.

They had come across fresh tracks from a group of about ten riders. It looked as though they were moving east, opposite Roache's group. The concern came from not knowing if there were more men in front of them.

Their forward motion was cautious. Roache spent time ranting about the loss of the map. He reminded them it was a good thing he'd taken the time to memorize it, or they'd be wandering aimlessly in the woods.

The day passed uneventful. Caityn was strapped to the saddle and exhausted. Maybe it was a good thing she'd been secured, else she might very well have fallen off. It was dusk, and she hadn't slept well the night previous, having spent a good part of the wee hours thinking about Idra.

She considered the possibility she was feeling something akin to worry, but the sentiment was only vaguely familiar. She knew Idra must have made it. She had to be alive, because the other man, Zaide, the one who threw knives with dexterity, came back empty handed and in a sour mood.

She also thought about what might happen to her when they found Nox . . . or he found them. She had no idea what his plan was or why he would want her enough to hire these criminals to capture her. Her contemplation was more out of curiosity than fear, however. Now that Idra no longer needed her protection, she didn't care what happened to herself.

The train of horses and riders came to an abrupt halt, jarring Caityn's mind back to the present. She stretched out as far as she dared, hoping to get a look at what had caused their sudden stop. She was unable to see around the men in front of her, but she had no problem hearing the ensuing conversation.

"This woman had better be worth it, Nox. I lost a few of my men in the process of bringing her here."

"Oh, she's worth fifty of the likes of your men, Mr. Roache."

She still couldn't see the man, but his slimy voice sent a chill down her spine, as though she'd heard it in a nightmare.

"Well, if you want her, you'll have to provide me with another bag of gold. The other girl didn't make it. I lost good men, and I want full payment," Roache demanded.

"That's not my problem. We made a deal, Roache," Nox said with incredible calm.

"The deal was I get the other girl and the gold. If I don't get what was agreed to, then you don't either." Roache sounded a little too smug.

Caityn looked up in time to see Roache moving in her direction. He untied the ropes holding her in place and reached up to lift her from the saddle. Her hands were still tied together, but it didn't stop Caityn from taking a swing at him as he grasped her waist. She could see the anger in his eyes. Instead of saying anything, Roache adjusted his grasp on her to avoid the blow and deposited her on the ground.

When Nox saw her, he swore under his breath. "That explains the dull glow."

Caityn struggled in Roache's tight grasp, but she said nothing. "Is this the one you wanted, Nox?" Roache asked.

"Yes." He walked closer to them and removed his hood. He grinned at Caityn. "Do you recognize me, Princess?"

She glared at his wrinkled face and rotten teeth. His laughing response was mirthless. "It seems your prince really does care for you. I suppose I should not be surprised your youth and outer beauty have been restored. Even your filthiness cannot hide it." He stared into her unblinking eyes. "At least I still possess the most important part, although it would have added countless years to my life to have your youthful outer beauty as well," he said. The furrowed look on his face transformed into one of angry regret. "Tis too late now."

"I want my payment, Nox," Roache said, pulling Caityn back and handing her off to Zaide.

Nox narrowed his eyes to imperceptible slits. Caityn could see the tension in Roache's shoulders. Maybe he was afraid of the little man.

"Very well. Follow me." Nox spun around and disappeared into the forest.

Roache regained his hold on Caityn. She gave one retaliatory tug back, but he ignored her defiance, dragging her off the trail and into the woods. The other men took the horses' reins and followed their leader on foot. An hour later, Nox stopped at the base of a massive, gnarled cypress tree. What was left of the dead, old tree hugged the mountainside. Its roots were a tangled mass, wrapping round and round in a maze of chaos.

"Roach, you bring the girl. The rest must wait here."

Roach pulled Caityn against him, his hold tight enough to leave fresh bruises on her upper arms. She glared in annoyance at both men and struggled in Roache's grasp but to no avail.

"How can I trust that this isn't a trap, Nox?"

"Don't be foolish, Roache. My allowing you entrance here is a privilege, one you should not take lightly. I have no reason to harm you or your men. I only mean to give you that for which you've bargained: the gold. If you'd rather wait here, I'll take the princess in and bring your gold back to you after I've secured her."

Roache loosened his hold on Caityn and shoved her forward. He spoke to his men without taking his eyes off Nox. "Stay here and guard this spot. Keep a sharp lookout for the high prince or any other guard units."

"Yes, sir," Zaide replied.

The Beauty Thief located an opening between the tree roots and ducked into it. Roache hesitated for only a moment before he shoved Caityn headfirst into the relatively narrow opening. Once they were inside the root system, darkness engulfed them. Caityn could feel Roache's presence directly behind her. She smelled his sweat mingling with the damp scent of earth and sensed his hesitation. In less than a minute, Nox had lit a lamp. From the eerie glow, he beckoned them forward.

Roache nudged Caityn along as they followed Nox down a set of crudely-carved steps. They descended only a short distance before the tunnel changed and headed in a new direction. The incline was so gradual it took Caityn a minute to realize they were going up. No one spoke in the dank stillness.

The tunnel's ceiling was high, so even Roache could stand up straight as he walked. The walls were no longer dirt, but made of intricately patterned stones in a multitude of colors and textures, many of which Caityn was unable to identify. Every once in a while, they saw an unlit torch affixed to the wall, but otherwise the passage was bare.

They'd been slowly ascending for at least an hour when Roache spoke up, irritation apparent in his voice. "How much farther, Nox?"

Their guide turned around with such rapidity that Roache bumped into Caityn. She took the opportunity to elbow him in the ribs but was disappointed when he seemed to ignore her.

"We will be there when we get there. Would you like to wait here?" Nox asked. He gestured to the dark chamber they'd entered a few seconds before.

Roache did not answer, but a soft growl of frustration passed his lips. Meanwhile, Caityn memorized the layout of the cavern before being ushered out through the middle of three tunnels. She wanted to remember which one they'd gone in and which one they'd come out of in case she might escape. The thought, though, struck her as sad and funny. She laughed despite her gnawing disquiet.

"What do you find so amusing?" Roache said in hushed tones.

She chanced a glance over her shoulder and tried to spy out Roache's face in the darkness. With some difficulty, Caityn could make out the lines of his features which spoke of his anger boiling just below the surface.

"I wasn't laughing. I was thinking, it would be not difficult task to become lost in this place. I wonder if it would be worse than what Nox has planned for me. But I don't care what happens to me anymore, so it really doesn't matter."

He lowered his voice when he answered. "I value my existence, so it matters to me."

All conversation ceased. The only notable deviation from monotony was the stream trickling through the second tunnel they entered.

Eventually, another chamber loomed before them. Nox, took the far left tunnel. There were steps carved in to the hard ground, but they were steep enough one had to crawl up them like a ladder.

When Caityn looked up from her awkward crawl, she saw a tiny speck of light. It resembled a grain of sand. The image flooded her with memories of the idyllic stream near her home. She was jolted by something strange: a desire to go home. She missed it. She missed her family. The foreign appeal of her longing caused Caityn to slow her momentum.

"Get moving, you stupid girl," Roache grumbled as he shoved her from behind.

Her new emotions left her reluctant to move, but after another bout of prodding, she picked up the pace again.

* * *

"We're almost there," Nox called to his guests as they crawled quite a distance behind him. "You will be pleased by what you see when you arrive at my domain." He couldn't mask the pride he took in his home, though he'd played no hand in its ambitious construction.

While he waited for Roache and the princess to join him on the landing, Nox removed his outer robe and flung it into a nearby corner. He caressed the amulet. *Soon! Very soon!* As the clatter of footsteps echoed in the chamber, Nox focused his attention back on the doorway, a wide grin in place.

He relished the look of awe on Roache's face as the mercenary took in the beauty and grandeur of the room. Nox looked around again, with fresh eyes, as if seeing it for the first time.

Nox's wonder was think upon him as he admired the opalescent walls, the beautiful carved-stone floor, the enchanting murals on the curved ceiling, and the imposing half moon fissure facing south, providing a picturesque view of the Saddle Ridge Mountains. The escarpment's edge immediately dropped off below the opening and descended hundreds of feet, like a balcony with no rail. And in the center of the room, stood the Seat of Honor, as he liked to call it, where he would receive the precious gift of renewed life.

After taking it all in, relishing his power, he welcomed them as though he was some magnanimous king. "Please come in and be enveloped in the beauty of my abode. You are welcome here."

He walked over to Caityn, who seemed mesmerized by the shimmering walls, and took hold of the ropes bound around her hands. "Come, my dear, you must see the view." He was gentle with her while he pulled her to the opening in the chamber wall. Instead of admiring the view, he watched Caityn as she took in the scope of everything before her.

Nox was not disappointed to see the lack of amazement on her face. Even the sheer drop-off did not disturb her. It was obvious she was surprised, but it gave him comfort to see her inner beauty had not been restored. Anyone who knew love could not help but be in awe of the sight before them. The prince may not have as much love for her as Nox had assumed after first seeing her on the trail below.

"Come! I have a special place for you while we wait for the eclipse. You will have a lovely view of the whole splendid finale of our joint tale, princess," he cooed.

Caityn didn't resist as he pulled her across the room. Without untying her hands, he pressed her to a sitting position on the cold floor. Nox held her hands palm-up in his own as he examined her rope burns. He brushed his thumbs along the open wounds and enjoyed watching her shiver of pain.

"My, but you are accommodating, Princess. Thank you for not struggling." His smile was full of evil, but he would have called it the wisdom of the ages.

She looked up at him. "Prince Theiandar is on his way here," Caityn said without an ounce of emotion. "He will stop you. My heart will be restored. You cannot win."

Nox remembered the dream he'd had days ago in Larue — the one in which the dastardly prince had stab him in the chest. Though set off-kilter by her confident words, he was determined not to show it. "No. It is impossible for that imbecile prince to find his way here. You're doomed, my dear." He spoke with more confidence than he felt.

Roache interrupted their conversation. "Well? Where's my gold?"

"But, of course. A deal is a deal, is it not?" Nox gave Caityn's chin a tweak and crossed the room, disappearing through a narrow door, cleverly hidden in the wall.

In his hands he carried three bags of gold. He could see the look of greed on Roache's face and offered up a devious-looking smirk in return.

"What would you say to earning a third bag of gold, Mr. Roache?"

Roache looked intrigued. "I'm not opposed to the idea. What would it entail?"

"Killing a prince. *The* prince, in fact."

"That can be arranged. But I must be paid up front, or 'tis no deal."

Nox smiled in triumph. He'd known all along what the mercenary would say. "Of course. What you require would only be right. Is it a deal then?" He held out the three bags of gold.

Roache reached for the bounty. "Yes. We'll ambush him, making quick work of it."

"You will do this, Roache, or I will hunt you down and kill you myself."

Roache laughed as his fingers wrapped around the tied tops of the bags. He opened one and inspected the gold within, the color of it glinting in his eyes, before he shoved the satchels into the pockets of his jacket. "I'll take care of him. Now, how do I get out of here?"

CHAPTER THIRTY-ONE
Captive Audience of One

The lunar eclipse was only three days away. It would start just before midnight of the third day and end a few hours into the night. The feelings of urgency were growing and hope was dwindling.

Theiandar and his men had gone to the village at the crossing the day before and checked on Idra. She seemed to be on the mend, though she was asleep when they'd arrived. The women attending her explained all they'd been able to ascertain from Idra's fever-driven ramblings.

Idra woke up for a short time, and Theiandar assured her they were doing everything possible to find the kidnappers and rescue Cait. The High Castle guards did not stay long. Theiandar thanked the women and asked them to continue their care of Idra until the soldiers returned for her. Saar left the same three guards to protect Idra and the villagers in the event the kidnappers returned.

The two guard units split up. Saar went south along the river, and Theiandar headed across it on the shepherding trail leading into the mountainous regions of Wyeth. He hoped Ahmad was certain of the location of Ophira's Peak.

He seemed confident, though he consulted the map multiple times. The reticence of the men increased. They spoke amongst themselves less often since they'd crossed the river. Other than the rustle of the map and various observations, they were silent.

Theiandar had the impression they were being watched. He peered deep into the trees, searching, but saw no one. In fact, he saw no woodland creatures, either. And then it struck him. There was nothing disturbing their trek but the eerie, all-encompassing silence.

"Gavin, have you noticed the lack of animals in this forest? Why, I haven't even heard a bird chirp for over an hour. What do you make of it?" Theiandar slowed his horse to let Gavin ride beside him.

"I'm not sure, Raz, but I was thinking the same thing. Tis odd this uninhabited area would be free of even birds and squirrels. All I know is it has me on the edge of my saddle."

Agreement rippled through the unit, but the silence surrounding them persisted. Another half hour passed. At first, the change was imperceptible.

Ahmad stopped, signaling for the others to fall in line behind him. The horses stamped in place, restless, sensing what was to come. From up ahead and to the left, they heard the faint hum of hooves pounding the root-besieged woodland. Theiandar signaled for the men to dismount and prepare to fight.

He spied an adjoining trail up ahead and motioned his men to form an arc in the bushes around the other trailhead.

Theiandar and Ahmad stayed centered with the horses, ready to call the attack.

Saar emerged from the other trail head and was startled to see Theiandar and Ahmad standing there.

Theiandar's tension eased. "Stand down, men! Tis Captain Saar."

Saar smiled and jumped down. "That could have been exciting, Sire!"

"To say the least. We've had strange misgivings about these woods all day. I'm assuming you didn't find the kidnappers," Theiandar said, a hint of disappointment in his voice.

"No, Sire. The only signs of life were hoof prints and a place where blood had been spilt. It was north of there where we found they crossed the river. They tried to cover their tracks, but the ground south of here is extremely soft. It was easy to track them after we made the assumption their destination ran in this direction."

"This is where the trail led?" Theiandar asked.

Saar pointed to the west and a little south. "Yes. I'm sure if we continue this way, we'll find more of their tracks. They must have had a hard time finding the right path, though, because it looked as if there was a game trail south of here—a more direct route."

"Probably thanks to the work of the thief. Our assumption is he provided the map for them to follow. It leads down this winding path," Theiandar replied.

"By my calculations, we have a day's worth of travel left to reach the peak, but the mountain is substantial, Sire. How will we know where to go once we arrive?" Ahmad said.

"Captain, do you recall coming across a grotesque sort of tree?" Theiandar held out the map for Saar to inspect.

The captain studied the tree on the map. "Yes, I do remember a tree something like it. Actually, it was extremely out of place in this forest. No other tree in the area like it, and it was obviously dead. Is that where the map leads?"

"Yes," Theiandar replied. "Do you think you could take us to it?"

"I can, Sire. It would be a privilege to do so."

"Good! Then let's use the daylight we have left."

* * *

Caityn tracked the passing of time through the opening in the side of the room. It faced south and allowed in the warmth of the sun after a cold night spent trapped on this mountaintop.

Nox lengthened her chains to give her room to move about in a limited space. He also set out a bucket of water and a stale loaf of bread. "Can't have you wasting away before our time, now can we?" he'd said.

An emotion—*anger?*—caused her split-second decision. She'd kicked the bucket of water. It landed on the bread, soaking it to mush. His backhand to her face was instantaneous. She'd touched the new damage inflicted to the bruise given days before. *So much for that healing*, she thought.

"Do not forget!" he said through clenched teeth. "I only need you until the eclipse is complete, then you are nothing. *Nothing!*" He'd grabbed the bucket and disappeared through the hidden door. Caityn cried, but she didn't understand why.

The confidence she showed before had been false. No one would find her. No one would save her. She was lost. Part of her accepted that; there was nothing she desired to live for anyway, not even herself.

Her heart had no love in it. She knew she should care, but how long could she keep up the act without the desire? A dull ache was beginning to invade the numbness of her soul.

After a while he'd returned with a fresh bucket of water and a piece of fruit. "You ruined the last of the bread. This will have to do," he said while handing her the apple.

She'd already dried her eyes. Instead of knocking the fruit from his hand, she reached out for it. "Thank you," she said, thinking of how Idra would respond.

He'd disappeared through the door again and she did not see him all the rest of the night or the next day. Now the sun was setting and the room lost its warmth in slow increments. Caityn shivered.

But instead of curling up in a ball on the floor again, she took a turn about the room, as far as her chains would allow, in an attempt to loosen her stiff muscles. Caityn stretched closer to the opening, but her restraints prevented her reaching it. The only thing she could get to was the enormous stone throne standing in the center of the iridescent room.

"Do you like it?"

Caityn jumped, startled to find the Beauty Thief had returned unnoticed.

"Did I scare you, my beauty?" he said with a chuckle. He walked closer, licking his wrinkled lips, and Caityn backed toward the wall. Something about this pint-sized man actually frightened her. "Do you like my Seat of Honor?"

"No. Tis not honorable. It only deceives the one who sits in it. Your time will come, Nox, and that chair will be destroyed. It will only serve as a reminder of the coward who feared death."

His eyes narrowed as she spoke, but he said nothing in reply. In a sudden move, he changed direction, settling himself on the throne. He leaned over the edge to look at her while he spoke.

"In little more than a day, my *chair* will prove my power is great. Then you will die, never to reveal my greatness to the world. This is the bane of my great power. It must stay hidden from the world! Others would vie for this amulet's power. By no means can I allow that."

Enlivened all of a sudden, he said, "Oh, I almost forgot my little present for you, Princess." He climbed down from his perch, hurried over to the hidden door, and leaned into the darkness. He returned with what looked like a blanket and mattress stuffed with feathers.

"For your last night of rest you should have a bed fit for a queen." He held them out to her, but she refused to reach for them. Nox threw the bedding at the wall. "Have it your way. Good night, *Princess*."

She kept her sight trained on him as he walked out. When she was sure he was gone, Caityn picked up the mattress he'd tossed against the wall. She took her time laying it out on the hard stone floor. She worked at poking the protruding feathers back into the cover. Once she was satisfied with her work, she reached for the blanket. The scent of musty dirt and mold filled her nostrils, but she wrapped the poor excuse for a blanket around her chilled shoulders and sat down on the feathery bed.

Caityn stared into the approaching darkness. There was no light to keep her company except the rising moon, but still, she whispered into the night. "I'm ready to go. Take me now. I can be done with this and stop this man from getting what he wants. Let Theian stop him from hurting anyone else. Please, Most High. I'm tired of being this girl, this wretched woman I've become. My only hope lies in you."

Sleep was slow to come, but when it did, it was a deep, peaceful slumber. The night slipped by, the moon watching over her through her prison's gaping window. Its bright aura shimmered with magic—a wonder to behold, if only a heart could feel the depths of its mystery.

CHAPTER THIRTY-TWO
The Trail's End

The men waited in their camp, vigilant, under the deep cover of darkness which surrounded them. Unwilling to have his men ambushed, Theiandar increased the number of soldiers standing guard throughout the night.

He was certain they were close to their destination, and his anxiety grew with each passing hour. He tried to pray, but it was more of a plea. Though it was difficult to find the words, a blessed peace filled his heart, and memories of his sweet Caityn crowded out the unknown. He remembered her on horseback, grinning from ear to ear, her riotous hair coming loose from the pins that struggled to tame it. He remembered her two nights before the wedding, her smile bright, a twinkle in her eye as she teased him. He pictured her determined look when, as a child, she remounted the horse from which she'd fallen. His cruel mind tried to linger on the fear he saw behind the courage, but it was trampled out in the face of her strength.

Theiandar squeezed his eyes tight and tried to keep the frustration and fears at bay. He wanted what the memory held—not just her outer beauty, but all the love, joy . . . grace .

. . hope . . . all of the best of her, emanating from within. Caityn was a precious gift. He knew he didn't deserve her love, but she'd been willing to give it all to him. He'd do the same for her, no matter what the cost.

As the approaching dawn turned the black sky to gray, Theiandar found a place to lay his head and dreamed of a future he knew might already be lost forever.

* * *

The sun's early rays bounced off the iridescent walls, shooting arcs of brilliant color across the room. The moldy mattress had grown hard over the course of the night, and a damp chill had settled in Caityn's bones. She pulled the smelly blanket close around her shoulders and huddled against the wall.

It was a terrible sort of quiet here, as though death reigned. She should feel afraid. Instead, her mind perceived something almost foreign to her. It took some time of thought, but she decided it was tranquility she was feeling—or at least an awareness of peace. Maybe it was acceptance of her situation and forthcoming death. *It really wouldn't be awful to die*, she thought. Maybe dying would alleviate the pressing darkness. And yet, something kept tugging at her.

The distant song of birds interrupted the pensive moment. Her ears perked up at the tune, and she realized how long it had been since she'd heard nature's resplendent music. She struggled to her feet and moved as close to the open wall as her restraints allowed, her arms taut behind her. "Hello!" she called out, quietly at first and then with more volume. "Hello?" The birds stopped singing. All was quiet once again.

* * *

Theiandar sat up straight, his eyes darting about as he scanned the nearby forest. "Is everything all right, Raz?" Gavin said.

"Did you hear that?"

Gavin looked confused. "Hear what?"

"The shout. It sounded like 'hello' or 'help' . . . or something."

"No, Sire, I didn't hear anything. The forest still seems unusually quiet, especially for this time of morning."

Theiandar chose to ignore his intuition. "We need to get moving as quickly as possible. I'm sure we're close, but we have no time to waste. I'm not sure what the tree on the map means, but 'tis obviously important. Let's head there to get our bearings." He looked up through the leafy cover to see Ophira's Peak, monstrous and majestic.

"Please, Mighty One, let us find her," he whispered.

The men wasted no time devouring their breakfast and prepared the horses for more travel. Theiandar rode next to Saar, sharing the lead since the trail had widened. They discussed the fact that while the map did not show it, the trail actually appeared to veer away from the mountains and would likely turn north toward the kingdom of Emlyn.

"What do you think about leaving the trail?" Saar asked.

"I was considering the option myself, captain. Perhaps we should be looking for a trail leading to the south."

Before Saar could respond, an arrow whizzed past Theiandar's head, grazing his temple. "Ambush!" he cried as he dismounted, wiping the trickle of blood from his ear. As the other men gathered about, Theiandar scanned the area but saw no one at all.

They were completely vulnerable. None of them were familiar with the terrain, and the enemy was well hidden. Theiandar removed the sword from his saddle, his eyes focused in the direction from which the arrow had come. At first he saw no one, but then someone stepped from behind a tree and took another quick shot. He missed again, but Theiandar got a good look at him as he stood thirty feet away on the south side of the trail.

"Over there, men!" Theiandar's shout was followed by a host of assailants charging out from the trees. They were trapped between their horses and the oncoming assault. The sounds of battle filled the once-silent forest, as shouts, grunts, and the clang-clang of metal-on-metal echoed into the distance.

Theiandar had no time to assess the battlefield. No sooner had he called out to his soldiers before a large man was upon him—sword raised high, eyes alight with bloodlust. With only the breadth of a heartbeat to spare, Theiandar raised his blade up to block the full-force, downward strike of the other man.

His confusion turned to anger when he realized who was attacking them. "You! You're the kidnapper?" Theiandar said as he pushed back against the other man's sword.

Roache pulled back and sneered. "I am a man of business. It just so happened that your business crossed paths with another customer of mine. It has really worked out quite well in my favor!" he exclaimed while swinging his sword in a wide, sideways arc toward the prince.

Theiandar blocked the blow and swung back with all his might.

"What have you done with Princess Caityn, Riggs? Or is it, Roache?"

Theiandar's question roared out from the depths of his gut as he jabbed his sword toward Roache's stomach, missing by a hair's breadth.

Roache laughed. Theiandar was appalled to see the other man was actually enjoying himself.

Theiandar pulled his dagger from his boot. With his sword raised above his head as a distraction, he jabbed his knife toward Roache's face.

His opponent saw the glint of the blade from the corner of his eye and swung his free arm out to dash Theiandar's hand away. He was a second too late. The knife sliced deeply into Roache's cheek, sprinkling blood through the air in its wake.

The kidnapper cried out in pain, all traces of amusement gone. Roache bent at the waist and rammed into Theiandar like a madman, knocking the prince to the ground.

Before he could drive his sword into Theiandar's gut, Saar blasted into Roache's ribs, knocking him sideways.

They landed in a heap of grunts, arms and legs flailing.

Theiandar was quick to regain his feet. He scanned the area, finally able to assess the situation. There were several men lying about, either dead or injured, and still a few fighting. His inspection came to the two men on the ground.

Roache squeezed Saar's neck in a death grip.

Theiandar swung his sword around and pressed it into Roache's back. The brigand paused in his dirty deed.

"Let go and get up, Roache," Theiandar ordered.

As Roache's hands loosened their grip on his neck, Saar hooked his fist into the fresh cut on Roache's cheek causing the big man to cry out in pain.

Theiandar pressed the sword harder into Roache's back. The mercenary stood up from his position over Saar.

Having retrieved his knife, the prince stepped closer to Roache where he then placed the tip of it against Roache's back and swung the sword around to lie on his neck.

"Saar, send some men to round up the horses and find some rope for our new guests. Gavin, do a headcount. I want everyone accounted for."

Yes, Sire!" Gavin said, gripping his shoulder and worn from battle but ready, as always, to obey.

In the meantime, Theiandar turned his attention to more important matters. "What have you done with the princess, Roache?"

Roache laughed. "Well, if you must know, Nox wanted that little prize all to himself. Of course, now I still need to earn the last bag of gold. You'll not be seeing her again once I kill you."

With a touch more force, Theiandar pressed the knife into Roache's back. "I think you'll be disappointed there, Roache. Now, you're going to lead us to this Nox."

"Easy, friend," Roache replied. "I'm a simple businessman. I'm happy to make a deal."

"No deals," Theiandar replied through clenched teeth.

After Roache's hands were shackled, Theiandar released him, overcome with weariness.

He knew he'd have to regain his strength quickly in order to handle the situation. If he couldn't be strong, he'd need to at least appear so. Theiandar replaced his knife in his boot and his sword in the sheath.

Gavin approached. "Raz, all the men are accounted for. Zaccur's chest injury has opened up again. Lieve took an arrow to the shoulder; Daray is working to remove it. One of Saar's men was killed, and there is one injured assailant as well as two dead. It would seem, though, some of the attackers have escaped."

As Gavin gave his report, Theiandar kept his eyes on the man he had first known as Riggs. It was almost imperceptible, but he didn't miss the look of rage as it flitted behind the captive man's eyes.

"Thank you, Gavin. Roache is going to lead us to the princess. The only deal he'll get is he won't hang today. Gavin, you and Ahmad are in charge of this prisoner. Daray will stay here to care for the wounded; Wade and Florian will remain to stand guard in case the others return. Wait here for us. Saar, you and your men bury the dead attackers and prepare your fallen soldier for the return trip home. See if you can track the escaped attackers on the way."

"Yes, Sire. Thank you for letting us return Iggy home," Saar replied, solemnity infiltrating his words.

"Of course," Theiandar said, placing his hand on Saar's shoulder. "He deserves a proper resting place and to be honored for his great courage and sacrifice."

Saar nodded, unable to speak. Theiandar watched him go, knowing his pain and feeling wretchedly unable to relieve it. Instead of dwelling on it, though, he took a deep breath and used the sun to gauge the time. It was past noon now.

He knew they must be close to the gnarled tree, and time was of the essence. The horses were rounded up.

Theiandar took the lead, followed by Ahmad who had a rope secured between his saddle and Roache. Gavin brought up the rear.

"Roache, where do we turn off the trail?" Theiandar said.

"What? You don't know the way, Prince?"

"Heed my words, Roache, both these men are excellent trackers. You may as well make this easier for yourself, or death will come swifter than the night."

"You'll get no help from me. Nox may seem old and harmless, but he is not a man to be trifled with, let me assure you," Roache said.

"Roache, I'd dearly like to kill you and be done with it. But if you really are the businessman you claim to be then look at this situation as a way to redeem yourself. You can avoid the death penalty. Help us, and I'll make sure you're not hung for your crimes."

"That smells like a deal, Highness."

"Tis as close to one as you'll get."

"What difference does it make to me? Rotting in prison is just as bad as hanging." He was silent a moment. "What guarantee do I have you'll keep your word? What about Nox?"

"As High Prince of these realms, my word is my bond, Roache. We would not be here now if that were not true. You'll not die for your crimes."

"You've offered no guarantee against Nox. He'll kill me if I don't kill you first. You see my dilemma, don't you?"

"You get us to Caityn, and we'll protect you against Nox," Theiandar said.

"I suppose I have little choice, but mark my words: Nox is not what he seems." He leaned sideways to look around the horses. "About one hundred feet ahead is where we'll leave this path. The trees are thick. You'll have to dismount and lead your horses in."

Two minutes later, they arrived at the spot and dismounted. Theiandar brought Roache to the front and gestured for him to lead them into the thicket.

More than an hour later, they emerged from the thickness of the forest to find themselves standing under the eerie, twisting branches of the cypress. "You'll have to leave your horses here and find something to light the torch inside the entryway," Roache said as they reached the clearing. "Tis going to be dark from here on in."

They gathered their weapons, Gavin taking special care to retrieve the bow and arrow. He guarded the prisoner while Theiandar slung them on. The four of them ducked through the opening, caution keeping their movements slow.

Ahmad slipped the blowdarts and dart gun into his inner pocket then found the torch. He used his flint to light the end. It burst into a bright orange flame. They noticed a lantern farther in on the dirt wall opposite, and Ahmad lit it as well. Theiandar placed his knife in his belt for easier access and took hold of Roache's upper arm.

"Let's go," he said.

CHAPTER THIRTY-THREE
In the Belly of the Beast

The inky darkness enveloped them, increasing with each step they took. The hard, dirt stairs ended at the beginning of a tunnel. It looked like a hallway within an ancient castle.

Theiandar prodded Roache to move forward again. They walked with cautious steps, aware that their every move faintly echoed through the hall. There was little chance their approach would go unnoticed.

"How much farther?" Theiandar whispered to Roache.

"We have a ways to go," he replied, a slight quaver detectable in his voice. "It took hours to ascend."

Theiandar finally released his hold on Roache's arm, any concern he might run, dwindling. They entered a chamber, halting when Roache's steps hesitated. In the deathlike silence of the room, the rhythmic hiss of breathing made for a ghostly companion.

"Well, which way?" Theiandar asked, his patience wearing thin in the face of the possibility Roache was looking to lead them astray, to follow a path that would take them farther from Caityn and any possibility of her restoration . . . salvation.

"That way, I think."

"You think?" Gavin said. He didn't bother to restrain his irritation, evinced by his words echoing through the cavernous space. "That's not good enough, Roache. We don't have time to waste. Are you certain?"

Roache glared at him. "I'm as sure as I can be." Sweat trickled down his neck, glistening in the torchlight.

Theiandar once heard you could smell a man's fear, and at this moment, he believed it. *Is it possible he's not afraid of the place, but the man we're set to find?*

Trusting Roache was proving to be next to impossible, but his word was all they had to go on. They moved down the far left tunnel. Easily twenty minutes passed before the mercenary stopped at the edge of a shallow creek crossing their path.

Roache shook his head. "This isn't right."

"What?" Theiandar asked.

"This creek. I mean, it was here, but we didn't have to step over it."

"We don't have time for this, Roache. Which tunnel did you take first?" Theiandar ground out the words between clenched teeth.

"I think it was the second tunnel the first time and the first one the second." He paused in consideration. "Yes, that's it."

"We'll have to make up for lost time." Theiandar grasped Roache's arm again and pressed him into the lead.

They moved at a fast clip back down the tunnel for a good ten minutes before a startling cackle halted their progress. Too late, Theiandar regretted allowing his senses to be dulled by the quiet of the place.

Without warning, the tunnel exploded in front of them. Rock and dirt crashed down. Theiandar hesitated only a second before he pulled back on Roache's arm with all his might, dragging him away from the collapsing ceiling. When the dust finally settled, it was pitch-black and deathly quiet.

Theiandar assessed his own condition. His forehead was bleeding, but other than that, he was relatively unscathed. He called out to the others but received no response. He tried again, a little louder this time. "Gavin, Ahmad, are you well? Answer me! Roache?"

A rock tumbled in the dark, followed by a groan. "I'm fine, Raz," Gavin said.

Gavin had been behind them in the tunnel, thus avoiding most of the avalanche. "Ahmad?" Gavin called out.

It was too dark to see anyone or anything. There was another groan near Theiandar. He reached out to physically inspect the place from where the sound had come. His fingers came in contact with cloth and leg. "Ahmad? Is that you? Are you unharmed, my friend?"

"Yes, Raz, I'm here, but I think there's something on my arm. I can't move it."

"Be still, we'll get it off."

Theiandar crawled on hands and knees, keeping his hands in contact with Ahmad's body. Feeling around Ahmad, Theiandar's fingers came in contact with the rock crushing his friend's arm.

"Tis not impossible. I think Gavin and I will be able to remove it," Theiandar said, finding it difficult to sound encouraging all while thinking it could be much worse than his hands could ascertain in the darkness.

Gavin could be heard shuffling his feet through the debris as he attempted to move in their direction. "Keep talking so I know where you are," he said.

"You're almost to us, Gav."

The next thing they heard was Gavin's grunt. "Maddening rocks," he mumbled.

"You're next to us, Gavin. Just reach down," Theiandar said. "Let's get to work." Both men were grunting and huffing as they strained to remove the fallen piece of ceiling. They were able to lift it enough for Ahmad to pull his arm out.

When the rock's weight was lifted, a cry escaped him as Theiandar imagined the rush of pure agony brought on by the freedom. Ahmad rolled to the side and cradled his broken arm against his body.

"I'm out," Ahmad said between gasps.

They dropped the rock, sending up a cloud of dust. Gavin coughed. "I still have my lantern over there, but the light was blasted out. Maybe we can try lighting it again."

"Do it," Theiandar said. He kneeled beside Ahmad and rested his hand on his shoulder for a brief second. "I'm going to see if I can find Roache."

Gavin stumbled back the way he'd come. In the dark, it was almost impossible to tell which direction was which. "Found it," Gavin said, triumphant.

"Ahmad, let Gavin have your flint."

"Tis in the right pocket of my jacket," Ahmad replied through clenched teeth.

In the meantime, Theiandar searched the darkness near Ahmad, expecting to locate Roache. The brigand had not uttered a sound. It didn't take Theiandar long to find him, though. He paused and waited for Gavin to light the lantern.

When it was lit, he could see Roache's upper body was free, but he was situated facedown. Theiandar tipped the man's head to the side and found his eyes wide open, blood dripping from his lips. Death hung on him like a fog.

"We're trapped." There seemed to be nothing else to say. Theiandar's body sunk down, weighted by despair.

Gavin didn't bother to acknowledge what Theiandar had said. "Ahmad's arm is broken. I'm going to splint it. Find the other torch, Raz."

The prince searched the area near where Ahmad had fallen and was able to pull the other torch from beneath some debris. He took out his sword and broke off the end.

Ahmad, always the encourager, said, "All will be well, my friend."

Theiandar wanted to believe him with every fiber of his being. He placed his hands palm-down on Ahmad's shoulders with firm pressure.

"Take a deep breath, Ahmad. Let it out slow," Gavin said.

Gavin waited for Ahmad to comply. Before another word was uttered, he pulled, twisting Ahmad's arm back into place. A bone-grating pop followed by Ahmad's agonized scream were the only sounds in the cavernous space.

Theiandar removed his weapons and outer garments. He took his shirt off and ripped it into lengths, handing them to Gavin who then used them to secure Ahmad's damaged arm to his body.

Theiandar put his vest and jacket back on. He stared at the bow and arrow for a long time before he slung them over his chest once again. "We have to keep moving. Maybe this tunnel will lead out of here."

Once they'd pulled Ahmad to his feet they hobbled down untested section of tunnel. They came to the spot where the stream intersected with their path and stepped over it. After continuing down the path for another hundred feet, they entered a chamber no bigger than a kitchen larder. There were no exits from the otherwise-empty room.

Gavin slammed his fist into the wall and laid his head against the cold stone. Ahmad, weakened by his injury, slumped against the wall just inside the entrance. Theiandar closed his eyes and silently cried out to the Mighty One for deliverance. Silence, desperation, and an inkling of hope mixed with despair surrounded them.

Minutes passed in what felt like hours. "Raz? Of course! The water . . . didn't Roache say the other tunnel had a creek just the same?"

"Yes." His eyes brightened as he realized what Gavin was thinking. "You don't think they're connected do you?"

"I don't see why not. It would be a tight squeeze, but I can't help thinking there's a chance we could crawl through. If I'm right, we could end up in another passable tunnel."

Hope surged through Theiandar, having welled up from deep within. Two choices were before them: stay here and die, or try the stream. Then he remembered Ahmad's injury, and the hope faded by increments. Theiandar looked at his wounded friend. Could he even ask him to attempt it?

He never had to pose the question. Ahmad pushed himself off the wall and smiled at them to cover his discomfort. "It wouldn't be the first time a beast walked on three legs. Don't worry. I can do this, Raz."

With nothing more to delay them, they headed back to the interior creek.

* * *

Caityn hated to admit it, but hunger was gnawing at her stomach with a vengeance. She stared at the apple on the floor in front of her, contemplating the dull, red skin. The sight of it made her dry mouth yearn for water, but she'd had nothing to drink, either. The thought of not letting this evil little man have his way kept her from quenching her thirst and satisfying her hunger.

The only thing able to distract her from her raging appetite was a thunderous *boom* from the mountain and the quaking that followed. She listened for a long time, wondering at the commotion and ensuing stillness, but nothing else happened. Wild ideas flitted through her head. Could it be the prince coming to save her?

When she heard quick steps ascending from below, she perked up in anticipation. Upon hearing Nox whistling a triumphant melody before he appeared in the doorway, Caityn slumped to the ground.

"Ha! I have assured success!" He reached for the chains securing her hands and pulled her to her feet. She looked at him with confusion but said nothing in reply.

He was obviously put out by her lack of response. She was startled when he yanked her close to him, pulling her face down to meet his. He licked his lips with his snake-like, slimy tongue and kissed her full on the mouth. She shrieked and recoiled in disgust as she pulled back against his vice-like grip.

"You stupid girl! I always get what I want!" He released his hold on the restraints, and she fell to the floor. He moved over to the wall and unlocked the chains from the ring to which they were secured. With a firm grip on the icy metal, Nox walked across the chamber, dragging Caityn behind as she tried to stand. He didn't bother to give her the chance, though, and laughed as she spent the move sliding on her knees or skidding along the floor. When he reached the other side of the room, near the gaping hole in the side of the cave, he reattached her chains to another ring.

"You'll have a much better view of the show from here, Princess."

"Prince Theiandar will stop you, you monster," she murmured. She was exhausted to the point of total weakness. Even her words lacked strength.

"Oh no, my pet. For you see, I have just killed your prince in the tunnels below. There will be no savior for you. As I said before, I always get what I want." His laugh made her skin crawl.

"I'll kill myself before I let you have what you want!" She spat at him as angry tears streamed down her cheeks.

"Trust me, my deluded princess, you shall have no chance of that."

Before she could say or do anything else, he pulled her to a standing position, taking her shackles and attaching them to another chain. Nox walked a short distance and reached into a hole in the wall. Swiftly, Caityn's arms were pulled above her head.

Caityn watched as Nox strolled confidently from the room. Any inkling of hope she harbored dissolved like acid-covered limestone. "Oh, Theiandar," she whispered as she watched the sun disappear beyond the horizon, "I'm so sorry."

* * *

The tunnel was dark and tight. The surface of stone under the slow-moving water was slippery with slime. The three men resorted to crawling on their bellies, pulling themselves through with elbows, knees, and toes. Theiandar kept the light raised out of the stream of frigid water. Ahmad was struggling, but he swore the cold water helped relieve the pain in his arm. They kept their pace, moving as quickly as they could.

Just when Theiandar was sure they would never make it out alive, he noticed the tunnel widening ahead. The well of hope he carried in his heart surged with renewed energy. He shimmied faster through the icy stream. Sure, enough, he emerged into an open tunnel area.

He pulled his body into the open space and stood in the middle of the gentle stream. After a short assessment of the new tunnel, he bent over, offering his hand to Ahmad who took it with his good arm. "We made it! This must be the other tunnel. Tis as Roache described it."

Ahmad, relieved to be standing tall once again, smiled through his pain. They were shivering with the cold, but pure elation at having escaped a sure death overrode every other feeling.

Gavin scrambled from the water and searched the darkness much as Theiandar had done. He pointed in the opposite direction of the way they'd come out of the water tunnel. In this mountain corridor, the stream ran parallel to the walking path as opposed to perpendicular. "Let's head this way."

"Sounds reasonable," Theiandar said. "Let's move!"

They fell in line, moving with purpose and strength of courage once again.

CHAPTER THIRTY-FOUR
Total Lunar Eclipse

Night fell and the full moon rose higher, its intensity growing with each passing hour. Over the course of time, Caityn's arms went from tingling discomfort to aching pain and numbness. She was chilled to the bone, exhausted, and hungry. She thought of little else.

When Nox returned to the chamber, he ignored her presence there as he went about preparing for the upcoming eclipse. He hummed as he draped rich purple cloths over the stone throne and unrolled a lush, red carpet in front of it, stretching all the way to the precipice open to the night sky. He lit two torches, but they were not sufficient to dim the shimmering moonbeams which danced across the walls.

Caityn watched him work, wallowing in the despair and darkness within her.

"I see you staring at me, Princess. I've seen such a look before. Others have been here—many, in fact—but I must admit, you have caused the most trouble. No other man has ever made it into my lair. I suppose his near-success is only proportionate to your exquisite loveliness." He retrieved a cup of water and held it to her lips. This time, she drank greedily.

He stopped talking and looked out at the moon. "Ah! So it begins. I will be back shortly. I'm sure you'll wait patiently." Nox chuckled at his joke as he waddled out, leaving the door ajar in his wake.

* * *

When they emerged from the tunnel into another chamber, Theiandar was confident they were on the right track. He had no idea what time it was or if they were too late. Time didn't exist for them in the darkness. He assessed the placement of the entrances before him and strode toward the one to the left.

Theiandar stopped just inside the doorway and held up the lantern. The stairs were steep, and the walls were close. He took a deep breath and began the slow, steady ascent. He was exhausted but fought against the weariness. They had to be close. He could feel it.

Mightiest, you've carried us this far. Please take us the rest of the way. Give us strength. Please save my Caityn! They continued to climb and minutes passed. Theiandar saw light up ahead—almost like moonlight, but the color was all wrong. It was a strange shade of red. Then it hit him: the moon might appear red during a total lunar eclipse! Were they too late?

"Cait!" Theiandar bounded up the steps with renewed energy, his companions forgotten somewhere behind him, and burst through the entryway at the top of the stairs. His eyes searched the red-tinted, iridescent room. What appeared to be a throne sat at the center, illuminated from behind by two torches, their flames an unearthly crimson. The moon was huge in the sky, centered perfectly in the opening of the wall.

"No, no, no!" he cried. "I can't be too late! Please, Almighty, I can't be!" He ran toward the throne and spun in a circle looking for any sign of Caityn or the Beauty Thief. In his frenzied desperation he almost missed the sight of her hanging limp against the far wall, hidden in the shadows.

"Cait." He breathed her name in a sigh of relief. The distance between them became excruciating. In no time, he crossed the expanse to stand before her. Theiandar's relief was short-lived. Her frail body, bathed in the orange-red glow, hung limp. Her eyes were closed, her head bowed. She was still.

He reached out to cup her pale, lifeless face. "Oh Caityn, sweet Cait! It can't . . . I can't live without you!" He lifted her head. Denial hit him like a brick. They had come so far and gone through so much to get here. "I'm so sorry, my love. I failed you." His voice was thick with unshed tears, and he couldn't swallow; the lump in his throat was too big. Theiandar closed his eyes and leaned his forehead against hers, feeling the coolness of death upon it. "Forgive me."

"You're alive," she whispered.

Theiandar's head popped up, eyes wide. "You're alive!" Overcome with wonder, he kissed her with all the love that had been held prisoner by his pent up fear and rage. He cared for nothing else except this: she lived.

Breathless, she stared at him. "I thought you were dead. Nox said he killed you."

"He's a thief and a liar. But there's no time. I've got to get you down from here!" Theiandar's eyes traced the course of the chains by which she was bound.

"Theian, look out behind—"

He wheeled around, his arm up in defense. A blade edge sliced his forearm before the weapon sailed over his head.

"You'll not stop me, Prince!" Nox snarled, baring his ugly teeth. "You will never get the amulet! You will never save your princess. She belongs to the dark! Her life is mine!"

Before Theiandar could make his move, Gavin sprang from the shadows and jabbed something minute into the Beauty Thief's neck. The evil man swung his head around to stare in shock at his assailant before he crumpled to the ground. Gavin bent at the knees, winded but smiling nonetheless.

"Ahmad lost the dart gun somewhere," Gavin said, "but he still had the darts. I figured there was more than one way to thwart a demon!"

Theiandar's smile was from the heart as he clapped Gavin on the back. "Well done, my friend! Thank you!" He noticed Ahmad leaning heavily against the wall. "And you as well, Ahmad. Rest for a time. We'll take care of the princess. Gavin, find how to lower Cait down while I look for a key on this deranged imbecile."

Gavin made short work of locating the lever and lowering Caityn. She wept as relief mingled with pain where blood flowed back into her arms and hands. Gavin scrambled over to her collapsed form and rubbed her tingling upper arms, attempting to relieve the pinpricks of sensation.

"Hello, Caity. Sorry to keep you waiting," Gavin said, doing his best to make light of a tense situation.

"Thank you," she whispered.

He leaned in, resting his forehead against hers. "There's no doubt, my fair cousin, you would do the same for me."

Theiandar found the key to the manacles and dashed over. He couldn't contain himself and enveloped Caityn in his arms, pressing her to his chest where his heart beat out a frantic rhythm.

"Cait. My Cait!" He breathed the words into her dirty, matted hair. Theiandar allowed himself only a scant minute to enjoy the pleasure of holding her in his arms. He knew the window of time was limited. Theiandar reluctantly let go of Caityn and removed the shackles from her wrists.

As soon as her wrists were freed from bondage, he took them in his masculine hands. Gentle as a dove, he massaged her injured wrists, examining the rope burns. Theiandar could only wait so long before he pulled her back into his arms. He'd almost given up hope, and he prayed she was more than a figment of his imagination.

"Raz, I think we have a problem!" Ahmad said from across the room.

Before Theiandar could respond, Nox was on his feet, running at the prince and Caityn and screaming like a banshee. "You will never stop me!" He squealed in rage as he dove at the prince.

Theiandar shoved Caityn at Gavin and rolled to the side, avoiding the impact of Nox's body by a scant half inch. Nox stumbled and smashed into the wall in a drunken heap. Dazed, he rose to his feet and tried to regain his composure.

"I thought you said the darts last half an hour!" Theiandar said.

"The water in the tunnel must have reduced their potency!" Ahmad said.

Nox set upon Theiandar, his desperate arms reaching for the prince's throat. He snarled like a wild dog. Spittle flew from his lips.

Theiandar reached for Nox's throat, too, but with intent of an entirely different sort. His eyes were fixed on the crimson glow of the amulet, crying out to him like his own soul. He was shocked at the level of strength the diminutive, older man possessed. Ahmad tried to come to Theiandar's defense, but he was quickly knocked aside as the other two men fought dangerously close to the opening in the wall and its sheer drop-off.

"Theiandar, watch out!" Ahmad yelled as Theiandar backed toward the cliff.

Gavin ushered Caityn as far from the fighting as possible and rushed across the room in time to see Theiandar yank the amulet free from Nox's throat. Nox was thrown off balance. He tripped on the red carpet.

The others watched Nox attempt to regain his footing in agonizing slow motion. Theiandar reached out, endeavoring to halt the Beauty Thief's momentum, but then it was done. Nox dropped from the face of the cliff, his screams echoing off the rocks, through the mountain valleys, before all was silent.

No one moved as reality sunk in. The eclipse had reached its zenith in the midst of the fight. Time would not wait for them to finish their task.

Theiandar limped back to where Caityn leaned against the wall. She stared at him, her look unreadable. He held the necklace high, as if to place it around her neck, the amulet suspended between them.

Caityn lifted the amulet, examining the flowing, red liquid at its core. The fluid shimmered of its own accord. They could feel the depth of her captive love, its power radiating from within as it pressed against its prison walls.

Caityn wrapped her fingers around the amulet and gave a gentle tug. Theiandar released his hold on the chain and watched her lift it over her head. She laid the amulet gently against her breast before she looked up into his eyes.

"I'm afraid, Caity. I can't believe how fearful I am. If I miss, it will kill you. I don't think I can do this!" He was ashamed of the dread and despair in his voice.

"You must, Theiandar. If you don't, I'll be lost forever anyway. The darkness is growing stronger. Before you came, it had already seeped into my soul." She paused and let sorrowful eyes plead with him. "I don't want to be . . . just a beautiful, empty shell. I cannot live like this when I know what I once was. Who can live without the pearl of her soul?"

He couldn't look away from the supplication emanating from the depths of the abyss in her eyes. Theiandar knew she was right, but the fear of losing her was overwhelming.

She stepped closer and leaned into him, her weakness visible in the shaking of her raised arm. But instead of hugging him, like he thought she would do, she plucked the arrow from the quiver.

"You must do this," she said. "Please, Theiandar." She pressed the ruby-tipped arrow to his chest.

"Caity," he said, taking her hands in his. Her fingers were still wrapped around the weapon she held between them. His mind was taken back to the day he'd made his promise to her. He repeated his former vow. "My love for you is steadfast and strong." He lifted her free hand to his lips. He lingered there for a moment as he breathed in the scent of her bruised and batter knuckles. He smelled the blood crusted on her hands and guilt swept over him like a wave.

Gavin cleared his throat, reminding them of where they were and what must be done. Theiandar took the arrow from her and stepped back a dozen long paces. He watched Caityn back herself toward the wall which still glimmered with the reflection of the red glow.

He brought the bow up over his shoulder and tested its strength before placing the nock on the string. Theiandar pulled the arrow back in tempo with his intake of breath, aiming with great care and trepidation.

As he exhaled, he released the arrow.

He couldn't take his eyes off Caityn. He couldn't breathe.

She was dirty and disheveled, but stood with regal posture. His heart, in that split second, said a thousand prayers for this to work, for Caityn to be unharmed.

The arrow flew straight and true, piercing the amulet's center. The force of it knocked Caityn to the ground.

The three men rushed toward her. Theiandar reached her first, and gently touched her chest where the amulet had rested. The chain, still intact, spilled across her neck and pooled on the cavern floor. The amulet had exploded, and the crimson liquid covered her pale skin in tiny, shimmering droplets, splashed about as if an impassioned artist had created a bloody masterpiece.

Before their very eyes, the red glow intensified until it was shining, white light. It was too bright. Theiandar covered his eyes and turned his head away. The light vanished as quickly as it had come. The room was again lit only by the dissipating red blaze of the moon and the matching torches.

The amulet's liquid had disappeared from Caityn's chest. Theiandar let his hands drift over her heart in search of a wound but found none. He stared at her pale, still body and feared they were too late. He lifted her in his arms and cradled her lovingly against his chest.

Into her hair, he whispered, "Caity, come back to me."

* * *

Caityn's eyelids were heavy, as though she'd just woken from a long, pressing dream. She could feel the strain of Theiandar's muscles as he held her against his chest. The rapid beat of his heart thumped against her ear. "There you are, my prince," she said as she opened her eyes and gazed up at him.

Theiandar's eyes shimmered with unspent tears. Caityn knew the droplets would not fall. The tense muscles in his jaw took time to unclench, but once they did, he whispered, "I thought I'd lost you."

She pressed herself away from him, wanting to better see his face. Caityn was tired beyond anything she'd ever imagined, but she smiled. The eclipsing moonlight cast a strange shadow across Theiandar's features. "You almost did. Somewhere deep down I knew you would save me, though. Something wouldn't allow me to let go completely. And . . . I remembered your promise."

Theiandar kissed the top of her head, his words muffled by her hair. "I love you, Cait. I couldn't live without you."

"I love you, too, Theian. It feels so good to love."

"And be loved," he said, the smile he wore unmistakable in the tenor of his voice.

Caityn didn't notice Gavin and Ahmad's quiet exit through the secret door. She was too wrapped up in the comforting pleasure of Theiandar's arms. She clung to the emotions flooding her soul. Her senses were alive. She reveled in compassion and guilt at the scents of sweat and blood spent on her behalf. If not for his love and for the help of his men, she would be lost. If it had been possible for her to cry, she would have.

Knowing the complete depth of her unworthiness in the face of such personal sacrifice was overwhelming. Indebtedness welled up to the point of choking her. Thank you, Most High.

She wasn't sure how long they stayed huddled together on the floor of the cavernous room. It didn't seem long enough to her mind. She wanted to stay forever wrapped in Theiandar's steady embrace.

Again, Gavin interrupted them. "Theiandar, you won't believe what Nox has stored here. There are trinkets from all over the world down this hall. There's also a locked room we can't get into." He didn't wait for a reply before he exited back through the open doorway.

Theiandar never took his eyes off Caityn. "We need to get you out of here and send word of your safety to High Castle." He helped her to her feet.

Gavin and Ahmad came out through the hidden door again. Ahmad carried a jewel-encrusted dagger, its sheath and handle bedecked in a myriad of precious gems. Gavin had a round shield slung over his arm. It was also covered in jewels, with glittering diamonds arranged in the shape of a lion.

Gavin's face transformed to reveal his great relief when his eyes met Caityn's. He set the shield down and stood before her.

If it was even possible, his smile grew. "I'm beyond relieved you're safe." He didn't wait for her to say anything else before he hugged her tight.

"I love you, Gav," she whispered. "I will never be able to thank any of you enough for what you've done."

He released her and raised her hand to his lips. "My sweet cousin, it has been an honor to serve you. I would do it all over if it meant seeing your radiant smile again."

He gave her hand a gentle squeeze and released it as Theiandar wrapped his arm around Caityn. Gavin shifted his gaze to the prince. "Raz, there are a few more weapons down there. We were unable to open the locked door, though. It might be wise to return later and explore this place."

"Hmm, yes. For now, we need to get Caityn and Ahmad somewhere to take care of their wounds. The journey back to the river is long, but the rest of our unit should still be on the trail where we left them."

Caityn realized Sir Ahmad stood alone by the doorway. She chanced a glance at him, and for the first time, noticed his immobilized arm.

Weak, but determined, she closed the gap between them. Her head felt light and tipsy, but she concentrated on moving one foot in front of the other until she was less than two feet from Ahmad.

Caityn wanted to say thank you, but two entirely different words spilled out of her mouth. "Your arm."

He chuckled and touched his broken arm. "Yes, 'tis still attached."

"Oh, Sir Ahmad, I'm sorry."

"I'm only relieved you're well enough. Don't worry about my arm. It will heal."

She took him at his word, knowing he meant what he said. "Thank you."

Ahmad smiled at her and dipped his head.

"Gavin, light some torches. We're getting out of here," Theiandar said.

Caityn wandered over to the precipice. She looked out into the night. "Do you think he's dead?"

Theiandar took Caityn's elbow to help steady her. She leaned heavy upon him. "No one could survive so far a fall," Theiandar replied without hesitation. "I didn't realize how close to the edge we were. I wish there had been another way. Our intention was to take him captive."

"Tis a wonder and blessing you didn't go over with him." She shuddered at the thought.

Gavin picked up the shield he'd set down and spoke from across the cavern. "Raz, here's a torch for you. Would you like me to take the lead?"

"Yes, Gavin. Caity and I will bring up the rear." She looked up at him, exhaustion clouding her sight. "Come on, Cait."

She wrapped her arms around his neck as he picked her up. "You're tired, too, Theian. You can't carry me all the way out of this mountain."

"That's probably true," he said with a wry smile.

Caity pressed her face into his shoulder and rested in the circle of his enduring strength and love. He carried her to the top of the stairs and set her down. Soon they were making their way out of the mountain's labyrinth, Theiandar sometimes carrying Caityn. It proved much less difficult than their ascent.

Eventually they emerged from the bowels of the mountain, ducking through the roots of the cypress and out into the diminishing moonlight.

Caityn stood in the clearing before the tree and breathed deeply. She relished the scent of musky forest. It was heavenly to be able to appreciate this simple thing again.

The early-morning air was chilly, and she wrapped her arms snug around her waist, trying to hold in what little heat she possessed. She shivered and smiled in contentment. Caityn's eyes closed tight as she savored the tumult of feelings that rushed over her.

"Thank you, Most High." The words were whispered like a sigh and carried away on the breeze. She was startled by a blanket being tossed around her shoulders.

"Come eat a bite or two. Then you can rest while we get the horses ready," Theiandar said.

Caityn leaned into him. "Oh, Theiandar, how are Adair and Idra? Where is she? Is she safe? Who is with her?"

"Whoa, there. Don't get all worked up. They're both recovering. Lady Idra, by some miracle, made it to the village at the crossing."

Caityn could hear the exhaustion in his voice. "I will never deserve any of the sacrifices made for me. I . . . how will I ever repay everyone?"

"You don't have to, my love. Come here." He pulled her into his arms again. "There is nothing to repay. We know you'd have done the same for any of us. Let your gratefulness speak for itself."

* * *

The horses were prepared, and Ahmad's injury had been secured as much as possible for the journey home. Theiandar saw Caityn curled up on the ground, wrapped tight in the blanket. She was sound asleep.

Seeing her tranquility, it was almost impossible to believe she'd been through this uncanny ordeal. He touched her hair, matted and grimy, and felt a swell of love for her burgeoning up in his heart, its breadth and depth far beyond what he'd known before.

Her eyes fluttered open and she gave him a dreamy smile.

"We're ready, my love," he said.

Theiandar didn't wait for her to stand. He took her up in his arms and carried her to the horse, unable to ignore her frailness. "Lay on the horse's neck. You must keep your head down here, as the forest is thick. I'll join you after we leave the dense grove."

She obeyed without a word but reached out to touch his cheek. Her fingers were warm against his skin, soothing and inviting. Caityn's expression, the silent words spoken through her eyes, was enough. He leaned into her hand, savoring her gentle touch, grateful to the marrow of his soul.

Epilogue

Three Weeks Later

After one more peek out the window, Caityn finally fell back against the carriage seat, a restless breath whooshing past her parted lips.

Idra laughed. "Caity, we're almost there. Are you excited to see your family, or is it something else?"

Caityn closed her eyes and placed her fingertips on her eyebrows. "Yes . . . to both. I'm anxious about seeing everyone after how I looked and behaved before. What if that is what people always remember most about me? What if people blame me for the deaths?"

Idra was quiet in contemplation for a moment. "Well, I suppose that's possible, but you shouldn't dwell on it. I think everyone will be celebrating the prince's success. Besides, even if there are some people who think poorly of you, 'tis only because they don't know the real you. Given time, you'll prove them wrong."

"I hope you're right, Idra."

As the carriage bumped along, her mind traveled back to the days since she was rescued. They had reunited with the remainder of Theian's guard and some of Captain Saar's men. She was surprised by their shouts of joy when she was escorted into the camp just before dawn. Saar's remaining men were sent in search of Nox's body but returned empty-handed.

It took a couple days of slow travel to return to where Idra was recuperating and waiting anxiously for new of Caityn's life. The woman who was caring for Idra didn't waste a breath before she set to work checking wounds. She concerned herself over Sir Ahmad's arm, in particular.

Even now, knowing he was riding outside the carriage, one arm bound tightly, Caityn couldn't help but admire his strength, both of body and spirit. He never once complained. It reinforced her deep admiration for this man who served both his king *and* the King of Kings.

Her mind wandering back to the present, Caityn peered out the carriage window. Her brother, heaven help him, had made his way to Wyeth as soon as the doctor had cleared him for travel.

Adair and his unit of men arrived two nights before and, by chance, had met Caityn and her group on the road between the village and the castle. It had been the most tearful reunion. Caityn had clung to her brother and cried out all the tears she hadn't been able to release before.

Being brought back from her reveries, she jumped in surprise when he tapped on the little glass window. Caityn unlatched the pane and swung it open. Adair leaned forward a fraction to peer in.

"The castle is up ahead, Caity. Father and Mother are waiting impatiently, I'm sure. The messenger said Mother and Brennan arrived two days ago."

She poked her head out the window, straining to get a view of the castle. "I'm anxious to see them. I thought I was done crying, Adair, but I can feel the tears already."

"I'll pinch you when we get there, Sis. That way you'll be too annoyed to cry."

He sounded serious. She looked up at him and smiled when she saw the grin on his face. "You'll do no such thing! Besides, at this point you'd have to tell all my secrets to truly upset me. And anyway, a pinch would reassure me that I'm not dreaming."

"Oh, you're not dreaming, Caity! This day is a miracle and a blessing. Now, get all those tears out of the way before we get there." He sat up in the saddle and prodded his horse forward.

Sooner than Caityn realized was possible, they arrived at the castle. She was afraid to look out the window, but heard all the cheers erupting from the castle folk. The carriage wheels ground to a halt on the cobblestone courtyard of the keep. Before she could even begin to turn toward the door, it burst open. Her father, King Othniel, was there. He grasped her hand, pulled her from the carriage, and then wrapped his arms around her in a loving embrace. She heard her mother's voice behind her just before another pair of arms crushed her body.

"Oh dearest!" Ismene's cry of joy swept through Caityn's hair like a warm breeze. The three stood there, locked in each other's arms. You couldn't tell where one body ended and another began. This was another sensation Caityn would never take for granted again.

Two Months Later

Ismene watched Idra place the last flower in Caityn's hair. Caityn couldn't help smiling at her mother's reflection in the mirror. "Mama, your eyes will be red if you cry."

She chuckled as her mother reached into the bosom of her gown and pulled out a handkerchief. Ismene snapped it in the air and then used the corner to dab her eyes.

"My heart is about to burst. I could have lost you forever, and I cannot imagine never being able to see your smile again, or feel your love, or witness this day. I'm joyful, but I'm afraid something terrible will happen."

Caityn took her mother's hand. "I almost couldn't rest last night for fear of what might happen, but I prayed myself to sleep." Caityn couldn't keep the serious look from passing over her face. "Men died because of me. *Idra* almost died because of me. I will never forget it. Just like the scar on my chest, my gratefulness will always be there, but we cannot let fear rule our lives. It will stamp out the hope and joy."

Idra stepped up next to her cousin and wrapped her arm snuggly around Caityn's waist. "The Almighty's sure to use your grateful heart to lead this kingdom with love and devotion. Now, I hate to change the subject, but your bridegroom impatiently awaits your arrival."

Upon opening the door, they were met by her beaming father. Adair stood next to Othniel. He offered his arm to his mother. His other, he held out to Idra. Caityn took her father's arm, and the two trailed a short distance behind the others.

"Caity, you're a vision," King Othniel said. "This is a joyous day, indeed! I'm sorry we were unable to have the wedding at home, but High Castle is beautiful in its own right."

"Tis fine, Papa. This is more central to all the realms anyway. And after word spread of what happened to me . . . well, the legend of it has caused quite a stir. Many more people are here than before, and there's no way we could have accommodated all of them at Taisce. Theian says in a few months we'll be able to visit, though. I do miss it! But I think I will love it here, too."

Caityn didn't notice the dark look that passed over her father's face when she mentioned the stir which had rippled across the realms due to the ordeal she'd experienced.

They proceeded in silence. Caityn's younger brother, Brennan, stood by the carriage, ready to hand his mother and Idra in. Othniel assisted Caityn up and climbed in behind her. Adair and Brennan mounted horses behind the carriage.

Because a great number of people from every station of life wanted to witness the wedding of their beloved Prince Theiandar to his princess bride, they held the ceremony outside the castle walls. The spot they'd picked was beautiful. It sat at the foot of rolling meadow hills. There was a lane of trees on either side leading up to the ruins of the ancient castle of the realm, in use before the twelve had been united as one. From the carriage, Caityn could see the castle walls—still standing in places, crumbled in others. The sun was setting behind the ruins and silhouetted the grand old place with a halo of dazzling radiance.

Well-wishers lined the path. Some cheered and threw flowers before them. Caityn was overwhelmed by the greetings and had to fight back tears as she waved at everyone.

When they arrived at the ruins, Caityn saw Theiandar's guard unit. They were dressed in their finest clothing, swords held aloft, making an arch for her to walk through.

Gavin stepped out and took Idra's arm, preceding Caityn to the base of the grassy knoll. Caityn had to tamp down the panic rising in her gut. Her thoughts spun in and around reassurances of her safety.

The moment her eyes met Theiandar's, her fear melted away. She didn't even notice as the others parted in front of her and her father gave her away. She was floating through a dream, a beautiful dream, and her heart was full to bursting.

* * *

Idra watched from her place of honor next to the bride, and let the joy of this occasion engulf her. She didn't notice the eyes looking only at her, the eyes that echoed a longing to snatch her away. Nor did she notice the other man whose heart was full of adoration for her of an exceptionally different sort.

All other eyes were trained on the bride and groom. No one noticed him or the darkness that surrounded him as he looked on with uncanny patience—not for revenge, but to establish his domination and control. He'd not wasted the past two months, but now he'd wait until the time was right. She would not best him in the end. If all worked according to plan, no one would discover his handiwork for quite some time. He smiled and lifted his glass as they toasted the prince and his beautiful, new bride. Yes, it would be worth the wait.

Available Now

CAPTIVE HOPE

Book Two

in the Chronicles of the Twelve Realms

ACKNOWLEDGMENTS

This has to be my favorite page to write. It is a testament to the love and support of the people in my life. And who wouldn't want to give a great big thanks to their biggest supporters? You must know I'm thankful to you for reading my book. It means the world to me that you chose to pick it up and dive into the Twelve Realms. I also can't go without saying a huge thanks to my editor, Susan Hughes. Your professional attitude, kind encouragement, and honest feedback are such assets! You rock! Merci, mon cher—my husband, Karl. You applied plenty of positive pressure to keep me moving in the right direction, not to mention loving me through thick and thin, but mostly thick. Ha! Love you! Big thanks to my kids who've not always understood my dedication to writing but have supported me in the endeavor anyway. Can't finish off the round of thanks without saying how grateful I am for Sheila and Cherie. Without these two ladies, I never would have been able to clean up the manuscript enough to make it worthy of an editor's time or your eyes. Thank you, my friends! Other people who helped out along the way with support, encouragement and/or feedback—deserving a big thanks—are Stephanie, Jeremy, Lizzie, Samantha, Dawn, Tara, and Job! God is good and I'm grateful He blessed my life with people like you!

*A second edition was made to fix minor character perspective issues and a few typos. None of the main/essential content or story have changed. I hope you enjoyed the book and will continue reading the Chronicles of the Twelve Realms.

"Do not let your adorning be external . . . but let your adorning be the hidden person of the heart with the imperishable beauty of a gentle and quiet spirit, which in God's sight is very precious."
1 Peter 3:3-4 (Bible ESV)

Connect with Rachael on
Facebook: http://www.facebook.com/WritingRaci
Twitter: http://www.twitter.com/RachaelRitchey
http://www.rachaelritchey.com

CPSIA information can be obtained at www.ICGtesting.com
Printed in the USA
BVOW11s1215060316

439265BV00001B/1/P